A VAMPIRE'S GUIDE TO SURVIVING HOLIDAYS

VAMPIRE INNOCENT
BOOK EIGHT

MATTHEW S. COX

DIVISION ZERO PRESS

ISBN (ebook): 978-1-950738-20-5

ISBN (paperback): 978-1-950738-21-2

CONTENTS

1. Adulting is Overrated — 1
2. 1001 Uses for a Vampire — 16
3. The Absent Professor Montgomery — 33
4. Weird — 42
5. Hunter Hunted — 50
6. A Moment to Think — 61
7. Another Lifetime — 66
8. Politics Always Ruins Everything — 74
9. Homework and Banishing Spells — 91
10. Tmi — 99
11. Thanksgiving Miracle — 119
12. A Little Helpful Prodding — 125
13. Every Family Has Secrets — 129
14. Pie — 135
15. The Hunter in the Ointment — 140
16. Nothing is Illegal if You Don't get Caught — 151
17. A Girl's Gotta be Careful at Night — 161
18. Cats and Dog — 170
19. Near Miss — 189
20. Conflict of Interest — 199
21. Underestimated — 202
22. Vampire Delivery Service — 212
23. Unlife Isn't Fair — 222
24. Caught Red-Handed — 228
25. Air Ambulance — 233
26. Mission Complete... Sorta — 236
27. Fog and Kittens — 247
28. Not Quite Dead — 254

Acknowledgments — 260
About the Author — 261
Other books by Matthew S. Cox — 262

ADULTING IS OVERRATED

Anxiety has a way of making people rearrange their priorities. For me, I find myself worrying a lot more about the lives of my family and friends than my own... considering I've already lost it. Generally, I've come to terms with becoming a vampire and things are even starting to feel second nature. But, dammit, the Universe is just not done screwing with me yet. Every day that passes without me getting sucked backwards through the inner workings of a pan-dimensional chaos machine counts as a victory.

Today's the first day since a pack of vampires from LA kidnapped my little brother and his friends I haven't noticed any trembling in my hands during moments where my attention isn't focused on anything specific. No, the shakes didn't come from fear, more restless energy and anger. Like an itch never quite exactly where I scratched, a sense of impending retaliation haunted me. Still kinda does. Completely out of sorts for my personality, I'm worried we hadn't killed enough of those LA vampires. It would only take one getting away alive—well, unalive—and holding onto a grudge to create problems down the line. So, yeah, lots of looking over my shoulder.

The feeling of dread I always had haunting me whenever I went somewhere alone at night in life had come back, and dammit—it's not right! I'm a creature of the night. We're not supposed to be jumping at shadows. And let me tell you, jumping at shadows is a real pain in the ass when your eyes can't see them.

Unlike before my death, I'm not worrying about some random creep looking for a girl to assault. Now, I keep expecting angry vampires to drag me into an alley or stuff me in the trunk of a car. My pants aren't going to be what they try to separate from my body— more like my head. Maybe they'll chain me to a tree and let me wait for the sun to rise. Given a gloomy enough morning, the joke would be on them. Ultimately though, it feels exactly like it used to feel to be alone at night. And this bullcrap is something I'd thought no longer applied to me. Getting away from living in permanent fear for my life had been the second best part of becoming a vampire.

Yes, flying is awesome.

Anyway, finding myself scared in the dark again has me in a near permanent state of being pissed off.

For the most part since the 'LA incident,' I kept up a normal face around my family, especially the Littles. Sophia is too empathic for her own good. She knows how bothered I've been. Pretty sure she's the reason behind Ashley and Michelle taking me to TGI Friday's for a girl's night out. Is it weird to go to Friday's on a Sunday? Do they have laws about that?

Anyway, a week and a few days without any sign of trouble from LA vampires could mean I'm in the clear. Not like we pissed off anyone old, powerful, or politically important... basically they'd been the vampire equivalent of a street gang. The most potent vampire involved, Armand—yeah, I know... but it wasn't his real name—had only been a vampire for roughly forty years, not even as old as Dalton. He'd also taken a sun bath, so he's not a problem anymore. The bigger worry is him having a sire or progeny who'd be looking for payback.

If someone ever killed Dalton, the idea of me going off on a revenge quest doesn't seem likely. For one thing, I'm not a violent person—mostly. Dying has definitely given me new confidence. For another thing, any vampire who could kill Dalton would completely spank me. Any chance for me to avenge him would rely on sneakiness combined with a boatload of luck, and as the spyglass incident proved, my attempts at being a thief don't pan out.

By the way, I mean thief in the sense of the roleplaying games Dad and Sierra like. You know, like character classes and fantasy stuff. Those thieves don't necessarily all steal; they're good at stealth. At least, that's how Sierra plays hers. Kinda strange how she regards taking property as 'something bad guys do' but she has no problem ambushing and killing the enemies. Like, theft is bad but murder isn't? Guess it's kinda like people who watch a movie with massive amounts of violence, rape, drug use, or similar horrors, but only seem to have a problem if the characters use bad words.

I'm astounded Sam brushed off the entire incident like something he'd seen in a movie. I mean, for real... my little brother had a vampire's severed arm dangling from his neck like a tie. As far as he's concerned, the whole experience had been a cool adventure. And yeah, I looked into his head to make sure he didn't crack and go nuts. Despite being scared during a few close call moments, he really did regard the whole situation as exciting. He'd been more worried about *me* being hurt than himself. Fortunately, he's not in any hurry to go on another 'adventure' with murderous vampires.

It seems my new normal is spilling over into my siblings' definition of ordinary, too.

I mean for crying out loud, Sophia has a teleporting kitten she made from mushroom dust.

So, anyway, Ashley and Michelle showed up at the house earlier and whisked me out the door the way they used to do when we'd go hang out together before the bad thing happened. No, I'm not talking about my almost-murder and becoming a vampire. The 'bad thing' is us growing up—or at least starting to. Thoughts like this shouldn't be in my head considering I'm eighteen. Then again, undeath is quite a shock to the system. Hell, it made me appear a few years younger, so it's probably powerful enough to alter my brain, too.

A girl my age shouldn't feel nostalgic. I haven't had enough life yet. Well, I mean 'life' metaphorically there. And it's not like I'm having a crisis like my parents where they've become so overwhelmed with responsibilities they want to jump back to being fourteen again. My 'nostalgia' takes the form of missing the time from like seventh grade to junior year in high school when the three of us had been old enough to enjoy a little independence while remaining young enough to dodge any true responsibilities. Dad is pretty sure vampirism did something to my head since he only started missing those years after he turned forty.

And, while getting frozen looking like I'm somewhere between fourteen and seventeen depending how the light hits my face has more than its share of annoyances, I'm never going to get any older or fatter or worn out. Yeah, being a vampire is pretty damn amazing. Just wish the price of admission wasn't so damn high.

Sitting at a table in Friday's with Ash and 'Chelle reminds me of like a year or two ago. None of us really appreciated the drastic changes we'd all crash face first into once high school ended. Like blind lemmings rushing for a cliff, we only thought about having fun until one day, society expected us to grow up. The nerve.

And yeah, through no fault of my own, I wound up slamming on the brakes at the cliff's edge watching my friends fly past me over the side. They're going to cruise headlong into the rest of their lives while I'm stuck as a teenager for eternity. My parents—once they got over the emotional rollercoaster of nearly losing me—tease me constantly about being jealous. Mom's job stresses her out so much, she flat out said if she could go back to being a teen, she'd do it in a heartbeat. She didn't really mean it, though. Mostly, she wants a break from stress.

Sure, I've thought about grabbing Ashley and Michelle's proverbial hands to stop them from flying off the cliff, but I can't bring myself to do it for several reasons, not the least of which is Dalton never showed me how to make someone else into a vampire. Ash wants to be a mother someday, and she couldn't have kids as an undead. In Michelle's case, her parents are overly religious and would never be able to handle the mere concept of vampires. They still don't know about me, and it's going to stay that way even if I need to erase their memories. If Michelle turned, she would have to go through with the normal process and allow the mortal world to believe she'd died. This would also have the effect of making it a pain in the ass to hang out with her.

The third and most compelling reason: neither of them asked me for the Transference. Forcing it on them is totally wrong. I'd have enough trouble doing it to them if they both wanted it *and* were already going to die through some other cause. No damn way could I ever ambush them against their will.

As cool as it would be for my little circle of friends to be frozen in time, it's not right.

Is it weird I'm an actual teenager but have to force myself to think like one? Stopping myself from worrying about a future more distant than a few hours takes effort. I fail at teenagering. That's me. Weird. But at least I'm not 'ten-foot pom pom of death' weird. My sister has some issues. Maybe there's something out there sillier to be morbidly terrified of than a giant puffball, but darned if I can think of what.

Our waiter is a skinny, tall, dark-skinned guy only a few years older than us named Jordan. He's gotta be a theater major since he's the most extroverted, friendly person in the entire state of Washington. He has a hint of a foreign accent, but I'm not sure what it is beyond cool sounding. We skip appetizers and go right to the entrees. It still feels wasteful for me to order normal food, but at least I can enjoy the process of eating and tasting it.

"No inferno bites?" asks Ashley. "You, like, *always* get them."

I squirm in my seat. "Umm. They don't like me back anymore."

'Chelle and Ash peer quizzically at me.

"Ever see the movie *Fire Down Below?*"

"That bad?" asks Michelle.

"What does the movie have to do with chicken?" Ashley blinks at me.

While I *could* tell them it felt like having a lit candle an inch away from a place a lit candle should never be, we're about to eat. "Food doesn't process, remember? Not the movie, just the title. Kinda burns on the way out."

Ashley covers her mouth to muffle a laugh. Michelle gawks at me while squirming.

"Yeah. Exactly. I can't do spicy anymore." I exhale. "So, what's going on with you guys? Haven't seen you much lately."

We talk about random stuff, mostly their college courses and jobs. Michelle grumbles about living at home and can't wait until she's able to move out. She's stuck in a fairly awkward situation. Her parents are loving and take good care of her, but Michelle's nowhere near as into the churchy stuff as they are. The big problem, though, is how her parents consider LGBT people 'sinful.' I'm not the only one keeping a secret from Mr. and Mrs. Gerard. No, not Michelle either. Ashley's bi. For the most part, she's out—except for Michelle's parents.

I can't help myself but chuckle.

"Exactly what is funny about my parents?" Michelle raises one eyebrow.

"It's not funny," I say between chuckles.

"So why you laughing?" asks Michelle.

"Trying to figure out what would make your 'rents freak out more: learning about Ash or discovering I'm a vampire."

The mild annoyance in Michelle's expression fades to a blank look. Bet she's trying to legit come up with the answer.

Ashley grins. "They'd probably spontaneously burst into flames if they got near a gay vampire."

I'm done. Head down on my folded arms, I laugh myself to tears.

"Guys!" Michelle pats the table. "We are not making jokes about my parents being on fire."

"It's okay," says Ashley. "Don't feel awkward. It's not your fault how they are. Besides, if you went to an out-of-state school where you had to dorm so you could escape being dragged off every Sunday, then you wouldn't be able to hang out with us, so it wouldn't matter."

"Maybe Sarah could change their mind?" Michelle sips her soda.

"Whoa." Ashley stares at her. "You're seriously... didn't you tell her to leave them alone?"

"Yeah, well." Michelle frowns at her pre-dinner salad. "Dad went off on a screed this morning about the decay of the country's moral fiber. Somehow, he connects just about every problem to the mere existence of gay people and/or non-believers. I love him, but I'm just *so* tired of hearing that stuff. I don't mind the peace and love part of it, but they're forgetting it for the fire and brimstone."

I fidget. "I dunno, 'Chelle. Seems wrong to just go around mind controlling everyone. If you think your father's going to hurt someone, or if they find out about Ash and flip, sure... I'll fix it."

"No way. My dad would never hurt anyone. All he does is complain." Michelle teases a fork at her salad. "I don't think he'd even say what he thinks to someone's face."

"Sorry," whispers Ashley.

"Maybe you could at least get them to stop wasting three hours of my Sunday morning?" Michelle stares pleadingly at me. "I have so much damn work to catch up on, it's not even funny."

"It's kinda bogus they force you to go. You're eighteen." Ashley shakes her head, then takes a sip of her raspberry iced tea.

"It's not a 'force' type of situation. It's a 'stop paying for school and letting me live there rent free' type situation." Michelle rolls her eyes. "And my mother would be crushed if I told her I didn't believe."

My parents never did the religion thing. Mom's parents are kinda spiritual, but they, too, never went to any organized church. They both believe in a higher power, but didn't see any purpose to large, formal groups. Not once in my life have I been dragged out of bed early on a Sunday. Weekends are sacred holidays of rest. I pitied Michelle for only having one day a week where she didn't have to obey an alarm clock.

Ashley's in the middle of reassuring her she doesn't hold it against her parents and is okay with keeping that secret from them when our food arrives. Jordan hands out the plates, asks us if we need anything else—Michelle gets a refill on her drink—then walks off.

Since I don't have to worry about putting on weight, I ordered a pasta dish with chicken and a cream sauce. It's probably like 2,000 calories. I'm eating for the taste; might as well have something I'd actually enjoy. Also, my plan is to have about a third of it and bring the rest home for the Littles to share. If I ever fed from Ashley, she'd absolutely taste like a grilled chicken sandwich with cheddar cheese and bacon. For as long as I've known her—and she's been old enough to not order from the little kid's menu—every single time we've been out to eat, she tries to get it. The only time she eats anything different is if whatever restaurant we went to doesn't have a grilled chicken sandwich with cheddar and bacon. She even abbreviates it as CBC (cheddar, bacon, chicken).

Michelle got a giant steak, way too much for any normal human to eat in one sitting. She always does that when we go out—orders huge and brings at least half of it home for tomorrow.

"Oh, I forgot to tell you." Ashley wags her eyebrows at us over her sandwich. "Mom's out on a date tonight."

"Whoa, really?" asks Michelle.

"Yeah. Someone from her work. She didn't tell me much about him yet."

"Nice." I smile. "Think it'll work out?"

Ashley shrugs. "No idea. I haven't even seen the guy. Never thought she'd bother with dating again after Dad left."

"Sorry." Michelle gives her a pitying look.

If I see Mr. Carter again, I might break my rule and mind control him to do something embarrassing at the Boeing holiday party. The guy up and left them, deciding he simply didn't want to be married anymore or deal with the responsibility of having a daughter. Weird thing is, he didn't cheat. The guy probably has some kind of mental condition where he can't process emotions properly and lacks any understanding of the effect his leaving had on Ashley. He's an engineer, one of those guys who finds it fun to sit in a lab for fourteen hours in a row. Mrs. Carter once joked that she did lose him to another lover: work.

Meh. I guess it's not really his fault how his brain is wired. Funny how nature operates sometimes. How can a man with the emotional range of a Vulcan have a daughter like Ashley, who has *all* the emotions? It makes sense how he became frustrated though, even if it had been his fault. I remember being over their house as a younger kid and watching Mr. Carter try to talk to Ash like a tiny adult or becoming all awkward whenever she hugged him or tried to seek any sort of affection from him. He always made this 'why is she touching me' sort of face and hunched up his shoulders like someone spilled something cold on his shirt.

Some people just aren't cut out for being parents. Still, it could have been *way* worse. He never forgot her in a hot car, for example. Or hit her, or did anything to actively make her life worse beyond lacking any ability to express love. Never told Ashley this, but my internal nickname for her father is 'the crash test dummy.' They have about the same personality, two steps less lifelike than that android guy who owns Facebook.

"It's fine." Ashley makes a face at her dinner. "I still get to see my father once a year when Boeing has their Christmas party. It's so bizarre. He treats me like someone he used to work with, not his kid."

"Aww," says Michelle.

Ashley shoves 'stop hand' in my face. "I finished crying over him years ago. Now, I'm just annoyed. His loss."

"You gonna ask Sarah to sniff your mom's new guy out?" Michelle grins and slices off a bit of steak. "Gotta be sure, right?"

I so feel like an inventory item right now.

"Dunno. Maybe." Ashley shifts her eyes toward me. "Depends on if Mom sees him more than once. But forget about it for now. Tonight is supposed to be fun."

"Fun." I smile. "Yeah, that's still a thing, right?"

Ashley sighs at me while Michelle laughs.

"Thanks, guys." I twirl pasta onto my fork. My relationship with food might be fake, but having this time with my friends is anything but. "Glad you could get away tonight, 'Chelle."

"Seriously." Ashley stares at her. "You're as bad as Mrs. Wright. What is it with lawyers and ridiculous hours?"

"I'm not a lawyer… yet." Michelle wags a forkful of mashed potato at her. "The hours are ridiculous until you make partner. Then the hours are ridiculous, but you make a ton of money."

We laugh.

"Finally finished sorting the records room." Michelle eats the potatoes from her fork and points the 'weapon' at me while she chews. "I swear if your sister summons more of those things…"

"She won't. At the time, she didn't know it could happen. Just a kid doing something spooky for Halloween. The imps surprised her, too."

We chat about the disastrous costume party as we eat, which segues into the topic of holidays in general. Ashley gets kinda quiet, but Michelle grumbles about having to go with her parents to New York for Thanksgiving next week and visit her mother's side of the family.

"Five days of near total boredom." Michelle rolls her eyes and proceeds to grumble about having no one on the east coast even close in age to her. Mostly, she'll be surrounded by aunts and uncles in their late thirties, all of whom have small kids, plus a bunch of old people. Since she doesn't count as a child anymore, she'll probably end up either watching the toddlers or sitting alone for hours each day.

Except for the meal itself, she expects Thanksgiving Day to stink, being trapped in a house full of men watching football. I can somewhat sympathize with that part of it. While neither of my parents care at all about sports, the grandfathers and my Uncle Ricky —Mom's little brother—adore watching games of all kinds.

For as long as I can remember, the living room television has always blared football all day long on turkey day and Christmas. Naturally, Sierra despises this tradition since it kept her off the PlayStation. Christmas is worse if she gets new games as presents and can't play them because the guys need their football. Last year, Sam surrendered his bedroom so she could play the new game on his system.

Hearing Michelle complain about being forced to spend time with her family makes me think about how close I'd come to losing mine. I kinda nod along with her, pretending agreement, no interest at all in starting a sappy argument about how she should value them while they remain alive. Not everyone has the same kind of relationship with their family that I do. Michelle has no siblings and her relationship with her parents is more strained than Bree Swanson trying to stuff her boobs into a corset. Knowing Michelle really would be happier on her own is sad. If the Universe had any sense of fair play, it would've been her who ended up as a vampire. She might have maintained contact with me and Ash, but definitely would've let her family believe her dead. To her, undeath would've been total freedom. Honestly, it is really surprising she hasn't asked me to do it to her.

Sure, my family situation hadn't been perfect before my death, but we'd been a lot closer than Michelle and her parents. Mostly, the strains I had involved my siblings and me being selfish and too much in a hurry to grow up. Except for Sophia. She's never been selfish or in a rush to be older. Fate has a weird sense of irony. Nothing like being murdered to turn me clingy.

"Hey, Sare?" asks Ashley.

"Hmm?" I mumble around a mouthful of pasta.

"I volunteered to pick up a dog from a vet place out of state. He's a surrender case. It's a bit of a ride so I wanted to ask if you'd go with me."

"Surrender case?" Michelle neatly aligns a mushroom on her steak before cutting a piece off.

Ashley nods. "Yeah. The original owners couldn't afford the medical bills, so they surrendered him to a vet place in Portland. Someone here wants to adopt and is willing to cover the cost of the remaining surgery, so they're sending the dog to us. Normally, the adopter would go pick the animal up, but Hershey still needs surgery, so he's gotta go straight to the hospital."

"Hershey? Doesn't chocolate poison dogs?" I blink.

"Yeah. He's a chocolate lab." Ashley furrows her eyebrows. "Anyone who names a chocolate lab 'Hershey' needs to be slapped. Like, seriously, ten million other people haven't already thought that would be clever."

Michelle and I laugh.

"So, umm, you wanna go with me? I'm kinda scared to take the ride alone." Ashley smiles cheesily at me.

"Sure, if you can do it later in the day."

Her eyes widen. "Oh, crap. I forgot. Umm. I'll see what I can do."

"You're not gonna fly?" Michelle swirls her last mouthful of soda around her glass, then knocks it back.

"No. Remember the part about volunteering? If I flew down there to collect the dog, I'd be paying for the airfare myself. On short notice, the tickets are super expensive." Ashley sighs. "But, they're going to consider the time I'm on the road as being at work and pay me for it."

"That's cool of them." Michelle stares at her meal with a face like she's deciding if she should stop now or eat another bite or two.

I pull out my phone and check maps. "About three hours each way."

"Four, the way she drives," deadpans Michelle.

Ashley raspberries her.

"Well, if we leave around four, we should be back by eleven or so. Not impossible," I say. "Are you thinking of doing it on a weekend?"

"Ash is always thinking of doing it," deadpans Michelle.

I throw a napkin at her. "Taking the ride, dork."

Ashley laughs. "Yeah. Hershey's not quite ready for a trip yet. He's still recovering from the first surgery. But, I have classes, too. So they're okay with me going down there to pick him up on the weekend."

"What's wrong with the poor guy?" asks Michelle.

"He got clipped by a car and suffered a diaphragmatic hernia. He had major surgery already and still needs work on his back leg."

"Aww, poor little guy." Michelle frowns.

"Eek," I mutter.

"They say he's happy, like he already knows there's someone who's going to give him a good home." Ashley beams. "So, we just need to go there, pick him up, and bring him to my clinic. They should be okay with a ride later in the day."

"Great," I say.

"Adulting sucks," grumbles Michelle.

"Totally." Ashley whistles.

They spend a few minutes complaining about having to work jobs while going to school, leaving little time for hanging out together like we used to. We start reminiscing about 'the good old days,' namely like sixth grade when our biggest worry was teachers taking away our Silly Bandz or if the boys we secretly liked even noticed us. Ashley shocks us with a confession about making out with Melanie Francis in the latter half of eighth grade—*at* school.

"Wow," says Michelle. "You got the popular cheerleader."

Ashley snort-laughs. "Yeah for an hour. We only kissed. And she wasn't very popular then, not like she was for junior and senior year."

"Never realized Melanie's into girls. Isn't she still dating Keith what's-his-name?" I ask. "The baseball player?"

"I think so." Ashley shrugs. "At the time, she was curious what it would be like to kiss another girl. Pretty sure she liked it, but she's terrified of her parents. Honestly, I think she's bi but won't admit it to herself. I feel sorry for her. She's stuck trying to be what everyone wants her to be, and not who she is."

That's Ashley, feeling sad over some girl she kissed in grade school and barely looked at twice since.

"Sucks," I mutter.

"Yeah." Michelle prods Ashley's arm. "You should call her."

"Oh, no way. We haven't talked since then. And I'm not pining for her or anything. Just feel bad she's scared to come out. Neither one of us really understood anything about anything back then. And, yanno, maybe she really was just exploring and isn't really bi."

"Back then," says Michelle with a bit of a chuckle.

I laugh. "We fail at teenaging."

"Huh?" Michelle peers over her fork at me. "What?"

"We're not supposed to be feeling nostalgic until we're past thirty. When was the last time you had an argument with your parents over something stupid like not picking up clothes?"

Michelle sits up straighter. "We—my parents and I—have different opinions as to what constitutes a stupid reason for an argument."

"I don't really argue with Mom that much," says Ashley, staring into her empty plate.

"You're a goody two-shoes." Michelle winks at her, clearly trying to cheer her up.

"Not as much as Sarah." Ash points at me. "Your secret identity, Follows Rules Girl, is exposed."

"Pot. Kettle." Michelle shakes her head. "At least she doesn't feel guilty for days whenever she argues with her parents."

Ashley sticks her tongue out.

"I kinda do now," I say in a distant voice. "Or I would if we argued. Haven't really clashed with them even once since, you know. Came too damn close."

"You both fail at being teenagers." Ashley gestures at Michelle. "You're already a lawyer and Sarah's like some old wise woman with the insight of the immortals."

"At least I'm not stuck being twelve," mutters Michelle.

Ashley and I exchange a glance, unsure who she meant.

"I don't look like I'm twelve," I grumble.

"You ain't far from it." Michelle laughs. "But I meant Miss Raspberry there. She keeps showing me her tongue."

"I'm not going to make a joke out of that. Even though you walked right into it." I wag my eyebrows at her.

Ashley goes scarlet in the face. "I don't act like I'm twelve."

"Oh?" Michelle leans closer. "*How* many unicorns do you have in your *pink* bedroom?"

"But they're cute!" squeals Ashley, totally sounding like a tween— which I'm sure she did on purpose. "Collecting unicorn stuff doesn't make me twelve."

"No, having a frilly pink bed covered in stuffed animals does," says Michelle, her expression barely managing to stay fake serious. She glances at me. "Right? Too much rainbow unicorn pink. She's still twelve."

I shrug. "My mother collects little figurines. So do both of my grandmothers. Some women just get this strange urge to accumulate things. So, Ash likes unicorns."

"You're both nerds." Michelle grins.

"Hey, it could be worse," says Ashley. "We could be flipping burgers or delivering pizza."

I toss my napkin at her, nailing her right in the face.

Ashley pulls it down, blinking at me. "What?"

"I *have* delivered pizza." My turn to stick out my tongue—you know, since we're being totally mature tonight.

"Really?" Ashley stares. "When?"

"Wow, no kidding? I thought you were too good for a job." Michelle makes goofy eyes at me.

"Hardly." I smirk, making her laugh. "So, yeah, delivered by air. Made a decent amount of money. Not too long ago." I explain bribing Blix with a video game to exact revenge on Mr. Neidermayer for calling the cops on the Littles.

Ashley gets a bad case of the giggles. "Oh, wow. You know, somewhere, there's an ancient and fearsome elder spinning over in his tomb over you using your powers to deliver pizza."

Jordan returns, asking if we want any dessert or coffee. Despite being immune to calories, I'm stuffed. Ashley has a lucky combination of metabolism that largely lets her get away with eating whatever she wants, plus she doesn't really care too much if she puts on a little weight. Considering she never seems to actually put on weight, she might only be claiming not to care, but who knows. She drove quite a few other girls in our high school crazy since she's so blasé about her eating and exercise habits yet looks fine. Michelle, however, is militant about managing her weight. For her, it's all about having a professional appearance. If her father didn't have fitness equipment in the house, she'd no doubt cram gym time into her already hectic schedule.

We all end up passing on dessert.

While waiting for the check, we discuss what to do with the rest of our Sunday night. Eventually, a decision is made: go full on nostalgic and 'act like kids,' staying up a little too late hanging out at Ashley's the way we used to 'in another lifetime' when we'd been twelve.

2

1001 USES FOR A VAMPIRE

V ampirism has a predictably negative effect on my ability to be a productive member of society.

Mostly, it takes the form of making the idea of a day job impossible. Even though I can tolerate sunlight in small doses, it's impractical for me to consider doing anything that would require frequent exposure to the angry fireball in the sky. Every other bloodline shuts completely down at sunrise, unable to even open their eyes unless something attacks them—and forget direct exposure to sunlight, no matter how overcast. Even Dalton, who is by most standards, a nice guy, begins smoking instantly on contact.

A clear, sunny summer day will also cause me to give off smoke, but it takes a minute—and hurts like hell. Gloomy days are uncomfortable like it's over a hundred degrees, but no real threat. Still, my limited tolerance for the annoying day star is wholly incompatible with a traditional job. As inglorious as delivering pizza was, I didn't mind it. The hours work for my 'condition,' and considering how fast I can fly back and forth, the money turned out to be surprisingly good. Helps it's mostly under the table. The pizza place didn't pay me much officially, and cash tips leave no paper trail.

Cue evil laugh.

Yeah, I'm Follows Rules Girl, but it doesn't bother me to cheat the IRS a little. Not like losing the hundred bucks they'd get from me is going to matter when huge companies get away with paying zero. Guess it's kind of Robin Hood of me to think that way.

Anyway, my not working leaves me a ton of time during which I'm home alone. Well, functionally alone. The family doesn't keep vampire hours, so I have the house to myself after about eleven every night. I also fail at vampire, since I'm the exact opposite of a social butterfly and don't care at all about social politics. Maybe my attitude will change in a couple decades, but for now, I'm content to pretend at being normal. For me, a nice cozy night at home is more fun than hanging out at nightclubs.

I have three major time kills for the periods when I'm the only one awake in the house: studying, video games, and housework. Most teenagers are probably not fond of helping out with chores. I've caught myself trying to avoid them again, which could mean my mind is recovering from the trauma of being killed. However, the drudgery of cleaning when I could be having fun isn't what bugs me. I can't help but think about sunny afternoons of summers past helping Mom clean windows, and those once-happy memories get me maudlin. Not so much for being undead, but for growing up. I'm not a tween anymore. Those moments I had with my mother are forever in the past. Also, she'd been much happier back then before the promotion. Her job wasn't anywhere near as demanding, even two years ago.

And dammit, yeah I am doing this teenager thing wrong. I'm not old enough to be nostalgic.

Once Michelle and Ashley zonked, I slipped out the window and flew home. Can't exactly sleep over when the sun might crisp me in the morning. Also, it wouldn't be fair of me to ask Ashley to put boards over her bedroom window. They'll understand why I'm not there in the morning. Besides, it'll be Monday soon and they'll both be so busy scrambling to wake up in time to get to class they probably won't notice me gone.

One good thing about this situation, though. Taking on more than my fair share of housework has unburdened Mom of it, which lessens her overall stress load. Considering I'm not working and basically freeloading off them at this point, I don't mind.

I'm caught up on my classwork, so I putter around the house from about half past one in the morning until the approach of sunrise. The only thing I can't do is run the vacuum or change bedding. One makes way too much noise for the middle of the night, and the other... well, it's difficult to change sheets when people are *in* the bed.

Klepto, Sophia's kitten, follows me around. Most cats jump to high places, but this one teleports. It's a really long story, but the short version is my sister *made* Klepto out of powdered mushroom from an alternate dimension. Yeah, did I mention my kid sister has magical talents? Supposedly, she always did, but the ability lay buried deep inside her out of reach... until a sect of mystics peeled her soul from her body temporarily. Yeah, their spell had unintended consequences.

The kitten perches here and there observing me with a demeanor way more human than cat. I bemusedly call her my 'supervisor,' which elicits no reaction really. Whether or not this magical kitten has intelligence beyond animal level, I can't tell. It could be me simply reading too much into her unnatural posture. She is, after all, *not* an ordinary cat.

Keeping myself busy, either by cleaning or playing video games, occupies my thoughts away from the approaching holidays. When sunrise nears and I retreat to my basement bedroom, those thoughts crash into me hard. No, I'm not an emotional wreck, but a few heavy sighs happen. Lying there staring at my ceiling while I wait for the sun to knock me out, my brain circles like a buzzard around the idea this will be the first Thanksgiving after my death, the first major holiday where I'm not alive.

Sure, July Fourth is a major holiday, but people don't usually invite extended family over for dinner on the Fourth. Maybe an outdoor barbecue, but it's not the same as Thanksgiving or Christmas.

No, I'm far from being depressed at not being alive. While I do kind of miss the ability to go out on bright days, that's a pretty minor thing compared to all the benefits like *flying* or staying young forever, or not having to worry about cancer, disease, and so on. Yeah, I'll never have kids of my own, but I hadn't yet reached a point in my life where I'd even thought about it one way or the other. Except for Ashley, how many eighteen-year-olds in the modern era have already made up their minds to have kids someday?

What happened, happened. No point being upset about it. Besides, I have the Littles. Looking after my siblings is pretty similar to being a mother without all the annoying parts. If my sibs exceed my ability to cope with them, I have Mom or Dad to hand the issue off to. Hopefully, my mindset also froze at eighteen, so some decades from now, I won't get hit with a sad bomb over being unable to have kids. There's always adoption, and sure, no one in their right mind would allow someone who looks as young as I do to adopt a kid, but that's what mind control is for.

Downside is, I'd watch any potential adoptee go from kid to adult to old person and die. Not sure I want to put myself through an emotional rollercoaster, suffering the grief of losing a kid I raised. It's going to be painful enough watching my siblings suffer the march of time. Honestly, being a vampire is cool as hell, but it definitely has some negatives. At least those flaws are mostly emotional and can be dealt with via copious amounts of Rocky Road ice cream.

My eyes snap open at 2:36 p.m. Monday afternoon is pleasantly gloomy.

Hmm. Maybe next year for Halloween, I should dress up as Wednesday Addams? I'm not a disciple of the rain, really. Dry gloom is better than wet gloom. I find bad weather nice now mostly due to the absence of sunlight. Makes it easier for me to pretend at being normal. After a quick shower in the basement mini-bathroom, I head upstairs and spend some time with Sierra on the PlayStation.

She's in a particularly sour mood due to some grown men harassing her. At first, she rolls her eyes and mutters 'whatever' into the chat. A few minutes after the match starts, she begins snappishly saying girls can play games, too. This goes on for a minute or two before she calls someone a loser. A murmur from the headset makes her cringe and blush.

Over the course of the next two minutes, she goes wide eyed, then looks confused, flinches, gasps, and makes a 'holy crap' face. Not long after, she falls alarmingly silent, glaring at the screen.

"You guys are totally getting your asses handed to you by an eleven-year-old," says Sierra into the voice chat.

Her tone is nowhere near as confrontational as it should have been delivering that line, which worries me. I think she said it mostly to tell someone her age, not taunt them. Probably because they're getting crude with her. Even with my powers offline due to the daylight, I can tell she's furious. Minutes later, when the match ends—her team won by a few kills—she emits a gasp, flings the headset off, and shuts the PS4 off.

For a few seconds, she sits there on the floor, shaking. Okay, maybe not furious. She looks worried and a little freaked out.

"Sierra?" I ask. "You okay?"

She scrambles up to sit beside me on the couch. "Some guy said he was gonna find and, umm... *do stuff* to me."

I gasp, grab her tight, and whisper, "What happened?"

"At first, a bunch of guys whined about having a little kid in the game with them. When I told them I wasn't a little kid, they said 'girls don't belong playing these games.'" She rolls her eyes. "They started with the 'go make me a sandwich' crap. Then, I started kicking their asses, so they taunted me with like sexual stuff. I said they're having their asses handed to them by an eleven-year-old. They stopped saying the nasty stuff and switched to telling me I'm only tough over the internet and they'd slap some respect into me when they found me for real."

"They're only a bunch of man-children talking tough. You know, maybe you should take a break from the game for a couple days. Or skip the chat."

"I guess." She frowns, still blushing. "People on there don't usually say that icky stuff, just bad words."

"What sort of icky stuff did they say?"

She scowls. "What they thought a girl *should* be doing with her hands... or mouth, instead of playing video games. Asking me how big my boobs were, what I had on, if my boyfriend left me because I play games... and a bunch of other things I didn't really understand. If Mom heard that stuff, she'd ground me off the PlayStation forever."

"What is wrong with people?!" I fume.

"It's okay." She rolls her eyes. "My little innocent mind isn't broken. Anyway, those idiots seriously don't know how to threaten people. As if I'd cut my own head off and give it to them."

"What?" I blink at her.

"Killgod97 kept saying I should give him head." She scrunches up her nose. "What the heck does he mean?"

It means I'm highly tempted to play with her memories. But, dammit. I'm not online yet. Maybe later, I will. "It means I'm not explaining it to you until you're at least fifteen."

She sighs, frustrated at being treated like a child. "What is *wrong* with people?"

We commiserate for a few minutes about idiots.

"Why don't you give CoD a break for a bit? Wanna play that fantasy game?"

Sierra manages a weak smile. "Okay."

We spend some time co-op playing this dungeon crawl adventure type game, fighting goblins, giant spiders, and other fantasy standards. It's cartoonish and a good antidote to realistic violence plus unwarranted verbal abuse.

It's getting dark earlier, so I go online about quarter to five right as Sophia and Megan—her friend from dance class—come downstairs. No sooner do they reach the living room than Sam runs in the back patio door and hurries upstairs to change for his Taekwondo class. Seeing him reminds Sierra she's decided to attend martial arts as well. When she looks up at me to say 'gotta go change,' I dive into her head.

And... holy crap! The things those two guys said to her make *me* blush. Grr. She doesn't understand the really nasty stuff—some of it goes over my head, too—but she does know the P word. Swear, if a way existed for me to find those guys, I'd slap the hell out of them for saying that kind of trash to my kid sister. I'm so pissed off it's taking me serious effort to avoid doing damage in her brain. By the time I break off contact, she thinks those idiots spent twenty minutes calling her a cheater and cursing her out. To avoid creating any feelings of dissonance with her being more upset than normal, she remembers an extreme amount of cursing from a pair of knuckle-draggers who believe 'girls shouldn't be playing games'.

Mom's still at work—shocking, I know—so Dad winds up taking Sam and Sierra to their martial arts class while I drive Sophia and Megan to the dance studio. It's moderately rainy, so I pull up to the curb to let the girls out near the door, but they still squeal as they hurry inside. What are they, witches afraid of melting if they get wet? We arrived a little early tonight—class starts at 5:15 p.m.—so I don't get stuck parking all the way in the back. Between the gloom and November, it's already dark at this hour. Yay for me. Despite my vast cosmic powers, nothing about being a vampire protects me from the rain, so I use a collapsible umbrella.

I've apparently been here often enough now that a few parents nod in greeting as I take a seat by the window. It's still a few minutes before the class starts, so most of the girls cluster together and talk. This usually involves a few friend groups, but today, they form a large mega-cluster. I'm sure the Nature Channel could do some kind of documentary about the migratory patterns of dance school students. The reason for the big group appears to be a new arrival, a tween girl who's as extroverted as Sophia is sweet. She's got too-perfect blonde hair, brown eyes, and a suntan that is in no way natural for Washington State in November. Her parents evidently bribed some greater power. This kid could be a model, if she isn't already. Though, considering she's going to *this* dance studio, I doubt her family's rich. Not only do my oversensitive eyes pick up a hint of brown roots, I can smell the bleach on her from here.

Her first night here, and she's already talking to the others like she's promoted herself to the top of the pecking order. Bleach-blonde and going to a tanning salon at twelve? Yeah, here's a kid who's going to peak in high school. I'd compare her to Bree Swanson, but this girl doesn't have air leaking from her ears. Ack. Bad combination. A superiority complex is dangerous enough when wielded by someone like Bree. An actual smart girl thinking she's queen of the world is a whole other level of problem. Fortunately, I doubt the kid goes to the same grade school as my sisters.

She'd totally pick on Sophia for being too sweet... and Sierra would end up breaking her nose.

For the most part, I avoided drama during my school years. Ashley and Michelle consider me a 'stealth nerd.' Meaning, they think I appear to be 'normal' while really being smart and into geeky type stuff. Somehow, I avoided falling into the crosshairs of any mean girls in our high school, just another invisible face in the crowd. Fine with me.

Neither of the two cougars are here, likely in Vegas by now. One has a granddaughter, an overly mature fourteen-year-old who *is* here, and the other's a friend. With nothing else to do, I study the faces of the parents around me trying to find the girl's mother. *Someone* had to bring her here since her grandmother's on vacation. Eventually, I spot her in the front row with her nose buried in a Kindle. Haven't seen her before, but she's got a strong resemblance to the daughter.

The teachers run the kids through some warm ups, then spend about fifteen minutes demonstrating a new technique involving partners. One kid will jump up and do this back arching pose while the other one supports them by the hips overhead for a brief, slow spin. It's got something to do with swans. Everyone watches two of the younger teachers demonstrate the move several times while explaining how to grip and support their partner's entire weight.

It's a little nerve-wracking, but the floor is nicely padded today.

For a while, they work with a mannequin as the 'jumper' to get the form down. Roughly half an hour into the one-hour class, the instructors have the kids pair off to attempt the maneuver for real.

The new girl, Lindsey, glances over at Sophia and Megan with a huge grin.

I wouldn't call Megan obese, but she's a little heavyset. Sophia is easily the skinniest girl in the class. Again, thanks for the wonderful genes, Dad. Lindsey whispers, elbowing her partner while gesturing at Sophia and Megan and muttering something about 'moose and squirrel.' The girl next to Lindsey stifles a laugh. Other kids around those two slow their practice to watch.

Sophia is the 'swan' at first, which predictably works out just fine. My kid sister floats like a pixie into the air, her weight barely noticeable for Megan who holds her aloft, spins around once, and lowers her back onto her feet.

Did I mention Soph *loves* dance class? She really throws 110% into it and she nailed the pose. If she'd been wearing a stage costume with faerie wings, she'd totally have appeared to be flying.

"Watch this," whispers Lindsey. "The fat girl is going to crush her."

Grr.

The next twenty seconds happen in slow motion for me.

Megan and Sophia circle each other as per the dance routine. I can practically see the debate going in my sister's eyes as to whether or not she should magically lighten Megan again. The last time she did, the poor girl floated like a helium balloon. She doesn't make up her mind before Megan jumps. And okay, I have to give it to her. For a big girl, she *can* jump. Sophia braces her hands on Megan's hips and tries. Oh, dear, she tries so hard.

But... Sophia is a twig.

A dawning look of horror widens my sister's bright blue eyes. She manages not to scream as Megan flattens her into the padded mats, Sophia's skinny legs sticking up on either side of her like something out of a Wile E. Coyote cartoon. Lindsey's laughter explodes over the mostly silent room while Megan's face not-so-gradually turns beet red.

"Excellent form, Tubby," calls Lindsey. "Don't feel bad, even Darian couldn't hold you up."

A few other girls near Lindsey sorta laugh. Most of the class stops in stunned silence, staring at her in shock for saying something so mean. Sophia flails like a hiker trapped under an avalanche. Her evident panic only makes Lindsey laugh even harder. Annoyed, I burrow into the new girl's thoughts, wondering what sort of damage she suffered at home. Maybe this is another Alexis situation. Seriously, do twelve-year-olds bleach their hair and go to tanning salons by their own choice?

Turns out... yes. At least in this case. The girl doesn't have an aggressive, pushy mother or even a bad home life. She's merely arrogant and self-important—just like her father. Ugh. As soon as Megan sits back on her heels, already crying, Sophia flies to her feet and zooms across the room to get in Lindsey's face.

Whoa. Like what the hell? This is like watching a little bunny rabbit roar.

"Shut up! Leave Meg alone. She's my friend and it's not right for you to be mean to her."

Whoa. I can count the number of times Sophia has shouted at someone on one hand. And three of them have been her screaming 'look out' as a helpful warning. When someone is mean to her, she's usually the hide under a desk and feel sad type. At the outburst, Megan stops crying and stares in awe.

"She squashed you like a bug," says Lindsey. "Your legs were sticking up like—"

Sophia shouts, "I said, stop picking on her! It's mean."

The whole class is stunned at seeing my sister get loud. Guess they know her fairly well. A few girls near Lindsey tug on her arm with a 'c'mon, forget it' sort of attitude.

Lindsey rolls her eyes and goes back to her partner. "Who thought it's a good idea to teach a whale to dance?"

Megan—and about half the girls plus some parents—gasp.

Snarling, Sophia hurls herself at Lindsey, but Darian—one of the two boys in the class—catches her before she makes contact. My sister would definitely get her butt kicked in a fight, but I'm tempted to think it would've been a better idea than holding her back. With her physical attack foiled, she's going to seethe for the rest of the night and probably do something magically nasty to Lindsey.

Two of the instructors run over to Lindsey, no doubt giving her a 'talking to' about conduct in class. Megan doesn't know if she should cry, sulk, or quit ballet entirely. She's leaning toward quitting, ashamed of her weight and for 'crushing' her friend. Megan has nothing to feel bad about. She jumped higher than several thinner kids.

Darian and Sophia try to cheer Megan up. He's thinking about offering to attempt the move with her, but isn't completely sure he's strong enough. While he wants to make her feel better, he's afraid if he fails to hold her up, it'll make the situation worse. For an eleven-year-old, Darian is quite muscular and athletic. I'm sure he could support an adult woman—were she skinny enough. Heck, he could support me even without me fly-cheating.

Alas, he chickens out and goes back to his partner.

Megan stares forlornly at Sophia, not wanting to even try again. They murmur back and forth while everyone else resumes working on the move. Sophia refuses to find a different partner and rambles about it being totally okay that some moves are too extreme for every dancer to pull off while taking all the blame on herself for being too weak.

Oh, hell with it.

I'm already in a tee and sweat pants. I kick my sneakers off and walk over to them. The girls look at me in bewildered awe.

"I got her." I smile.

Megan stares, fidgeting. Her expression is more terrified than a politician asked an unscripted question. "But you don't dance."

"The move doesn't look too hard. Been watching you all long enough." I take a position in front of Megan, mostly matching how the girls set up before the move.

Lindsey glances at us and snickers. "Tubby's gonna flatten that kid, too."

Her dance partner whispers, "Aww, don't worry about it. Leave her alone."

Little does the priss know, I could toss and catch Megan in the air like I'm making a pizza. Granted, I'm sure she wouldn't appreciate me doing so.

Sophia, quite aware I'm a lot stronger than I look, grins. "Go for it, Meg. You deserve to fly, too. It's super fun."

Darian gawks at me.

Yeah, so much for staying low-key, right?

While I might not have practiced this at all, having superhuman agility comes in handy sometimes. Like, now. I pull off the admittedly straightforward footwork for the 'base' position. Megan spins around me, doing a few fancy small jumps, then commits to the big one. I catch her at the hips, then raise her up over my head with all the visible effort as though I'm lifting a Styrofoam dummy. Sensing the confidence and stability of my grip, Megan loses her trepidation and arches her back into a graceful swan pose.

Sophia claps.

The distraction of watching me support Megan so easily causes Lindsey to falter. The girl she's presently holding up over her head falls on top of her, taking them both to the padded mat. More of the class laughs at their crash than when Megan flattened Sophia. Lindsey scowls, and seems about to flounce right out the door, but sits still, likely not wanting to worsen her embarrassment.

Megan grins from ear to ear as I finish the spin and set her gently on her feet. She stares up at me, caught halfway between wanting to cheer and cry.

"It's okay to be who you are. Magazines and Barbie dolls are unrealistic," I whisper. "You're beautiful already. And you're athletic enough to pull off every maneuver this class teaches."

"Yeah," adds Sophia. "It's really my fault for being too weak. I'm the one who really shouldn't be in this class." She pinches her noodle arm. "I couldn't even hold Lindsey up over my head."

"No way. You love it so much." Megan sniffles. "That girl's right. Who ever heard of a fat dancer?"

"There are a lot more dancers with meat on their bones than you'd think." Ms. Ramirez, the head instructor, runs over to us. "Wow... Sarah is it?"

"Yep."

"Your form was excellent. Where did you study?"

Darian continues staring at me, mouth agape.

"Umm. Here, I guess." I scratch the back of my head. "Just watching this class."

"Remarkable." Ms. Ramirez smiles. "Have you ever considered dancing? You are amazingly flexible for someone who doesn't practice at all."

I shrug. "I'm not really a fan of being in front of people."

"Dance isn't for showing off. The best dancers do it because they love it, not because they want to get famous or rich." Ms. Ramirez laughs. "There aren't too many wealthy dancers."

Sophia grins.

She and Megan do the move again with Sophia 'flying' this time.

The chip on Lindsey's shoulder for not instantly becoming queen of the class is big enough to see from outer space. I've found that if I stare at someone intently enough, they eventually sense it and look at me. When Lindsey makes eye contact, I implant a mental command to make her forget entirely about Megan. No matter what the girl does— she could trip, taking out the entire stage set and every kid on it in the middle of a recital—Lindsey won't be consciously aware Megan exists.

I also give Darian a poke of confidence, then since I have no intention of joining this class, suggest he work with her for this move. Sophia is unbothered, despite being close friends with Megan. They switch partners for the remainder of the period. Though his expression shows clear effort, Darian holds Megan up easily enough. Having another kid her age successfully do the maneuver bolsters her confidence.

Satisfied, I return to the parents' seating area and get a few back pats. I'm not sure if it's a good or bad thing Megan's mother isn't here to have seen what happened. She likely would have started shouting at Lindsey's mom—who, by the way, is mortified. The poor woman is the opposite of Lindsey and her father, being rather passive and non-confrontational.

Fortunately, the rest of class goes by without incident. At the end, Ms. Ramirez announces an upcoming fundraiser to generate money to help offset the cost of a recital the second week of December. The students will be asked to sell candy bars.

About two thirds of the kids cluster around Megan briefly once the instructors officially dismiss them. I choke up watching all the kids reassure her she belongs in dance class and think Lindsey was out of line. Like nothing at all happened, Lindsey approaches her mother, commenting about this class being 'passable' and the instructors seem to know what they're doing. Her complete indifference to Megan's existence comes off as arrogant to almost everyone.

Sophia and Megan run over to me.

"Sare," whispers Sophia. "Please change their minds so we don't have to sell candy. I don't wanna."

"Aww, it's fine." I pat her on the head. "I'll help you with it just like the Girl Scout cookies. Besides, Mom will take the order form to work and probably make twice your quota herself."

"That was awesome. Thanks, Sarah." Megan hugs me again.

"Starbucks?" asks Sophia with a huge smile.

Lindsey walks past us, not even looking in our direction.

"Such a bitch," whispers Sophia. "Lindsey is going to be a problem."

"Nah. I bet she'll ignore Meg entirely from now on, like she doesn't even exist."

Sophia laughs.

"What?" Megan blinks at me.

"Don't worry about it." Sophia tugs on her arm. "Sarah's right. Lindsey won't bother you anymore."

Heh. Yeah, somewhere there probably *is* an ancient vampire shaking his head at how I abuse my powers for such mundane things.

"Are you sure?" Megan fidgets. "She's going to want revenge."

"Not this time." I wag my eyebrows at Sophia so she gets the hint, then say, "Girls like her need to be in control. The Lindseys of the world look for easy prey. She was totally not ready for Soph to run up on her and shout like that."

When I stop to think about it, Sophia presented an unwinnable situation for Lindsey. She's so small and thin—and *so* sweet—if the girl had hit her, it would've turned the entire class completely against her.

"Heh. I still can't believe I really did that. I was *so* furious at her for making Meg cry." Sophia shivers. "It's stupid, but I'm scared now."

"Of what?" I ask.

"Saying anything to her. It's like I pushed the fear forward in time, yelled at Lindsey for being a butt, and *now* I'm feeling like I shouldn't say anything even though I already did."

I put an arm around the girls. "You're sticking up for your friend. C'mon."

We head over to the Starbucks, which is on the shorter spar of the L-shaped strip mall. Luckily, the stores on the way have enough of an awning we don't get wet from the continuing rain. After our three small hot cocoas are ready, we run to my car—I've inherited Dad's old Nissan Sentra. Sure it's ancient for a car, but it still feels cool to have one that's mine. It would probably feel *awesome* if I couldn't fly. Still, though, having a car is a major teenage goal, right? I shouldn't think less of it merely because I can get places faster without it.

The girls hop in the back seat and explode into chatter about the class, largely ignoring Lindsey and talking about how much fun they had 'flying.'

We're not quite all the way out of Woodinville when my rearview mirror lights up in flashing red and blue. What the hell? I definitely wasn't speeding. Didn't run a red light or stop sign. You know what sucks? Despite knowing I can mind control the cop to go away and leave me alone, the instant those lights go on so close behind me, my stomach does a backflip and tries to cram itself up into my throat. All I can think of is getting in trouble with my parents for receiving a traffic ticket.

As properly as possible, I signal and pull over. Seconds after the police car stops behind me, a bright light on the side door floods the interior of my car. Damn, that thing is strong. I'm afraid to look back lest my face ignite.

"What did you do?" whispers Sophia.

"No idea at all." I squint at the light in the mirror. "We weren't even going the speed limit. Maybe I've got a tail light out?"

"Are we in trouble?" asks Megan.

"I don't think so." My mind races for an explanation. This *could* be a fake cop up to no good. Maybe a horny cop seeing a young woman he wants to make a pass at. The car looks completely legit (full bar lights and marked) so if the cop is fake, it's gotta be a vampire or someone who stole a police car.

Crap. In an instant, I'm super anxious all over again about the LA vamps.

Via the side mirror, I watch the door open and a man in uniform hop out. His body language is somewhat casual, which relaxes me a bit. He ambles up to my door and taps on the window.

I roll it down and smile up at him, projecting as much innocence as I can past my irrational fear. "Is there a problem, officer?"

"Little young to be driving, hon?" asks the cop, Thompson according to his name tag. "What are you doing behind the wheel?"

"Bringing my kid sister and her friend home from dance class." I look him in the eye… and read his thoughts. Ugh. He is a real cop… and thinks I'm fourteen. Pulled me over because he thought he saw a child driving a car. "I'm eighteen."

He gives me a 'yeah right' face. "Can I see your paperwork?"

"Sure, hang on." I grab my license and registration from my bag, and fish the insurance card out of the glove compartment, handing them all over at once.

He studies the license, tilting it back and forth while thinking it's a damn good fake. "Are you sure you want to tell me this is real?"

"It is real. I know I look a little young, but I swear it's a legit license."

Officer Thompson still doesn't believe me. He's moved up to being annoyed at me for lying to him and rather than just take me home to my parents with a warning, now plans to drag me downtown as soon as the license fails to run. "Sit tight a moment."

"Yes, sir."

He walks back to his car.

I really ought to give him a compulsion to go eat a donut, but I don't. Damn my superhero alter ego. Follows Rules Girl won't let me have any fun.

We sit there for a frustratingly long time before Officer Thompson walks back. "I'm not sure how you managed it, but the license checks out."

"I really am eighteen, officer. Blame my genetics for giving me a young face."

"Wow, kid." Chuckling, he hands me back my paperwork. "You're going to get carded until you're forty."

"Yeah, probably. Lucky for me I don't drink." At least not alcohol.

"Well, I only stopped you because you appeared too young to be behind the wheel. Seems my mistake. You have a pleasant night and drive safe."

"Will do. Thanks."

Sophia and Megan exhale in relief at the same time.

I roll the window up and grip the wheel. Ugh. This is going to be my life for the rest of time. It won't be long before my lack of growing older makes my legit license look like a good fake ID. If my printed birthdate calls me thirty but I still look like I'm under eighteen, no cop in the world is going to believe their computer when it says the license is good. They'll think I'm my own daughter or something and I stole the license.

How messed up is that? I'm going to need a fake ID because the real one will be unbelievable. More likely, twenty or thirty years from now, it will simply be easier to avoid driving.

Ugh. I'd say first world problems, but this is even more trivial.

Whatever. I'll come up with something. Got a few decades before I need to mind control every single cop who wants to see ID.

3

THE ABSENT PROFESSOR
MONTGOMERY

Two surprising miracles occurred in my not-so-normal life.
Sierra didn't touch *Call of Duty* for two whole days, and I made it to the middle of the week without anything more alarming going on than Sophia encountering a surprise escaped frog. Only, I don't think it was much of a surprise considering it came out from under her bed. Klepto managed to steal it. Of course, the frog, being a live critter, decided not to stay put.

Wednesday afternoon, Sierra surrendered to her want to play CoD again. However, she changed her handle in the game and didn't speak over the chat system. Mom has an important case coming up she can't discuss with anyone not officially employed by Boeing, and even then, only with higher management. She has no trouble keeping confidentiality, but the long hours frustrate her. Apparently, they had to hit some specific milestone with preparation for the hearing before the Thanksgiving holiday. Dad took over dinner prep and some other stuff. Between him and me, Mom didn't *have* to do anything when she got home.

Speaking of Thanksgiving, it falls on Thursday of next week. My school is closed that day plus the following Friday. So, I get to miss philosophy for an entire week as well as half my computer science and intro calculus class time. Professor Heath has scheduled a fairly weighty test for us tomorrow but announced he would not be giving us any homework over the mini-break. The other two classes, I expect will cram a whole week's worth of work into next Wednesday.

Hopefully, Dr. Mercer and Professor Garcia aren't going to hit me over the head too bad tonight with the homework hammer, since I'll need to spend most of my time before class tomorrow studying for Heath's test. For his class, I actually have to study. Can't read his mind since he's a vampire. You know, the everyday sort of problem most college students have, a prof with an unreadable brain. And it's not like I make a habit of cheating, really. Though, shortcuts have been taken sometimes. When forced to choose between study time and stopping a pack of vampires from killing my little brother, I'm sorry, but the homework loses.

Dad asks me to take Sam and Sierra to Taekwondo since he intends to cook tonight. Sophia is torn between wanting to hang out with me and hating all the shouting there. She's kinda like Mom. Loud noises bug her. Unfortunately, the class runs from 5:30 p.m. to 6:30 p.m., which conflicts with my computer science class having a 6:00 p.m. start time. My annoying early class. Naturally, Dad responds to this crisis in his usual way.

No, not by tying a red necktie on like a Rambo headband. That's reserved for demon attacks.

He plans to order pizza upon their return.

Since it's November and dark before five, the irritation of my early class isn't so irritating at the moment. For once, pushing the clocks back an hour does something useful. Being 'online' before class means I can fly, skipping traffic as well as cops who think I'm too young to drive. Okay, it only happened once, but it's still annoying. Maybe I shouldn't get so upset about people mistaking my age. Like most people, I spent the first eighteen years of my life desperate to be older and gain some independence... but in a matter of a couple seconds one night back in June, the only thing I wanted was to stay with my family.

Pretty sure whatever decision resulted in me becoming an

Innocent vampire had already been made before I regained enough consciousness to think about how much I wanted to go home. For all my looking forward to independence, the first time something went wrong in my life, my first instinct was to run home to Mommy and Daddy. So, yeah, maybe I deserve to look young.

Could be worse.

I could be like an Old Guard or something and look like a walking corpse. Sure, they're nowhere near as grotesque as Shadows, but there's no way anyone is going to see an Old Guard and mistake them for being normal and alive—unless they want to be seen that way. Take Aurélie for example. She constantly uses up power on her appearance to be lifelike. Many do not, especially while in private or in the company of other vampires. Sophia took a picture of me when I'm 'sleeping,' and it's grim. My skin's pretty much grey and corpselike. Compared to being stuck like a walking mummy all the time, people mistaking me for a kid is getting off light.

And I end up sliding into a bad mood from wondering if going home to my family would even still have worked if my appearance had been ghastly. Mom and Dad can take a lot, but seeing me deathly pale with sunken cheeks, hollow eyes, and so on would have been rough on them. My mother still won't go near my room again when I'm sleeping, and not only because of the time she accidentally exposed me to sunlight and got a peek at my dark side. She doesn't want to see anything that reinforces the notion of my being undead.

Heck, I don't want to see it either and I'm me.

Am I making any sense at all? Bleh.

Since Sophia can't stay home alone at age ten, she's got no choice but to go with Dad to the Taekwondo place, even though she hates all the shouting there. She and Mom are both averse to loud noises to the point Sophia will reflexively whisper if trying to talk in a quiet room. I suppose that could also come from shyness, not wanting to draw attention to herself. Though, with the success of her last dance recital, she's started to ease back on being so self-conscious. Also, I suppose being caught eyeball deep in a huge fight with hundreds of imps helped her confidence, too.

Dad and the Littles leave at 5:30 p.m. I could delay more, but have no real reason to sit here alone. At most, I have fifteen minutes. Not enough time to do anything worthwhile and too much time to merely sit around waiting. The cold doesn't affect me anymore, but neither does dressing overly warm. I throw on a sweater mostly to appear normal, step into my sneakers, and leave the house only a few minutes after the rest of my family.

It's good cold doesn't bother me or I'd have to suit up like a motorcyclist for flying. Sure, my top speed is around 140 if I push it, which to some bikes is slow. However, I've got a much lower chance of wiping out in the sky. How silly is that? I'm a vampire and still too chicken to get on a motorcycle.

Guess Dad referring to them as 'organ donor machines' all the time has left a mental block.

⋙ ———————— ⋘

I ARRIVE AT SEATTLE CENTRAL COLLEGE ABOUT SIX MINUTES AFTER leaving home.

And yes, I'm still humming the song from *Frozen*. The one everyone either despises or adores. Only, in my case, the cold *used to* bother me. Going out the door early gives me plenty of time to get to the classroom. In no great hurry, I circle around in the air, waiting until there's no one on the roof of the Harvard Garage across the street from the school. While it wouldn't be a complete disaster if someone saw me fly in, I'd prefer not to start my night with memory alteration.

It helps me pretend to be normal after flying to school.

A small crowd of students gathers at the corner outside the parking deck, waiting for the light to let them cross Harvard Ave. I anonymously add myself to the back end of the crowd, following when they go like any other normal student. Most of them turn left as the crowd disperses, heading to the various campus buildings. Both of my classes tonight are in the Science and Math building, two blocks north from the parking deck. Howell Street is closed to traffic where it crosses the campus, so I don't need to worry about cars again.

Going to school at night still feels strange. That oddity is made worse by most other students being in their later twenties and older… all working adults squeezing college credits in after their day jobs. Not too many 'just out of high school' kids do the night school thing. In another lifetime, I'd have been in California now, attending USC far away from family and friends. Ashley's convinced homesickness would've dragged me back to Washington after one semester. Going to school a thousand miles away from home isn't as drastic as being murdered, but it's definitely a shock. She could be right. Still, I can't help but daydream about what things might have been like for me if I'd remained normal.

No point getting angry at Scott all over again. It's not unusual for a girl to rip their ex-boyfriend's head off during an argument, though I might have been a tad too literal in that regard. We merely had a normal argument after breaking up. He'd stabbed me in the heart so I'd burned his remains in a crashed Jeep. As far as I'm concerned, my response was reasonable, right? And, it's pretty final as far as F-you's go.

I had a long conversation with Coralie—the Oracle, the ghost I freed from the mystic's basement—about where spirits end up. Some of the stuff I'd read online said becoming a vampire destroys the soul, takes a person out of the cycle of reincarnation or whatever. Not sure I believe in that reincarnation stuff, anyway. But, Coralie said the soul-death thing isn't true. Vampires don't lose their souls at all. She cited me as proof. Were vamps soulless, no such thing as an Innocent could happen. Or at least not one like me. Our conversation about the nature of kindness and empathy being related to the existence of a soul would make for an amazing time in Professor Heath's philosophy class. Pity there's no possible way I could bring up vampires there. Sure, he'd be game for a one-on-one conversation, but philosophy is kinda like charades—much more fun with a bigger group. Wait, no, that's beer. Charades is only fun with beer.

Anyway, she thinks Scott is wherever he would've ended up had he simply died without ever becoming a half-vampire Scrap. Hopefully, the circumstances he grows up in during his next life won't produce such a jerk. Did I mention Coralie also thinks reincarnation is real? No idea why she's sticking around as a ghost if she could reincarnate. Maybe the wait times are brutal.

"Excuse me," says a relatively deep, silky voice while I'm trudging toward the school entrance.

I lift my gaze off the sidewalk to a black guy in a grey jacket not quite blocking my path. He's almost thirty, thin but muscular, and distractingly handsome. A short flat-top afro kinda makes him look like a budget *Blade*. Maybe his stunt double. He doesn't feel like a vampire, he's not holding any religious literature, and he looks friendly, so I stop and smile at him.

"Hi."

"I was wondering if you might be able to help me." He nods once in greeting and pulls a photo from his pocket a little bigger than a playing card. "I'm trying to locate a professor I once studied with. Been a while since I've seen him. Do you know Professor Montgomery?"

The name doesn't ring a bell, so I look at the picture—of Professor Heath. It has a strong dated quality, though he still wears the same style of shirts today. Mostly the hair makes me think early Seventies, maybe.

Nothing about this guy throws off any warning signs, but Heath is an Old Guard vampire, a little over 170 years old. From what he's told me, he's been teaching at colleges for a long time, relocating every couple decades to avoid anyone noticing he's an immortal. Maybe this guy knew him before he came to Seattle. It's plausible Heath called himself Montgomery in some other state. However, I'm suspicious regarding the motives of anyone would be trying to track him down here, especially a man who is clearly too young to have been alive when this photo was taken.

Something doesn't sit right with me about this guy.

I've never been a great liar, mostly due to an overdeveloped sense of guilt giving me a lousy poker face. Uncertainty forces me to at least try and play dumb. Maybe he'll take whatever my expression does to betray me as being upset over not being able to help him. And, I can manage things more by not technically lying.

"Sorry. I don't know a Professor Montgomery."

"Oh, no problem. I guess you wouldn't. Wow, I didn't think people did tours this late?"

I blink. "Tour?"

"Aren't you a high school kid checking SCC out before applying?" asks the man.

"No, I'm a freshman." I fake laugh. "Some people say I look young."

He chuckles. "Wow. Sorry. Thought you were a junior. Makes sense. No one tours a prospective campus at night." He salutes me with the photo and starts to walk past me.

I turn, keeping him in view. "Maybe I could ask around. Would this Montgomery guy know you?"

"He might. It's been a couple years since I had his class. Name's Damarco Miller." He offers a hand.

"Sarah Wright." I shake hands with him, staring into his eyes and— not reading his thoughts.

What the hell?

"Are you all right, Sarah?" asks Damarco, his eyebrows going up a little, conveying worry.

Geez, my astonishment at not being able to see into his thoughts must make me look like a scared kid. "Yeah. Just worried about being late to class."

"Of course. Sorry to take up your time." He smiles, offering a partial bow.

Handsome *and* polite, plus asking for Professor Heath with a potential old alias? Call me a pessimist but that proves he's up to something. Or maybe he's merely being nice to me because I'm a girl he thinks is young. I push a little harder on his thoughts, but find nothing more than a sensation like he has a metal shell encasing his brain. Never felt anything like this before. Inanimate objects give me no feedback at all, and as far as I know, hyper-realistic androids only exist in movies and books. He's not a vampire. One, he smells alive—

then again, so do I. Two, trying to read the mind of a vampire I'm not decades older than (at present, that is a grand total of zero vampires) feels more like running headfirst into a stone wall.

The encased brain thing he's got... I can feel energy flowing out of me and oozing around his mind bubble. It's squishy and awkward. Unpleasant even.

He's staring at me in an odd way, too. The look in his eyes doesn't imply he's about to hit on me. No, it's more like he thinks I'm cute but way too young. Not even getting a bad or dangerous vibe from the guy, merely a strange one. It's a real two plus two equals five moment. Damarco is *something* out of the ordinary, but exactly what, I have no idea. Oh, maybe he's a mystic from out of town. His interest in Professor Heath could be benign. I may be a newbie vampire, but I'm not an idiot. Without completely trusting anyone, it's foolish to give away secrets, especially important ones like Professor Heath's identity.

"I'll ask around a bit, but I only just started here and don't know many professors. The name Montgomery isn't familiar."

"All right. No problem." Damarco puts the photo back in his pocket, giving me a genuine smile. "Don't be late to class on my account."

I wave at him and jog the rest of the way to the Math and Science building.

My gut tells me Damarco Miller is more than he appears to be— and he's something weird.

And by weird, I mean supernatural.

Of course he is. This is *me* we're talking about. Ever since last June, I can't get involved with anything and not have *something* weird happen.

If I'd have known how strange my life would've become, I never would've led Scott away from the party alone into the woods so he could murder me in a fit of entitled rage where no one would see us.

Seriously bad decision making on my part.

Still though, becoming a vampire *is* cool. Can't say I'd have volunteered for it, but it happened. I'm more than dealing with it, I'm kinda loving it. Almost. The only real downside is all the strange crap constantly happening to my family and friends.

I pause at the door, peering down the street at Damarco flashing the picture of Heath at another student, a guy in his later forties. Damn. He's eventually going to find someone who has no reason to keep the prof's identity secret. Question being, *why* does the guy want to find him? For all I know, his intentions could be harmless.

Can't shake the feeling that whatever happens, it's going to be weird.

Hopefully, this time, I can at least keep the tornado of paranormal poop from splattering all over my family.

4

WEIRD

My classes went more or less as I expected tonight—dropped a ton of homework on me.

There's a saying about nature abhorring a vacuum. It has a little-known-of corollary: teachers abhor a vacuum, of work. It's like they can sense I'm all caught up so they make sure to hammer us. I've got Heath's test to study for tomorrow night and the homework they gave out tonight is due Friday. At least I know there won't be any homework from Heath tomorrow, so I should be able to finish this all Thursday night after the big test.

Tonight, I need to study.

After seeing Hunter for a date.

I do run over to Professor Heath's classroom in the main building, but he's not there and he's also not in his office. Can't say it's unusual since I'd never gone looking for him on a Wednesday night. Meh. I'll see him tomorrow and can mention Damarco to him then. I mentally grumble about the homework load on the walk back to the parking garage. Even though my car isn't in it, jumping into the sky from an elevated roof reduces the chances of me being seen. Also, the walk gives me a chance to look around for Damarco. One whole orbit around the campus fails to find him. Looks like he gave up and left.

It is kinda weird to walk around outside showing a photo to students rather than checking the website or calling the school. That has to mean he knows the man he's looking for isn't using the same name anymore. Hmm. Could he be a cop? Detectives run around showing people photos. Nah, can't be. Professor Heath doesn't seem like the sort of man who'd do anything to rile up the police.

Maybe with all the crap going on lately, my anxiety about Damarco is purely in my head.

Right. That's gotta be it. Only, I'm sure it's not.

HUNTER TAKES ME OUT FOR DINNER... TO MCDONALD'S.

He waits tables at Mi Tierra restaurant, which is a surprisingly good Mexican place. The only reason I say 'surprising' is they don't charge too much for the quality of the food. You'd think that would be his choice for dinner out, employee discount and all. Maybe he's sick and tired of smelling Mexican food? Or maybe he feels awkward stepping across the employee/customer barrier and having someone he knows wait our table. Anyway, even with the discount they give him, fast food is cheaper. I don't mind, honestly. There's no justifiable reason for me to ask him to pay for expensive food I get no benefit from. It'll go right through me. Sure, there's the whole 'enjoy eating it' argument, but I can wait until he's not barely scraping by. Bad enough the guilt I have from being undead and potentially stealing his life away from a living woman who could give him a real family. He says he doesn't care about my living impairment, and I believe him. Yeah, mind reading comes in handy. Sure, he'd have preferred me alive, but living me never noticed him in high school. Hunter had it *bad* for me ever since ninth grade, but had been way too shy to try talking to me more than once.

Dammit. At eighteen, I shouldn't have this many regrets in my life.

Enough bad thoughts.

We get our food at the counter and take a booth near the window in the back, sitting on the same side.

Hunter looks up from his tray, an impish smile on his lips. He's ever so slightly hesitant to look at me still. "Sorry it's only Mickey D's."

"Don't be. It's cute." I grab the collar of his shirt and pull him into a quick kiss.

He grins, trying to open the paper on his burger as 'politely' as possible.

I pretend fluff at my hair. "No guy has ever taken me to a place this fancy before."

"Only the best." He holds up a ketchup packet. "Would you care for some organic tomato relish seasoned with *sel de mer?*"

"Of course." I take it and squeeze the ketchup out on my fries. "It's an absolute must when dining on *lances de pomme de terre.*"

Hunter fights to contain laughter. "They say the *petit steak* served on a toasted brioche with a *cornichon* garnish here is exquisite."

That's me done. I crack up laughing. Never has a hamburger with pickles sounded so extravagant.

"Are you sure you don't want to try the *crème de chocolat parfait?*" He wags his milkshake at me.

"Bit heavy for me. A girl's gotta watch her figure." I stuff fries into my mouth.

He laughs. Not sure if he finds it funny because I *can't* gain weight now or because before vampirism, my metabolism had been so fast my butt remained skinny regardless of what I ate. Granted, I never went crazy with food… just ate reasonable amounts of whatever.

Hunter holds the cup out for me. I smirk at him, but lean in to take a small sip. He squeezes the cup, squirting a little milkshake onto my nose. The side eye I give him makes him laugh again.

Argh! Being with him is so damn pure I want to explode.

I wipe my face, then he lets me take a normal sip of his milkshake. He's in such a happy mood it's infecting me telepathically. When I look up at him after dealing with the momentary brain freeze, he's got a pair of French fry fangs sticking out of his mouth. The ketchup on them is the perfect accent. One falls out when he makes a biting motion. That makes me snort-laugh.

We talk about random stuff while eating, mostly about where our lives are at school wise. He's busy but not overloaded with his classes. I grill him about how it feels to go to daytime school. It's surprisingly mundane to me. Then again, my daydreams of going to USC involved more hanging out and having fun than actual schoolwork, kinda like I'd been used to doing with Ashley and Michelle. In hindsight, I'm positive being in California without my friends would have resulted in a significant lack of fun and a whole lot of loneliness. Not being anything even close to a 'party girl,' it hadn't made any sense for me to think of going off to college as a vacation.

Would have been nice if the Universe could have used something more subtle than death to help me screw my head on straight. Like, I dunno, maybe start with a car coming too close and covering me in a tidal wave of rainwater. Or even a broken leg in a car accident. But no. The Universe had to go straight to death.

Sigh.

"You seem really happy," I say.

"I am. Having time to spend with you is the absolute best. Not getting anywhere near enough of that lately."

"You're busy with school and work and helping your mother fix up the house. I understand. School won't last forever and we'll have time."

"Yeah. Just need to be patient, but you are always on my mind." He dips his hamburger in a puddle of ketchup on the open paper wrapper, putting on a fake air of high society.

"I think about you all the time, too." A silent sigh slips out of my nose. I *do* think about him often… whenever I'm not worrying about what manner of paranormal oddity is going to sideswipe me the instant I let my guard down.

He puts an arm around me. "Ronan's been unbelievable lately."

"Uh oh."

"No, I mean he's happy. Like, normal happy. Never thought I'd see that."

"Aww, nice." I smile. His little brother had been perpetually terrified of their abusive father. It took months, but sounds like he's finally accepted the bastard won't be back.

Hunter shakes his head, chuckling. "Even after the mess in Los Angeles. It's as if it didn't even happen for real. He talks about it like he'd seen the whole thing as a movie, not really lived it."

"Dalton and I may have had a little to do with it. We got rid of the scarier parts of those memories."

"Cool. Thanks. And thank you for helping out with Mom's interview."

I shrug one shoulder. "No problem. Least I could do. When does she start?"

"December first."

"Nice. Hope she'll be earning a bit more there."

Hunter nods. "Definitely. Not going to be rolling in money, but it's more than double what she was getting. Best part is she's actually going to be using her finance degree."

"Cool."

She'd been working for a smallish place as an executive assistant or something, or maybe data entry. Either way, I helped her get in the door at Starbucks Corporate. She'll be working with their accounting department. Amazing the effect using a vampire as a personal reference can have on the hiring process. Granted, I don't think their HR people were expecting a character reference to show up at their homes after dark.

Following our romantic dinner at a five-star restaurant—hey McDonald's is five stars to someone, somewhere, right?—we go to his house and make ourselves comfortable on his bed. He's got a smallish television in the room, but it's hooked up to cable. We put a movie on, kinda paying attention to it while cuddling. We're not doing anything more than cuddling because his mother is still awake, downstairs watching TV in the living room, and Ronan might still come wandering by.

'Beyond cuddling' is definitely on the menu for later—after everyone else is in bed.

It doesn't take long before we're paying more attention to each other than the movie. Hell with it. I throw a leg across, rolling to sit on top of him while peeling my sweater off. Despite both of us being dressed, we writhe against each other for a few minutes, kissing while our hands roam.

"My mom's still up," whispers Hunter. "She's going to look in here on her way to bed."

"It doesn't matter what she sees. It matters what she remembers." I wag my eyebrows at him.

He blinks. "Never even thought of that."

"Umm. I'm mostly kidding. I can hear when she walks up the stairs. She can't sneak up on me." I glance at the hallway. "But we should at least close the door."

Bad things happen inside me when I jump to my feet. A noise comes out of my gut more appropriate for a horror movie about Old Gods rising from the deepest, most forgotten pits of Antarctica. Apparently, fast food is even faster when inside a vampire.

"Umm." Wow, that's embarrassing. "Be right back."

"Okay."

I run down the hall to the bathroom. Normal food usually takes a couple hours before it wants out. Can't even blame grease since I've had greasier stuff than this and it's run the usual course. Must have been the bumpy ride on the bed. Ugh. Bad timing. If I've learned one thing about my new anatomy, it's never to make the internal plumbing wait. There is no waiting. Any vampire other than an Innocent who eats normal food is going to upchuck it within about ten minutes. Nothing they can do will hold it down.

In my case, it follows the usual plumbing, but the time varies. When it wants out, it's going to come out regardless of where I am, what I'm doing, or what I want. At most, I've got thirty seconds to react. Fortunately, the upstairs bathroom is empty.

Other than still smelling like whatever food it was, the process is remarkably the same as before.

Right in the middle of things, the mirror over the sink at my right glows blue. Ronan's head pops out of it, his blonde hair almost green in the magical glow. He looks left—right at me—and gasps.

Fortunately, the toilet is in the corner behind the sink cabinet, so he can only see me from the chest up.

"Sorry!" whispers Ronan, after turning his gaze away. He climbs headfirst out of the mirror and squats atop the sink like a capuchin monkey.

"Gah! You're as bad as Sam. What is it with little boys and personal space?"

"Really sorry I didn't look before jumping out. Something was chasing us."

"Us?" I blush a little harder, hoping to hell and back Sam isn't about to emerge from the mirror next.

Ronan shifts to sit on the sink edge, then drops to stand on the floor, his back to me. "The monster didn't look scary at all, but Blix freaked out."

"What was it?"

"A giant black puffball with teeny wings. An old lady with a walker could've run faster than it."

I cringe. "Umm, yeah. Stay away from that thing."

"Seriously?" Ronan almost turns to gawk at me, but catches himself before looking.

"Yes. If you touch one hair, it could kill you. You know the inverse law of monster speed, right? The slower a creature is, the more deadly."

"Never heard that before."

"Not surprising, since I just made it up. It makes sense in there." I gesture at the mirror. "Please trust me."

"Okay. Sorry again. Hey, are you eating McDonald's in here?"

"Ro?"

"Yeah?"

"Look at me a sec?"

He timidly turns his head around. The second we establish eye contact, he forgets smelling food in here. Some things are just too embarrassing to explain. Since he didn't see anything more mortifying than my bare knees past the sink, and I warned him to avoid Fuzzydoom, I let him remember seeing me.

"Sorry again. Please don't tell my mom I stayed out this late."

"I'm Switzerland."

"Huh?" He pauses at the door.

"Neutral party."

"Oh. Thanks! You're awesome." He dashes off down the hall.

I'm about to yell at him for leaving the door open, but he runs back and shuts it for me.

Blix sticks his head out of the mirror, floppy ears drooping. He rambles at me in his indecipherable language. Based on his expression, he's probably saying sorry.

"No problem."

The imp waves and retreats into the mirror, which flickers bright blue for an instant, then goes back to being a normal silver surface. Nothing unusual going on here, merely Ronan taking a shortcut home past his bedtime via the mirrorverse.

Wow. Just think… I used to consider the sight of Sierra wearing a dress to be what counts as 'extremely weird.'

5

HUNTER HUNTED

Mom's in serious need of a vacation.

It's Thursday and she's stuck late at work yet again. I swear, once this case is over, if she doesn't decide to take a week off to decompress... she's going to decide to take a week off. Once again, I bring Sophia to her dance studio. My philosophy class starts at eight, so I've got plenty of time. No big deal since studying for the test tonight can happen pretty much anywhere.

I don't pay much attention to the class, but the whole hour goes by without any screaming, bursting into tears, or any fistfights that abruptly turn into a full-on musical number. Ugh. Can you tell Sophia's been watching a lot of Disney movies lately? I must be absorbing the soundtracks in my sleep.

Don't tell Mom, but I flew Sophia to class.

Sure, it's awesome having a car to myself, but more and more, being stuck on the ground feels like a handicap. Gotta take advantage of wintertime darkness while it's here, right? Surprisingly, my scaredy-cat sister is completely cool with flying. A girl who can scare the crap out of herself with her own coat somehow has no worries about heights. Go figure. How does a coat scare her? Simple. She hung it up, forgot about it, and screamed at the shadow it made against her window when she saw it later, thinking someone had snuck into her room.

I'm actually more worried about Sierra. If someone *did* break into her room, the girl would try to punch him. Then again, maybe not. She's wound so tight over those shooter drills at her school who knows what she'd do. Our parents still haven't given in to her continued requests for a real sword, though Sierra is making some headway in convincing them to let her take lessons.

Dance class ends at six. We get home in time for dinner and I join the family at the table entirely out of a desire to pretend we're still a normal family. Mom looks halfway between wanting to strangle someone and a zombie. Second 'don't tell Mom' for the night—I prod her to get some sleep. Otherwise, she'd stay up late staring at work stuff. She is amazing at her job, but everyone screws up when sleep deprived. Three hours on a clear mind is better than eight in a fog.

Dinner is *painfully* normal. The only part of it that feels different from before is the lack of arguing among the Littles. Okay, not technically true. Sophia didn't usually participate in the arguing. She mostly yelled at the rest of us to stop. Sam drags Sierra into a debate about a character build for a video game they're both into. He stays entirely calm while she becomes progressively louder and screamier, insisting she knows how the game works and he's got it wrong.

Right at the point she's close to shrieking at him, he says, "You're right. I was saying it wrong on purpose."

"Why?" rasps Sierra, staring at him in complete disbelief.

"I wanted to see if you'd question yourself. Dad said you can make someone doubt the truth if you lie and act like the other person is an idiot for not believing you."

Sierra snarls.

Mom gives Dad side eye.

"It's true," mutters Dad.

Sam looks up from his plate, smiling. "You knew you were right and didn't doubt yourself."

"You are *such* a dork." Sierra huffs.

Dad and I deal with the dishes after dinner. He and Mom head to the living room to watch TV while the Littles go upstairs for homework or personal electronics. Time for me to go to school. Talk about another thing that makes me thrilled the Wheel of Vampire came up on Innocent for me. If I'd turned out as any other type, no way would my butt be even trying to fake normality.

On the flight to Seattle Central, I argue with myself about the whole higher education thing. Vampires don't need careers, or even jobs. Mind control powers solve a lot of problems, except for the icky feeling it gives me to steal. Honestly, we have no need to buy food. Rent isn't an issue, though years from now when my parents are gone, property taxes will be. It's probably easier to just pay it than try to magic my way out of it. Even the powers of an immortal vampire pale to the evil that is governmental bureaucracy.

So, some manner of income will be necessary. Don't need a college degree to deliver pizzas. Or I could do for myself what I did for Hunter's mom. Compel someone to give me a job with hours compatible with my continued existence. How did old-time vampires do it? They all seem incredibly wealthy. Like Aurélie, or Arthur Wolent. Both of them have tons of cash. She pays more in a month for rent on her place than the majority of working people earn in a month. Well, I suspect Aurélie married her way—multiple times—into money. She's got so much the interest is basically an extravagant salary. Can't fault her for how she got it. Considering the era she came from, marrying rich guys is what she believes to be normal.

No, she didn't murder anyone. Merely outlived them.

As for Wolent? I heard some rumors he has connections to like Raytheon or some defense contractor. Distant connections anyway. Maybe stocks, or something cryptic like owning a company owning other companies. Bleh. Don't know, don't care.

I stop for a quick bite a few blocks from school, ambushing an expensively dressed woman as she's about to get in a black BMW. She's got one of those little rat-dogs (my dad's term for them) in the back seat. Not sure what the breed is, but it's smaller than most cats. The dog snarls at me as I bite the blonde woman—anyone walking by on the sidewalk would think we're making out. As soon as I make eye contact with the dog, it stops growling and wags its tail at me.

The whole few minutes I slurp down strawberry shortcake flavored blood, the dog lets me skritch it under the chin. Deep inside her brain, I bet this woman is calling her pet a traitor.

"Good dog. You know I'm not going to hurt your mama, right?"

It yips happily.

Feeding done, I blank myself out of the woman's mind and add a little prod to give the dog a treat when they get home. This spot is close enough to the school that I decide to walk rather than worry about finding a stealthy landing spot in a few blocks.

When I reach Harvard Ave, I spot Damarco wandering around among students, showing the photo of Heath while doing the 'have you seen this man?' thing again. I still can't see into his head. Grr. This isn't normal.

I enter the building with the intention to tell Professor Heath about him right away, rushing down the hall to the stairs and into the basement-level classroom. The sight of a TA standing behind the professor's desk almost makes me scream in frustration. The twenty-something teacher's assistant is wearing a pea-soup-green sweater and brown corduroy pants. Oh wow, he's doing the beard and man-bun thing, too. Dude looks like he doesn't want to touch the test papers before confirming the pulp was ethically sourced.

Okay, now I'm seriously worrying. Strange guy outside looking for him plus Heath pulls a disappearing act?

Okay, Sarah, reality check. I've been a vampire for five months. Heath has been at it for decades. Why would I assume he isn't aware of this guy looking for him? The dude's mind is closed off to me, so he's clearly *something* supernatural. Not only has the professor been a vampire way longer than me, he's also a professor. That means he's smart. Well, probably.

I decide not to worry about it for the time being and deal with the more immediate crisis: the philosophy test. At least I didn't forget my earbuds.

GETTING THROUGH THE TEST REQUIRES I POKE THE TEACHER'S assistant in the brain.

Not to cheat, merely to make him ignore me wearing headphones. Apparently, the school is afraid someone might pull some *Real Genius* type stuff where students use personal electronics to get answers from an outside helper. Nope. Not me. Just music to drown out all the little irritating concentration destroyers normal human ears can't pick up.

All the studying I did pays off. The test doesn't exactly feel *easy* but it's not grueling.

I finish by 9:32 p.m. and head up to hand in my paperwork.

"Thanks. Have a nice holiday," says the TA.

"You too." I take a step past him, then pause. "Oh, do you know where Professor Heath went? I needed to ask him something."

The guy shrugs. "He didn't say. I'm not even sure how I ended up covering this period."

"How could that confuse you?" I blink.

A few students still taking the test 'shh' us.

"Because," whispers the TA. "I'm from the psychology department."

"Oh." I nod at him as if it somehow makes perfect sense, then head out.

Checking Professor Heath's office area gets me nowhere. Guess he really did go somewhere.

Upon leaving the building via the 'Harvard A entrance,' I spot Damarco hiding against the wall of the former church across the street. He's almost directly in front of me in such thick shadow it's doubtful a non-vampire would see him... so I pretend not to have noticed him, turn left, and walk in the direction of the parking garage.

If Heath did leave town, it's obvious Damarco didn't get the memo. I'm ready to walk away and trust older vampires than me can handle things, but something about the guy hawk-eyeing the building gets me curious. Given all the Eighties movies Dad makes us watch, you'd think I'd know better than to be the nosy kid... but dammit, I'm curious. Can I really expect the Universe to throw me right into a *Scooby-Doo* plot and walk away from it? Of course, with my luck, I'll peel Damarco's mask off and find a bloody skull. Whoops. Real face.

Anyway, I'm sure he's… *something.* Ordinary humans don't have shields around their brains.

Once I'm safely alone atop the Harvard Garage, I leap into the air, fly over the Lenawee apartment building plus three other smaller houses, and glide in to land atop the former church. Its roof is canted downward at an annoyingly steep angle. Fortunately, there's a tiny ledge that looks like a slice of medieval castle tower on the southeast corner of the building—like directly above the guy. I peer over the lip of the brick wall down at him.

Damarco stands there observing people exiting the school. In an effort *not* to be an idiot, I mute my phone so it doesn't ring and give me away, then send a few text messages, letting my parents and Hunter know not to worry about my delayed return. Naturally, saying 'following suspicious guy, don't know what to think of him' doesn't go over well with my mother.

Mom: ‹Leave it to the police and come home.›

Dad: ‹LOL›.

‹No, Mom. This is a v problem.›

Dad: ‹Weren't you just at the doctor's?›

The final evolution of Dad: Making me blush over 4G. I can just picture him laughing while Mom hits him with a pillow. I'd say something like 'not that v,' but my father isn't confused. He's mortifying me on purpose by remote.

‹B home soon.›

Dad: ‹Wear a headband.›

I almost laugh out loud, nearly defeating the point of muting the phone.

A minute later, Hunter sends me a quick ‹@ work› text. Oh, yeah, it's not quite ten.

I sit there watching Damarco watch students for a while, having an intermittent text conversation with Hunter about random things. Right as I start to feel foolish for wasting my night sitting on the roof of a de-sanctified church, a glint of moonlight flashes at his back. That's weird.

Careful not to make a noise, I lean out a little farther to look straight down at him. The guy's concealing a small, modern crossbow behind his back. What the hell? It's not loaded with a stake, but the arrow does look kinda thick… and red. Oh, shit. Is this guy a vampire hunter? That wouldn't explain his impenetrable mind, would it? He's no Shaolin monk. Could he be a mystic? Nah. I didn't have any trouble reading Darren Anderson's mind.

Hmm. Maybe this guy is from another order with different spells?

My thoughts jump back to the spirit Sophia accidentally released from a giant jar. Okay, maybe not an accident as much as naivety and overdeveloped empathy. Anyway, the spirit thing zoomed to London to seek revenge. Is it possible they sent Damarco here to… no. That doesn't make any sense. Nothing about ancient British ghosts would have connected to Professor Heath or my school.

I can't see much detail about what he's got loaded in the crossbow, but it can't be good. Normal people don't lurk in the shadows with a crossbow behind their back. Maybe he's got a perfectly reasonable explanation for it, but I'm hesitant to confront him directly. If this guy *is* a vampire hunter, he looked me right in the eye and didn't even flinch. Guess they don't have vamp-dar or whatever. Could be, he's as new at killing us as I am at being one. Speaking of which… if this guy is here to *kill* Professor Heath, does it mean I'm supposed kill him before he can hurt anyone? It *has* to still be wrong to kill people, even if they are willing to murder me without a second thought. Admittedly, I'm jumping a bit to conclusions about him being a hunter. Asking about a vampire using a wrong name and a photo from forty years ago while concealing a crossbow behind his back doesn't prove he's a vampire hunter.

But it's *really* damn suspicious.

Damarco seemed so nice and friendly, though. I can't attack him.

Ironic the 'monster' is more hesitant to kill than a human.

Dammit. Now I'm torn. If I tell Professor Heath this guy is looking for him, it could easily lead to the old man twisting Damarco's head off. In that case, how much of his killing would be my fault? Or, Heath could pick up and relocate. That would suck, too—though not as bad as a dude being killed. I like the old guy and it's nice having a kindly old vampire mentor here at school, a teacher who *understands* what I'm going through.

Things are starting to make sense. This guy doesn't realize Heath lives in the school building, so he's waiting for the prof to emerge or arrive. Maybe he plans to follow him home, or—more likely—will simply shoot him as soon as he appears. Having the crossbow out doesn't necessarily prove he intends to use it right away. Damarco doesn't look like an idiot. He's probably intending to at least tail Heath somewhere less out in the open. Unless, of course, he knows vampires—well some of us anyway—can fly.

Great. A vampire hunter, or so I assume. He looks a lot more competent than the last batch I ran into. Really, they aren't too much of a problem for me. It's extremely easy for me to blend into normal life. Innocents are rare enough it's doubtful hunters know about our ability to withstand weak sunlight. Watching me go out in daylight could very well erase suspicion. I could easily ignore this entire situation and be free of fallout.

Naturally, I don't.

Ignore it, that is.

A little after eleven, Damarco grumbles to himself. Sounds like he's giving up. He takes the fat bolt off his crossbow and replaces it with a bright lime green aluminum one, which he fires into the dirt at his feet, most likely to release the tension on the bow. After collapsing the arms flat to the sides, he tucks the weapon under his jacket, plucks the green bolt out of the ground, and checks something in the tree.

Glim showed me how to zoom in with my eyes—it's how he watches his ex-wife's TV from across the parking lot. I home in on the object, which appears to be a tiny GoPro type camera pointed at the door. Looks like he's tired of standing there and wants to let technology do the boring part.

Apparently satisfied with the camera, Damarco looks around, then smoothly walks out onto the sidewalk, trying to pretend he hadn't been standing there like a creep for the past three hours. I glide up into the air, not terribly happy with wearing white sneakers. My top and jeans are reasonably dark at least. Still, few people ever look upward unless there's a flash or noise. From the air, I follow him as he walks a few blocks over and gets into a small grey Toyota.

I follow him at sufficient altitude to avoid being seen, easily keeping up with his car. Maybe I could get a job as a police helicopter? Just give me one of those million-candlepower flashlights. He drives south for a while, eventually coming to a stop at a six-story hotel in the northern part of Beacon Hill. There's a Sheraton less than a mile from the school, but that place is probably super expensive since it's right in Downtown Seattle. This place doesn't look shoddy, but it's no five star. However, something about the building sends a chill through me the instant I look at it. It's the sort of feeling scary enough I'd have avoided going near the place without a good reason before the whole vampire thing happened.

Okay, it's just a creepy building. I'm already dead. No reason to be afraid of scary places. Maybe something bad happened here years ago or there's an angry/sad/freaky ghost around. I'm not going to let that stop me. Unfortunately, there doesn't seem to be any way for me to follow him inside without being noticed. I'll try doing things the hard way for now and if it doesn't work out, the desk clerk is getting mind controlled. Or at least mind-read.

While Damarco crosses the parking lot to the hotel's main entrance, I start a slow circling orbit of the building, keeping my eye out for any room lights turning on. Each room has a window with a small balcony, but almost every curtain is drawn shut. Worse, they're a hideous shade of cyan. A few minutes later, I notice a spot of light appear on the parking lot while I'm on the opposite side of the building.

Yay for super-sensitive vampire eyesight.

I race around to the south side of the hotel and try to remember which room wasn't lit up seconds ago. Instinct pulls me to a fifth-floor window, one in from the left corner. Trusting my hunch, I land on the balcony and try to listen. Definitely a man breathing inside. A few objects clatter, making me picture Damarco unloading a whole host of vampire hunter toys from under his coat and setting them on a table or bureau.

He dials a phone. Even though I can hear the tones, I'm not a computer, so the number remains a mystery.

"Hey there," says a woman. Hard to guess age, but she doesn't sound too old. Maybe twenties. "How'd it go?"

"It didn't. Bastard never showed himself."

Ooh. Damarco sounds angry. I bite my lip and lean my ear closer to the glass.

"You gotta stay calm. Nothing these things do happens fast. Less you think he's on to you?"

He sighs. "It's possible. I should've guessed he wouldn't be using his old name here. Ran into one dude who said the photo looks like a Professor Heath. But, there's nothing on the school's website about any teachers using the name. He's probably keeping a low profile."

"I would, too, if I did what he did," says the woman.

"Tiff, you wouldn't do anything like that." Damarco exhales hard. "I gotta stop this guy before he repeats himself."

"You need to stay on point. F'you wanna get vengeance, do what you gotta do, but dammit, I can't have you *joinin'* them in the afterlife."

Thumps on the floor tell me he's stomp-pacing. "This ain't gonna be like the first time. I figured shit out now. Got a method. Those things are predictable. You damn well know the last six went smooth as silk."

"Yeah, but you never took one on this old before." The woman, who I'm guessing is either his wife or sister, fights tears. "You know I support you, but better the one who did this to us gets away than you die, too."

Damarco stops walking around. "I can't let this go, Tiff. You know that. Stay cool. I have this handled. No plans to die."

I smirk. Everyone who says they have no plans to die usually always winds up dead. Damn. Talk about a conflict. Someone close to them both probably died to a vampire attack, so I kinda feel bad for him. The notion of Professor Heath murdering anyone doesn't at all feel right to me. He seems like such a kindly, sweet man. He looks just shy of fifty but carries himself more like a grandpa. Granted, Aurélie looks like a harmless doll-obsessed twenty-two-year-old French runway model… right up until she plucks a man's heart out of his chest like she's grabbing an apple from a branch.

Could Professor Heath be lying to me?

"Hang on… I think I'm being watched," says Damarco.

Crap!

I dive over the balcony railing and swoop around to hide under it, flattening myself against the concrete slab. Above me, Damarco pulls the sliding glass door open and steps outside. The mild impacts of his feet on the stone transfer right into my back. It is *so* freaky having an amplified sense of touch. Feels like he's walking on me.

"Watched?" asks Tiffany. (I assume that's what Tiff means.)

A faint creak comes from the railing. "Yeah. Thought I saw a shadow on the curtain. Huh. Either I'm getting jumpy or there are ninjas in Seattle."

Tiffany laughs. "You ought'a consider coming home."

"Yeah, yeah." Damarco grumbles on the way back inside, slamming the door.

Whew.

She's got a good idea. Think I'll go home.

I drop away from the balcony and fly off toward Cottage Lake.

6

A MOMENT TO THINK

I only fly for a little while before second thoughts pull me back to the hotel roof.

It's the tallest building in the area, so it makes the most convenient hiding place where a girl can think. This is a crappy situation. The last time I ran into vampire hunters, it was easy to reprogram their minds. Those losers didn't have any strange force keeping me out of their heads. The idea mental resistance might be some kind of 'character class perk' of vampire hunters makes me laugh.

We're not living inside one of Dad's pen and paper games. Sure, it's possible the guy who shot me with a stake crossbow hadn't been a 'real' vampire hunter. However, real life doesn't have character archetypes. Someone wouldn't spontaneously generate mental resistance the moment they declare themselves a vampire hunter. Whatever is keeping me out of Damarco's head is unique to him.

It doesn't seem at all likely some random dude who wants to kill vampires out of revenge would have the meditative skills of a highly trained monk. I'm filling in a lot of blanks with assumptions here, but my impression of him is a vampire killed his parents some time ago and he decided to get revenge on us all. Since we're not in a movie, I make the further assumption he didn't pull a Batman and disappear to the Far East for several years to hone his martial arts skills and tap into his mystical chi powers. He's not from this area, so the Toyota has to be a rental. He's gotta be at least twenty-five. Maybe older. Some people don't look their age. Ask me how I know.

My guess is he lost family to a vampire attack. Possibly close friends, but he sounded a little too emotional for that. In my imaginary 'Damarco World,' I picture him around fourteen or so when he witnessed his parents die, old enough not to end up institutionalized afterward. Bet he tried to kill his first vampire at eighteen, maybe twenty, and barely survived it. It worries me he claims to have killed at least six more easily. Then again, a single well-placed bomb could do that. He does carry himself with competence and confidence. I'd be lying to say the idea of confronting him didn't scare me.

Innocents aren't known for our fighting capabilities. We're also rare, which means it's extremely unlikely any of those vampires he's killed before are of my bloodline. It also doesn't prove he's never run into a Fury or Beast. Pretty sure Garrett Alder would rip Damarco in half. Assuming, of course, he survived the conversion he attempted. The man might be a Fury now. Still, a Fury would squish a mortal.

Okay, I'm stuck treading water in too many information gaps to estimate how dangerous Damarco is. I can, however, guess he would kill me with little effort since I'm both new as a vampire and the weakest bloodline. There's also the slight problem of me not having any actual skill or training with fighting. On the other hand, maybe I shouldn't think of myself as overly weak. Aurélie's bloodline doesn't give her any help in physical combat—she's merely old as hell. If I make it to a few hundred years, I'd be as powerful as her, only without the ability to charm the free will out of everyone nearby. Innocents are considered 'weak' because we don't have 'cool' powers like *extreme* strength or shadow jumping, or mass charm, turning into wolves— still not sure that's really a thing for anyone. All my 'extra' stuff goes to being lifelike and my minor resistance to sunlight. That one's apparently a big deal.

And hey, yours truly is totally cool with it. Really. I *adore* being able to pretend at being alive... and flight? Who could ask for more? Well, the Old Guard probably. They tend to ask for more all the time. Still. I am happy. No desire for power, political or otherwise.

However, I also don't want to get myself killed.

Really, my bloodline has the *best* 'powers' to protect from vampire hunters. If he doesn't realize I'm a vampire, he'll have no reason to attack me. As Sierra would say, 'stealth builds are overpowered.' Yeah, she's talking about video games, but being sneaky is a massive advantage.

Anyway, I still have to figure out what to do right now. Telling Professor Heath he's got a vampire hunter sniffing around for him will have one of two outcomes: either the prof kills Damarco or leaves town. *I* don't want to attack him myself. For one thing, he seems like a nice guy with minor emotional scars and some compelling reasons to want vampires dead. He's also missing a lot of information. Namely, that not all vampires kill.

Speaking of killing, the idea Professor Heath murdered people in the past sounds impossible. I've watched enough crime shows to know some killers are great at pretending to be sweet and friendly. Maybe this is simply me rejecting the idea because I don't want it to be true. He's always been too sedate, thoughtful, introspective even. No, I just can't see Heath as a killer.

Ted Bundy was kinda charming, too... right up until he killed people.

Grr! I grab two fistfuls of my hair. My turn to pace around.

It's not like all vampire hunters are evil. As far as they're concerned, they're doing a good thing. The dude's a serious threat, but killing him feels wrong. I can't simply pounce on a guy and rip his throat out because he talked about killing vampires. That's not who I am. And to be technical, he didn't even say vampires. He referred to 'things.' The only way I'd ever kill anyone is if they hurt or meant to hurt my family... and doing it would still mess me up. If I had to end someone to save the lives of my parents or sibs, I'd do it without hesitating... and probably spend decades dwelling on it.

Weird right? I shredded a whole abandoned factory full of vampires. But vampires are already dead. Is that why it didn't bother me much? Or because they'd kidnapped Sam? Oh, damn. I really hope the reason killing them didn't mess with me is because I'm a vampire. Is it possible I *am* capable of killing live people without remorse? No. No way.

More pacing. Vampires are already dead. *Those* vampires were an imminent threat. Tried to kill me. Would have killed Sam, Ronan, Daryl, and Jordan. Just video game bad guys as far as I think of them. Totally different from pouncing on some rando walking out of Starbucks. Or some rando with a funny crossbow.

Something tells me Damarco isn't going to come after us with a stake-chucker. Whatever he had loaded in his mini-crossbow was too small to be a stake. Red, about a half-inch in diameter, eight inches long, taped onto a crossbow bolt. Not dynamite. Unless Hollywood got it wrong, that stuff's a lot thicker... like as big around as the cardboard center of a paper towel roll.

I might not have any idea exactly what the crossbow will do, but I *do* know getting shot by it is something to avoid. Okay, screw it. Telling Professor Heath might make me as guilty in Damarco's death as the professor—if he kills him. But, not warning him after discovering the truth is basically the same situation in the other direction. If this guy kills Heath, I'd feel responsible. Not telling someone about it might kill, telling someone about it might kill.

FML, right? Or FMU, rather. Unlife.

Okay, back to the school. Maybe the prof felt lazy tonight. A trained monkey could supervise a full-period exam. Probably why he sent a TA, they're less costly than skilled monkeys. Heath didn't need to be there personally.

It's already too late for Hunter to be awake, so it's not like I'm losing time being with him by going back to the school. And... hah! How messed up is that? A vampire dating a guy named Hunter. Heh. If he became undead, would it make him a vampire Hunter?

Ugh.

"Bad Sarah." I bonk myself on the head a few times. "Don't even joke about that. I will not kill my boyfriend."

A long, sad sigh slides out of me. No, I'm not going to kill him. I'm going to watch him grow old. The saying goes something like if you love someone, let them go. But, who am I to tell Hunter what's going to make him happy? If he doesn't want a living woman instead of me, one who can give him kids, it's his choice to make. No idea how I'll feel in seventy or eighty years when he dies—if he makes it that long. The world's a scary freakin' place. Everything and its mother causes cancer. Anyway, when he's gone, I may not want another emotional attachment of any kind. And if I *do* feel lonely enough, I'm going to find a vampire boyfriend. No need to feel guilty about stealing a normal life from him, and no need to worry about watching him grow old and die.

Of course, I could always get cats.

Chuckling, I jump into the air and fly back toward the school... thinking about Glim.

Nah. That would feel like dating my big brother.

7

ANOTHER LIFETIME

Professor Heath never revealed to me where he sleeps or spends his downtime.

He did tell me he doesn't usually leave the building. That will narrow down a search area assuming he didn't lie or joke. Since Damarco put a camera on one door, it's possible he has cameras on all of them. If he sees me on the video feed going into the school close to midnight, it might put me on his radar. At least I know he doesn't understand vampires can fly. If he did, he wouldn't have dismissed an empty balcony so fast.

Unless, he does know and assumed I'd be there listening to him and only said it to throw me off. Grr. I'm going to drive myself crazy. What is wrong with me? I am a 'spend an hour soaking in a bath bomb and curl up with a book' kind of girl. Not a 'track down a vampire hunter' adventure hero. Oh, right. Overdeveloped sense of guilt. Doing nothing at this point feels the same as helping Damarco kill Professor Heath. Not to mention what the rest of the vampires in Seattle would think of me if they discover I knew about a hunter and kept it quiet.

They all regard me as a useless kid. Maybe I should do the useless kid thing and tell a grown up, let them deal with it.

Nah. They'll kill him.

Sigh.

I slip into the school building via a second story window someone left open wide enough for me to get under it. It's nowhere near a door, so there shouldn't be any cameras on it. Once inside, it's pretty easy to make my way down the stairwell to the basement. Even though it's unlikely I'll find him there, I check the classroom first. Predictably, it's empty.

Next best idea is his office. We're *way* past office hours, but he is a vampire after all.

Can't say it surprises me not to find him there. However, I do hear voices… and music. Someone's watching a movie. It's quite faint. Even in the dead silence of the underground hallway, my ears struggle to pick it up. A normal person would never hear it. Spinning in place a few times gives me an idea of direction, so I head down the hall, deeper into the building than I've ever gone.

The movie soundtrack grows progressively louder, though still not to the point a human could hear it. Following the noise brings me to a boiler room. Specifically, the innermost corner. The sound appears to be coming from behind a giant metal tool cabinet taller than I am. One thing about having incredibly sharp eyesight and a sense of touch that can tell me if a coin is heads or tails by feeling it? I can find stuff like concealed doorways in a cinderblock wall. A narrow seam in the mortar outlines a passageway. Pushing on it doesn't do anything, not even rattle the obvious door. The sound isn't coming from behind the shelf, only a weird echo. It's coming—along with a faint breeze—out of the seam.

Must be a button somewhere.

For like twenty minutes, I look around the area for anything suspicious. Finally, I get the bright idea to fly up off my feet and check out the high shelf. It's packed with metal junk coated in such a heavy layer of brown dust it looks like it's been there for a hundred years. One object on the right side far in the back gets my attention due to a shiny spot. I have no name for whatever the hunk of metal is. It's kinda rounded on the top, gets wider on the way down and has a gear-like collar around the middle. If a machinist tried to make a model spaceship out of random parts, he'd create this thing. Maybe it's a boiler component or something from a car older than my parents?

It's got a little flange of metal bent into an L-bracket sticking out the top, and the short end of the bracket has no dust on it. That's about as glaring a clue as can be, so I push it. Doesn't move. Turn? Nope. I push harder, and the metal starts to bend, so it's not a vampire strength test. Pull up?

It lifts a quarter inch and clicks.

The slab pops out on the right side.

Nice.

I grab the edge and haul the door of cinder blocks open, revealing a small shaft going straight down. A few thin pipes and some wires run along the facing wall into an even more basementy basement. Interesting. I jump in, hover with flight, and pull the door shut. Wouldn't want anyone finding this place who doesn't belong here. You know, like me.

Once the door latches, I float to the bottom, a little deeper than one story below the normal basement.

Professor Heath is standing right in a doorway at the bottom, eyes wide like some kind of ghoul.

I about scream in his face from shock.

His posture isn't aggressive, more like he planned to memory wipe whoever snuck into his lair. He blinks, his expression of guarded defensiveness melts away to confusion. "Sarah?"

"Yeah," I whisper.

"What are you doing here?" He leans into the shaft and peers up. "At least you shut the door."

"Can we talk? It's important."

He nods, backs up, and waves for me to follow before ambling down a short hallway to a room that looks like it came straight out of a campy college comedy film. Pennants and random memorabilia adorn bare cinderblock walls. He's got a bed in one corner, some bookshelves, folding table with a computer on it plus an astounding amount of papers stacked—maybe students' classwork. If Mom let Sierra go six whole months without once nagging her to clean her bedroom, it still wouldn't approach how messy this place is.

"Whoa. You're literally Laslo," I whisper.

"What?" He glances back at me.

"Oh, something from a movie my dad likes. Some guy who lives under a college. Uhh, nice place." I walk in, looking around at like a hundred fat novels all with bookmarks in varying places. They're fairly thick, so either he's got a problem with commitment or he's trying to make them last. Fortunately, none of the mess in here is biological. No rotting food or mold. It's all books or old technology. "Whoa, is that a Commodore 64?"

Professor Heath grins at me. "Yes, it is. And it still works. I'm impressed you know what it is."

"Heh. My father's still living in the Eighties. Sometimes, I feel like I belong there."

"Nothing wrong with that." He hurriedly shifts the stack of books on the cushion of a brown plaid sofa, clearing enough room beside him for a second person. "What's on your mind?"

"There's a man here looking for you." I sit on the indicated spot, surrounded by the flavor of dust and old paper. "He's been showing your picture to students outside, asking if anyone knows a 'Professor Montgomery.' I think he's a vampire hunter."

"Oh…" Heath raises his bushy eyebrows, appearing genuinely confused. "That's surprising."

I explain eavesdropping on him. "He thinks you killed someone— I'm guessing maybe parents or some other family, and probably a bunch more people."

"Professor Montgomery was the alias I used while teaching in South Dakota… but that had been… at least forty years ago. You say this man looks around thirty?"

"Something like that. Maybe late twenties. Definitely wouldn't have been your student if it happened forty years ago."

Heath chuckles. "No. He's clearly lying."

"You didn't kill his parents, right?" I ask with my smile turned up to cheesy.

"No. At least barring some bizarre butterfly effect scenario."

I blink. "Huh?"

"It would be impossible to rule out the chance some tiny thing I did set in motion a chain of events that led to their deaths. But... I did not kill them directly."

"Ahh. You're just being you." I laugh.

He smiles.

"Have you ever killed anyone?"

"Once. It happened in 1908, just south of Richmond, Virginia. The place I'd been living then didn't have the most privacy. Some poor sod barged in on me before the sun went down. I'm certain his blood is on my hands, but I cannot claim any memory of doing the deed."

I nod. "Yeah. Sun freakout. Been there... oh shit."

"What?"

"Dammit. I lied to myself."

"How so?"

I fidget my hands in my lap. "Been saying I haven't killed any living people, but it's not true. Gang members. Had a sun freakout. Dalton and I got stranded in an abandoned motel when the sun came up. We hid in the back bathroom, but these guys showed up to do a drug deal. One of them had to use the toilet and he found me. They had all the blinds closed, so the outer room didn't hurt *too* bad. But the guy who was gonna deal with them whipped the door open and blasted me in the face with the sun. Next thing I know there are dead people. I really did shred this tall Jamaican guy and another one or two people."

He rubs my shoulder. "It is not completely a lie to separate the actions of the beast within from what your thinking mind does."

"Is that why it doesn't make me feel super guilty? I don't remember doing it? Or am I really a killer?"

Professor Heath lets out a long, slow breath. "It is due to your blackout. You didn't decide to kill them, nor do you remember doing it. It is little different than if someone else killed them and you found the bodies. I do not believe we become killers by nature, especially one such as you."

"That's good to hear you say… but do you believe it?"

"You did not kill this Damarco person as soon as you learned what he wanted to do?"

"No way. I didn't even consider doing it. Just plain wrong."

He grins and gives me the most platonic knee pat ever in the history of knee pats. "Then you are not a killer by nature."

"I want to make him forget you and go away but I couldn't do it. There is some kind of shield around his brain keeping me from accessing his thoughts."

"Hmm." Professor Heath rubs his chin. "If it is as you say and he is a genuine hunter, he likely has an amulet, bracelet, or other such trinket infused with vampire blood as a ward. That means he has made some contact with the Order."

"Order?"

He waves dismissively. "There are maybe two dozen of them in the world. From Europe. A group of vampire hunters who've been at it since the late 1500s."

"They're immortals?" I gawk.

"No, child." He laughs. "The *Order* is old, not the members. They generally only discover the vampires who lack discretion. Many of our kind overstate their danger. Some even refuse to speak directly about them out of a superstition it will attract their notice. Don't leave a trail of corpses behind you—or do flagrantly obvious supernatural things—and you will elude their notice. I'm quite certain they have no real comprehension of the true number of our kind that exist. The Order believes we are fiends who pop up here and there in small numbers, mostly as solitary individuals. If they possessed any real understanding of the actual scope of our society, they'd either disband or recruit their numbers into the hundreds."

"That's sorta reassuring." I clutch my knees, grimacing. "Still scary to think there's a whole guild out there devoted to wiping us out."

Professor Heath scrunches up his nose. "Pay them no mind. They do us a service, really. Clean up the ones who didn't deserve the

Transference. There are crazies and criminals among human kind. So, too, do deviants become vampires. The truly dangerous ones, we weed our ourselves, but the merely irritating ones, they handle so we don't have to."

"Almost sounds like a symbiotic relationship."

"In a way, you are correct. However, it's like working with dangerous chemicals. Need to be careful or you'll lose fingers." He winks. "Takes more than thick gloves to protect from the Order."

I glance around, biting my lip. Every breath down here tastes like moist dust. "Okay, so he's not simply immune to mind control. I'd just have to get the thing away from him."

"Precisely. The artifacts they use against us derive their powers from vampiric blood, using our essence to shield against our abilities. Because of that, the trinket would have no power during the daylight. You can go out in the sun, correct?"

"I can but… you know it takes *all* my energy not to catch fire. In the day, I'm basically a normal person. All the cool vampire stuff stops working. Any dark place where I'd come online would have the same effect on his bracelet or whatever."

"A conundrum, no doubt." He taps his fingers on a nearby hardcover book.

"What happened in South Dakota?"

He grimaces. "I do recall an incident at a hospital, though the details are spotty. A vampire, Beast if memory serves, lost control of himself. Thirty or so dead. His rampage is why I decided to relocate. That would certainly have gotten the Order's attention. And, I'd been there a while already. Almost time to move on to avoid people wondering why I hadn't become elderly."

"Are you going to leave here because of this guy?"

He holds up his hands in a 'what can ya do?' sort of gesture. "I might have to unless something is done about this hunter. However, for the short term, I will be careful. As I've no need to go outside, he shouldn't find me unless he gets into the building and finds the classroom. What does this man look like?"

I start to describe him, but Heath smiles.

"Thank you, Sarah. I've seen him in your thoughts."

"You can read my mind? Wow, you're old." I laugh.

"Not *that* old. You are simply very young." He pats me on the head. I playfully frown.

It hits me he taught in South Dakota forty years ago. My father would've been six. Talk about hard for me to even imagine, oddly more difficult than him saying he'd been around in the early 1900s. That's *so* far in the past it doesn't sound believable even though I know it is.

Heck, Sophia has no idea what CDs are. Dad teases me with cassette tapes sometimes. Like, seriously, what the hell does a pencil have to do with them? Why does he find it funny I don't understand how an ancient audio technology is related to an even more ancient writing technology? I might be immortal, but forty years ago doesn't sound real to me.

Guess I really am still a teenager.

8

POLITICS ALWAYS RUINS
EVERYTHING

riday evening at a few minutes past seven, I'm in the middle of something I vowed to stop doing—feeding in the bathroom at school—when my phone rings. My lips are attached to the neck of a woman in her early forties who's dressed like an office worker. Her name might be Sylvia. Think she works for a bank or something. Like corporate office, not teller. Maybe a branch manager?

Yanno how some people say they drink so much coffee it's literally flowing in their veins? Yeah, well, this woman's blood really does taste like pumpkin spice coffee to me. It's a little strange since it's not steaming hot, but it's hardly the worst flavor lurking in the depths of my subconscious.

Still drinking, I fish my phone out of my bag and hold it up to check the screen. The list of people I'd answer at a moment like this is short. Alas, it's Aurélie, and she's on that short list. I swipe my thumb at the screen to answer and hold the phone up as best I can to my ear.

"Mmm?" I mumble into the woman's neck.

"*Bonjour chérie!* Oh, this is a bad time. You are feeding."

I blink. "Mmm cmm smm mm?"

"*Oui.* Well, not see you, per se. *En tout cas,* I wanted to remind you to be here by 9:30 p.m. The soiree starts at ten."

"Smmm?"

"Yes, soiree. It has been a few months."

Oh, darn. That's right. The not-quite-monthly gathering of vampires in the area. I'd forgotten. Probably why she called. "Mmm."

"*Merveilleuse.* I will see you soon."

Full, I detach my fangs from the woman's neck and seal the bite with a swipe of my tongue. "Okay. Be there as soon as school's over."

She hangs up. I put the phone away and ease Sylvia to sit on the toilet, still fully dressed. Honestly, feeding in the bathroom is pretty nasty, but I'd wanted to save time tonight. Slipping in a meal between my classes means going straight home after school and having more time with the family. Friday nights are prime opportunities for Dad to put on old movies. Some Friday nights go to Hunter, but he's working until eleven and needs to catch up on school work. For whatever reason, he doesn't like staying up until sunrise to finish studying.

A minute later, Sylvia has no memory of seeing me and will think she slipped and landed on the bowl before she could drop her pants. What? It's plausible. I fly over the partition, glide two stalls away, and drop down. After a disguise flush, I wash my hands at the sink and return to the break room. Dr. Mercer's intro calculus class doesn't start for twenty-eight minutes, so I call Dad and let him know my presence has been *requested* at a social event. He's a little disappointed at postponing Eighties movie night but nowhere near enough to give me guilt. Plans change—he's going to let the Littles pick a movie and save the one he had in mind for us for another day, possibly tomorrow. While I don't think Aurélie would mind me bailing on the vampire social for a good reason, keeping her happy keeps my family safe. Also, I do like her and wouldn't want to be rude.

Sylvia wobbles into the break room a few minutes later. Oops. Might have been a bit hungrier than I realized. A quick mental prod gives her the urge to grab a donut or cookie from the machine. No idea if it really helps, but blood donation places always hand out cookies or orange juice. Figure it can't hurt.

The class feels like it takes less time than the fifteen minutes I spent waiting for it to start. This is due mostly to being busy, but also because of me setting Dr. Mercer on fast forward. For her, it means speaking like a normal person and not going ten to twenty minutes over the scheduled 9:00 p.m. end of class. She finishes the material with one minute to spare. It's kind of funny to listen to other students speculating why she sometimes has 'fast nights.' Most of the guys think she's got a date while the women are wondering what series just went live on Netflix she wants to binge watch.

Despite my rush to make it to Aurélie's apartment, I look around the entrance for any sign of Damarco on my way out, but it appears he's leaving surveillance to electronics for now. Expecting to be on camera, I act normal and follow the crowd down to the corner, breaking off with the group crossing the street into the parking garage.

Of the big cluster, only two guys follow me to the topmost deck, but they're not really *following* me as much as walking in the same direction to get to where they parked. I pretend to have trouble locating my car while they get into theirs and drive off. As soon as they're out of sight down the ramp, I jump into the air.

The nice thing about Aurélie's apartment is she's pretty high up off the ground. That lets me fly right to her balcony without having to look for an inconspicuous place to land. An even nicer thing is how I don't have another vampire chasing me into her place and trying to bash my head open with a statue.

Definitely a plus.

As soon as I'm inside, Aurélie whisks me down the hall to her dressing room. Yes, she has a separate room dedicated entirely to wardrobe. It's like we're backstage at a fashion show and I'm a model racing to swap outfits in time to go out on the catwalk again. That is to say, I change right in front of her while she helps me put on the elaborate bits. And, of course, she's a complete perfectionist so my modern underwear has to sit the night out, too. It would give her like some serious case of OCD otherwise. Some people find mixing colors gauche; she has the same reaction to mixing eras, even on stuff no one will see.

Sigh.

But, it's at once fun, casual, bizarre, and surreal. In minutes, she's dolled me up in an elaborate 1700s era gown, canary yellow with cream parts. If Sophia could see me at the moment, she'd probably scream 'you're so fluffy!' and squeeze me. I feel like a lemon meringue elemental.

Seriously, I could smuggle a middle school soccer team into an amusement park under this skirt. Why did anyone ever get the notion that dressing up to resemble a hand-bell was a good idea? Whatever. At least the shoes aren't too uncomfortable. I feel utterly ridiculous, but two things keep me calm. No one I know who isn't a vampire is going to see me like this… and none of the vampires will laugh at me because they all know how Aurélie is. It's possible they'll pity me or tease me for trading away my dignity in exchange for her protection. That *is* part of it, but also, how many people can say they've done something to make a vampire her age happy? It's kind of like how doing something nice for the elderly can make their whole week.

She yanks the corset a little too firmly.

Drat. I forget she knows what I'm thinking.

Aurélie peers over my shoulder with a coy smile.

"No, I don't think you're elderly. Just… it makes me happy to give you joy."

She giggles, then mutters in French too fast for me to keep up. The only word I catch is 'Marie Kondo.' It's impossible to look at her and even think of her true age. She's told me her Transference happened at the age of twenty-two, but she could pass for eighteen. With her high voice and the right cosmetics, she could shave another year off. She's also proof visible age means nothing in terms of a vampire's power.

It's kinda fun to imagine the stunned look on someone's face in a century or so when they mistake me for a harmless kid and find out the truth. Not that I have fantasies about hurting people or vampires, but by the time my body has anywhere near the kind of power Aurélie does, I'm going to be *really* damn sick of being mistaken for a child.

We hop in her limo, driven by one of her mortal employees, and soon arrive at the hotel where they hold these events. I still haven't figured out how many of the staff are under the control of vampires, *are* vampires, or simply get paid not to care. We aren't doing anything illegal, dangerous, or damaging. About the worst occurrence at these parties are the human hors d'oeuvres—mentally tenderized people who wander around aimlessly while being snacked on. It would bother me, but the older vampires who are apparently 'in charge' don't allow them to die. In a complete middle finger to most horror novels and movies, the majority of vampires try to *avoid* killing people. Body trails create suspicion and attract attention they don't want.

The chauffer, Louis, opens the door for us.

Aurélie gets out first. She laughs quietly to herself at the stream of naughty words floating across my brain while wrestling with my gown to climb after her. When these enormous skirts had been in fashion, people rich enough to afford them traveled by horse and carriage, which of course had enough room to stand up inside and walk down steps. The gown is not designed for a modern limo.

Louis grasps my arm and pulls me out of the car, setting me standing on the sidewalk like an overdressed mannequin. I follow her into the hotel and across the lobby. A bunch of norms hear the rustling fabric and gawk at us. The period fashion makes us stand out just a tad. A few go to snap pictures of us. I barely manage to look away so they don't get a clear shot of my face. Fortunately, we're out of sight down a corridor in only a minute, safe behind cordons denoting it a private event for invited guests only.

Aurélie heads for a set of double doors leading to a big convention area room.

Within a minute of us entering, two women glide over to say hello, Vanessa Prentice—a redheaded Fury who's got a serious case of envy for Aurélie—and Jennifer Ruiz, a blonde, tan Sybarite. Contrary to what Hunter tells me, I've never considered myself remarkable looks-wise. On the other hand, I've never felt ugly or that my appearance fell short of adequate, pretty much the typical 'girl next door' average. Maybe I'll accept being called 'cute'—more so now. I blame my bloodline.

But yeah, standing among these three women makes me feel like freakin' Quasimodo's uglier stepsister. The only reason anyone would even look at me is to stare at the old timey dress. The two women make the usual pleasant greeting conversation with Aurélie before even acknowledging they've noticed me. At least the simmering tension between Vanessa and Aurélie is absent tonight. My guess is Aurélie has been ignoring Vanessa's peacock act, which has given the redhead a false sense of security. Really, Aurélie's disregarding her because she knows there isn't even a contest as to which one of them is more beautiful.

Aurélie beams in response to me having that thought.

"Oh, what a lovely dress," says Vanessa, facing me. "Is the designer still alive?"

"*Non,*" replies Aurélie. "Marcel died in 1702."

"It's simply breathtaking." Jennifer walks around me.

I emit a wheezy chuckle while tapping the corset. "That's one word for it. Can't breathe in this thing."

The two women regard me curiously.

"Joke?" I smile. "You know, vampire… not breathing?"

Vanessa and Jennifer laugh. At least they're not catty with me. You know, the girl who's no threat whatsoever. Geez. Thought I'd escaped this BS when I finished high school. Never cared about who made it into the popular crowd back then, and I still don't.

"It's superb." Jennifer feels the material on the sleeve. "How do you keep it looking so new?"

"Guessing she uses something a little stronger than Febreze."

Aurélie laughs in that subdued sort of way the aristocracy always do in movies, hiding her mouth under her hand. "Marcel *designed* it, but this is not one he made. The garment is fairly new. However, it is *authentique*. Sewn by hand. No shortcuts."

For the next maybe twelve minutes, I stand there like a lemon tree while the women talk about where she had our gowns made. Aurélie's is equally elaborate, only rose pink and white. Vanessa slips in a subtle remark about outlandish coloration being a way for unremarkable birds to draw the eye of suitors. No doubt Aurélie catches the dig, but she ignores it.

She soon extricates us from the conversation and we migrate around the room, having brief conversations with other vampires. Ashton James and Henry Arnold are still hanging out as a pair, which gets me wondering if they're actually a couple. It's an odd combination if that's the truth, since Henry is an Old Guard and Ashton's a Beast.

Speaking of Beasts, he's nothing like Garrett. The man required a modification of the dictionary definition for 'huge.' Ashton, on the other hand, has a different kind of feralness about him. He's thin but muscular. Long black hair hangs to his shoulders around a rugged face with piercing ice blue eyes that remind me of a wolf's. Sierra would call him a fantasy ranger who's been dragged out of the woods and forced to dress nice.

Henry Arnold, on the other hand, looks and sounds like he belongs in high society, but without the old world snobbishness. More like the modern country club sort of person. Last time I saw him, he had a super short afro, but he's shaved his head bald. It has to be irritating for him, having to cut his hair every night.

Not sure exactly how it works, but vampire anatomy considers lost hair an injury and will heal it overnight when we sleep. Don't ask me why. Must be magic. Aurélie once hinted we can force it longer if we want, but no one has yet bothered to teach me how. Not that I need to make mine any longer. It's halfway down my back already. Both Aurélie and Sophia have hair long enough to sit on by accident if they're not careful. I don't know how in the hell they tolerate it. Me, I'd sit on it and jerk my head to the side *once* before hunting down a pair of scissors. Sophia does it to herself all the time and thinks it's funny.

It is—to watch.

The more we talk to these two, the less I'm sure what their

relationship is. They could be old friends. I'm not exactly a master of interpreting body language, but they don't display any outward signs of affection. They've probably just known each other for a long time, or could even be highly polite rivals. I suppose it makes them friends in a way. Maybe I'd care about what they are to each other if integrating myself fully into this vampire society mattered. I mean, it doesn't bother me to hang out with them or even be considered at the edge of their social strata. However, this girl will never be the one who obsesses over what the rest of society thinks about her.

Arthur Wolent more or less owns the entire interior corner of the room, surrounded by his close associates, a pack of hangers-on, and a bunch of others trying to suck up to him. After Aurélie, he's the next oldest-slash-most-powerful vampire in Seattle. By power, I'm mostly talking political influence, money, that sort of thing. He's a Fury, so it is likely he's *physically* the most powerful vampire around as far as I know. But, tons of raw muscle won't help him if Aurélie hits him over the head with her emotion hammer.

It makes me laugh to think, but it totally reminds me of how Sierra complains about wizards in the tabletop game they play. I'm nowhere near as into it as she or Dad, but I've tried to participate enough to understand the concept. Sierra likes warriors or assassins. At the start, both of them are quite a bit more powerful than wizards who are super easy to kill. Toward the later stages of the game, the wizards become ridiculously potent. Dad said playing a wizard is like a 'penance.' You deal with being weak for a long time before coming into strength. Warriors are relatively constant, never weak but never astounding either.

Aurélie makes faces at me like she's amused I think she's more powerful than Wolent but simultaneously baffled by the comparison to the game.

Another glaring thing I notice is the lack of Glim haunting the wall. He usually shows up at these events mostly to observe the goings-on and report back to the other Shadows. They're not interested in making any sort of political play; they merely like to stay informed. Could be a different Shadow is here tonight and he (or she) isn't inclined to reveal themselves to me. Gee, I hope he's okay. Holidays have to be a rough time of year for him. If I'd been turned into a vampire and forced to watch my family from the outside without them knowing I survived... that would completely kill me.

For a moment, it sounds like a good idea to invite him over for Thanksgiving dinner, but then I chicken out, worried he would take it the wrong way, like being patronizing. Also, we usually have a lot of relatives over and it wouldn't be right to ask him to join us but require he stays hidden from sight. And... people start arriving before sundown. Shadows can't wake up before sunset even if they're in a completely dark place. He probably intends to visit his family, anyway. Glim could totally stand in the room with them and remain unnoticed.

Oh, hell. I *should* ask him. He'll know there's no insult intended. And he could make himself invisible to everyone but me. Speaking of Glim, maybe I should ask his opinion on the vampire hunter situation. How messed up is that? I expected mild Professor Heath to react by wanting to kill Damarco but not Glim? Sure, Glim is quiet and friendly, but he's also a former soldier who would take a threat seriously.

"A hunter?" asks Aurélie. "Here?"

Oops. I cringe and rotate to face her. Now I really feel like I dropped the birthday cake while carrying it to the table. Talking about him to Aurélie could easily lead to Damarco being killed. However, I can't lie to her. Both figuratively and literally. I'd feel bad about trying to deceive her, and she's listening to my head. "Yeah... he showed up outside my school, looking for Professor Heath."

The lack of recognition in her expression to the name confirms the prof is sincerely committed to his policy of not leaving the campus. I start explaining how one of my college professors is a vampire, and about Damarco going around showing students a photo of him. A momentary ramble about his sounding like a reasonably nice guy and my not wanting him to die distracts me from the story.

Right as I get to the part about following him to the hotel and listening to the phone conversation he had with a woman who could be his sister or wife, Vanessa, Jennifer, Pascal Ivanov, Stefano Bianchi, and a few other vampires I don't know approach us. Pascal, an academic who often works with Eleanor St. Ives—the closest thing I have to a nemesis—doesn't seem like a bad guy. Academics aren't 'evil,' but it wouldn't surprise me if the guy would be okay with lighting a child on fire in the name of science. Pretty sure the *complete* lack of emotional depth or any sense of morality is *this* guy and not all Academics.

Stefano, on the other hand, is—pardon my French—an asshole.

"*Ce n'est pas français*," whispers Aurelie.

Her tiny smirk tells me she knows what I meant and cracked a joke.

Long story short, Stefano is not happy Dalton gave me the Transference. He liked it even less I didn't break contact off with my family. He also put my head through the wall here last time. That saying about having a 'stick up the butt?' yeah, this guy? The stick is so big it drags on the floor when he walks. I think his spine stopped flexing in 1790. To hear him ramble on, my parents and siblings being aware of vampires will result in every undead on the globe dying off in six months.

He *still* looks at me like I'm some barefoot rag-clad waif from the 1930s who walked into a five-star restaurant and expected to get a free meal. My mere presence here is something he wishes to scrape off his shoe.

I pick my eye at him… using my middle finger.

"What's this about a hunter?" asks Pascal.

Jennifer laughs. "Isn't that the name of the boy she's in love with? The *mortal?*"

Stefano narrows his eyes at me. Oh, this is a new layer of contempt. He's making a face at me like an antebellum father whose daughter just told him she fell in love with a dark-skinned man. Oh noes. A mortal. The sky is falling.

"I distinctly overheard her say this man is trying to destroy a professor at her college," says Ashton.

"There is a vampire at the college?" Henry Arnold raises one eyebrow. "How curious."

"She's feeding there to blend in with other young people?" asks Jennifer.

"No, she's *attending.*" Vanessa covers her mouth, snickering.

I give her side eye. "Not sure how it was when you were my age, but it's totally acceptable for girls to pursue higher education these days."

She bats a wave at me as if to say 'oh, stop.' "You misunderstand me. I find it simply adorable how you're clinging to your old life."

Her tone... she's not mocking me as much as she really does think I'm cute in an 'oh, look at that poor idiot pushing on the pull door' kind of way.

"If a hunter has shown himself here, he must be destroyed." Stefano looks among the other vampires, an imperious tilt to his head.

Henry steps up to him. "We do not even know if he truly is of the Unspoken."

Stefano frowns at him, then redirects his disdain back to me. "Is he?"

If someone explains what the heck 'unspoken' means, maybe I could answer him. The only reason I don't fire that taunt off out loud is the expectation someone would use it to find fault with Aurélie for not teaching me. Or maybe Dalton. Probably him since he's the one who gave me the Transference. Assuming, of course, vampires consider knowing what an 'unspoken' is a basic piece of important information.

Not wanting to throw Aurélie under the bus—or under the horse-drawn carriage considering our attire—I say, "I'm not sure."

Apparently, my expression and tone made it sound as though I hadn't figured out if Damarco is an Unspoken, not that I've no clue what it means. My gamble pays off as a heated discussion goes back and forth among the vampires about whether or not 'we' have a member of the Unspoken Order running around Seattle.

Ohhhhh.

Professor Heath referred to 'the Order.' Until a better idea hits me,

I'm going to assume they're both referring to the same thing, a 'guild' of vampire hunters. Wonder if they do fish fries on the first Friday of each month? Somehow, I doubt they're the VFW with stakes and crossbows.

This discussion evidently piques Wolent's curiosity as he wanders over to observe.

Crap.

While Stefano kinda looks like a Mafia don, Arthur Wolent basically is one, but not in the sense of being connected to organized crime. He governs vampire society in the Seattle area with the same sort of mindset: quite friendly and good to people he trusts, but fire will rain from the skies if he thinks you've betrayed him. Yeah, don't look my way. Just an innocent kid here. No interest in power. It is kinda odd though. Aurélie could be at the top of the food chain, but she's happy as an influential figure on the side, letting Wolent act like our de facto king.

Can't blame her, really. That much responsibility sucks. I guess having influence without having overt power is like hanging out with someone else's kids. When things get stressful, she can just hand them back to the parents and go home.

Aurélie muffles another chuckle and wags her eyebrows at me.

A few of the more established vampires call for Damarco to be 'put down.' Worse, they're demanding *I* do it since I'm the one who found him first. Stefano appears to take particular delight in the idea and massages it into some sort of gang initiation crap. His argument to Wolent is something like I need to 'prove myself' and earn my place among society.

No matter how intently I stare at Aurélie and try to mentally ask her to do something here, she remains quiet at my side. It's frustrating, but she wouldn't abandon me to the proverbial wolves. Certainly, she's biding her time and waiting for the right moment. It makes sense even though I don't like it. She can't shield me from absolutely everything all the time. That will only make it worse for me in the long run plus reflect poorly on her.

Arthur Wolent walks up to me, one eyebrow slightly up, his

expression dangerously close to 'what the heck am I supposed to do with you?' I really hope the next fifteen minutes don't end with my finger stuck in a cigar cutter. He appears to notice the dread in my eyes and adjusts his demeanor slightly more toward grandfatherly rather than displeased monarch.

"You don't know if this man is Unspoken," says Wolent. "What do you know?"

The rest of the crowd falls silent—except for the repetitive thumping of a snack human repeatedly walking into the wall.

"He was walking around outside Seattle Central College asking students if they knew a vampire there by showing them a photo, but he had the name wrong. I followed the guy back to a hotel and listened to him on the phone with someone who's either his sister or wife. Damarco blames the vampire for killing people close to him as well as multiple others in South Dakota forty years ago. But there's no way this hunter was alive then. He's too young. Professor Heath denied killing them. I'm not sure how the guy found out about the professor or his being in Seattle. I tried to read his mind, but it's blocked off. The professor thinks the guy has some kind of special item containing vampiric blood."

"Definitely Unspoken." Stefano frowns at me. "You should have told us."

Wolent rubs his chin.

"Having an item like that doesn't prove he's part of the Order." I hold my chin high. "Anyone could steal a police car. That doesn't make them a cop."

A few people chuckle. Stefano sneers at me.

"The girl has a point, if a weak one." Wolent smiles.

"He doesn't know some of us can fly." I explain him almost catching me listening in on him. "It didn't even occur to him a vampire might have been on his balcony."

Stefano shakes his head. "Or he said it on purpose to fool you."

"Sarah…" Wolent puts a hand on my left shoulder. "I think you should be the one to deal with this hunter."

The giant smug grin Stefano flashes is almost enough to make me slap him. However, it's probably a bad idea to get violent—even angry socialite violent—while our effective leader is right in front of me. They'd probably take it as a sign of disrespect. Well it is, but I mean of their society as a whole, not just Stefano.

Darn. This is exactly the position I didn't want to end up in. Hopefully, my best attempt at Sophia's 'can we please keep the kitten' face helps. "Is it really necessary to kill him? I don't want to murder a guy."

Most of the vampires 'aww' at me. Except Stefano, a few others, and Pascal—who has the emotional range of a desk lamp.

Stefano waves dismissively. "It seems this child wishes to be a cute little girl forever."

Four or five others near him chuckle.

He faces me again, sporting a victorious smile, but stalls before saying anything else upon receiving a displeased look from Aurélie. Pretty sure he intended to call me her doll, or fire off some remark about my dress making me look like I'm six.

I shrug. "Being thought of as a harmless kid bothers me less than killing a guy who's only trying to avenge his dead friends or family... even if he does have the wrong guy. There must be some other way to make him leave Seattle."

The group all start trying to talk at once.

"There is," says Wolent in a loud voice, trying to establish order. He pauses, waiting for the crowd to quiet, then continues at a normal volume. "There is one usual outcome when a hunter is encountered."

I can't help myself at hearing that... and daydream about kissing Hunter.

Aurélie titters.

"Something is humorous?" Wolent raises an eyebrow at her.

"An interesting coincidence." She smiles. "*Son petit ami s'appelle Hunter.*"

Wolent and about a third of the vampires chuckle. Stefano appears confused and a touch offended. I didn't understand her words, but the meaning is somewhat easy to guess.

Pascal leans closer to Stefano and whispers, "She has a boyfriend named Hunter."

"Oh, but of course. Another mortal," says Stefano, drawing it out. "Lives with her *mortal* family. Why shouldn't she have a mortal lover as well?"

The same small group that appears to like this guy laughs again.

Stefano strides closer, gesturing at me. "Surrounds herself constantly with the living. You'd think her ashamed of being a vampire... or at least partially a vampire."

"Aww, she's an Innocent, dear Stefano." Jennifer makes a tsk-tsk sound at him. "Basically a mortal herself, poor thing."

I force a smile. "Guess I missed the part of the Transference where people change from ordinary human to self-important prig."

Stefano's eyes flare. "You impudent—"

Wolent stalls him with a raised hand. "The girl may be of an underpowered bloodline, but she is still no Scrap."

"This one will expose us all." Stefano points at me. "She lives with mortals. She won't kill an Unspoken. She has no respect for traditions."

I fold my arms—a bit of a task in this dress and corset. "Traditions, I respect. But I don't respect a guy who needs to keep reminding everyone how much better than other people they think they are."

Aurélie puts a hand on my arm.

"Too far?" I glance at her.

"Approaching."

I face her. "Sorry. You know I've no interest in politics or what anyone thinks about me. But it's kinda lame how this guy can stand there insulting me and I'm the one who's wrong for talking back to him only because he's older."

"If you are so willing to remain a child, you should get used to it," mutters Stefano.

"It is our way." Wolent looks back and forth between me and Stefano. "While you could challenge him, it is not something I'd recommend."

Head bowed, I sigh. "Yeah. I know. I'm weak."

"This is not your college campus, girl," says Stefano. "You will find no preferential treatment here for being young, or female, or *enlightened* or whatever it is they call it in this era. Strength is the only thing that matters."

Fists clenched, I try my best to ignore him and hold my tongue—but still glare at him.

"Sarah, I will not insist—yet—that you slay this hunter." Wolent walks right up to me, leans close, and lowers his voice into a tone that *so* sounds like the Godfather doing an 'I love you like a daughter, but if you screw this up, you're dead' routine. "However, if this hunter kills any of our kind, it will be your responsibility. Deal with him however you wish, but see that you deal with him."

"Yes, sir," I whisper.

The group breaks up to resume their little conversation clusters. Stefano shoots me a smug glance before turning away. He thinks he's won. Either I'll end up forced to kill Damarco or I'm going to hesitate too long and a vampire will die. Then, I'll have to answer for it. Pretty sure Stefano is hoping for any outcome bad enough to blow up in my face, but would consider either one a win for him.

It freaks me out that it only takes me a few seconds to accept if it comes down to either Damarco or me dying, I'd kill him. However, I couldn't do that unless I like literally caught him about to murder a vampire and dove on him to stop it or ended up having to defend myself if he attacked me. It's still impossible for me to think of hunting him down and simply killing him while he's standing there not expecting it on the off chance he *might* hurt a vampire before I'm able to find a way to get him out of Seattle.

Gah! This totally sucks! All I want to do is keep my head down and live in as normal a way as possible, but I've landed in the spotlight behind the podium on Wheel of Misfortune—and I keep getting bonus spins. I glare at the back of Stefano's head. That guy seriously needs to go headfirst into a toilet. Would he be able to trace Blix back to me?

"*Pardonne-moi*," whispers Aurélie once we're more or less alone at the side of the room. "I did not think they would make such an event of it. Hunters are a minor nuisance."

I frown at nothing in particular. "It's not the hunter, it's me. Stefano is still pissed you won't let him kill off my family or force me to play dead." The thought of my family having to believe I'd died on top of my frustration at Stefano's smugness pushes me to the edge of breaking down in tears. Angry tears. Somehow, I keep a straight face. No, not somehow. I know exactly what's keeping me stone-faced. If Stefano sees me crying, it will make him even happier.

Not gonna let him have the satisfaction.

"I'm surprised he didn't try to get me in trouble for not telling everyone about finding a hunter right away."

She squeezes my fingers. "Why do you think I discussed it here? To get it in the open. There is strength in weakness. Or the appearance of weakness."

"Yeah. I know. As long as he keeps thinking of me as a helpless little girl, he'll underestimate me." I peer over at her. "Problem is, I'm not looking to hurt him. Politically or literally. I just want to exist in peace."

"Yes, yes. I know." She pats the back of my hand. "It is unseemly of a man in his position to openly attack the newest, and least powerful among us. It makes 'im seem weak and insecure. You are best off ignoring the man as much as you can."

"Easier said than done. Will your charm work on this hunter?"

"If this talisman is genuinely from the Unspoken, it would offer him a good deal of protection. 'Owever, few of our kind possess my combination of age and strength in that particular discipline." She bats her eyelashes. "It would be improper for me to interfere as your patroness, since you 'ave been given a task directly. But, if you become 'opelessly stuck, I may just so 'appen to be nearby and present an unintended distraction for 'im."

I grin. Aurélie *trying* to be a distraction? Wow. The guy would stand there like a tree staring at her while I did anything to him like take his stupid talisman. Okay, so my situation isn't completely hopeless—it's just going to be a bitch.

9

HOMEWORK AND BANISHING
SPELLS

S ooner or later, I'm going to need to do something Sierra-like to balance things out.

Friday night, I spent hours dressed like a giant porcelain doll at the vampire party, and tonight—Sunday evening—I'm sprawled on my bedroom floor with Ashley. We've basically gone back to being twelve, doing homework together. This girl has enough unicorn stickers on her books to have patched the hole in the Titanic.

I make the mistake of saying that out loud and setting off a thirty-minute debate about if the piece of wood had enough room for Jack. Ashley thinks he should have lived. She's always trying to be super optimistic. It's cute, except when it's tragic. I'm pretty sure she went into that movie hoping that the magic of Hollywood would have found some way to stop the boat from sinking and walked out of the theater heartbroken that it went down. Oh, she expected it to sink. She's not *too* bad. Ash merely hoped the movie might have taken some liberties to deliver a happy ending. One could say I went into the theater with a bit of a 'sinking' feeling because I expected the need to console her after.

My punishment for making Ashley watch sad movies has usually been serving as a cry pillow afterward. I swear the girl gets as upset over what happens to fictional characters as she does to bad parts of actual history.

Anyway, so attack of girlishness happened. There may have been some giggling involved. Between Friday and now, the needle's gone too far to the Sophia side. Oh, wait. I still have to deal with a vampire hunter somehow. Getting into a fight definitely counts as pushing the needle back to the Sierra end. My little sisters are like a pair of shoulder angels: the pink frilly faerie on one shoulder, and... I dunno, Sarah Connor on the other. I'd have said Lara Croft, but Sierra has no interest in finding relics, just blowing crap up—in video games.

In between doing our homework, we talk like we used to. Since Ashley's presently without a boyfriend or girlfriend, I attempt to avoid bringing Hunter up. She asks, but our conversation in that regard is limited to me telling her we had fun for a little while on Saturday, but the 'date' mostly consisted of doing stuff around his house. This leads to Ashley performing a reasonable impression of Tim Allen in some bizarre parody of *Vampire Home Improvement*.

Yeah, she's an oddball. That's why I love her.

I mention we invited Hunter, Ronan, and their mother over for dinner, too, but they already had plans to visit his mother's parents in Northern California, something they hadn't been able to do in years due to his jackass father.

Ashley's purse decides it can't take anymore and throws itself off my desk.

We're both stunned speechless for a few seconds until a small grey kitten with aqua eyes crawls out of it. True to her name, Klepto has a purple scrunchie in her mouth she's stolen from the purse.

"Hey, you." Ashley reaches for the kitten.

Klepto vanishes in a puff of faint light, but reappears atop Ashley's head. "*Mew.*"

She tries to peer up at the kitten. "You're going to take that, aren't you?"

"Mew." Klepto turns in a circle, then jumps onto Ashley's back, walking the length of her body. She squirms and bites her lip as tiny claws make their way over her butt and along her leg to the calf. The cat jumps to the rug, trotting toward my door carrying the scrunchie.

"What, no skritches?" asks Ashley.

Klepto drops the scrunchie out of our reach, then teleports in front of her, absorbing a few minutes' worth of petting before blinking back to the scrunchie, biting it, and disappearing entirely.

"So cute." Ashley wags her eyebrows. "And *so* weird."

I tap a finger to my chin. "I'm considering changing my middle name to Weird."

"It's already assumed." She waves me off. "No need to make it official. That would be redundant."

"Hah." I toss a wad of crumpled up paper at her, bouncing it off her forehead.

We work in silence for a few rare minutes before my thoughts randomly drift to this coming Thursday, and Thanksgiving. "Ugh."

"Hard problem?" She peers up from her book, gnawing on the end of her pen.

"It's calculus. They're all hard. But no, that's not why I'm grumbling. Just thinking about Thursday and Great Uncle Hank."

Ashley groans. "Oh, that man. Hey! This year, you can like look into his head and figure out why he's such a turd."

"Tempting… but the last thing I want to see is what's going on inside his mind. He's not happy unless he's making everyone else around him as miserable as he is. Swear he's surly on purpose to get back at Mom's parents for putting him in a care home."

She cringes. "Really not nice of them to do."

"They had no choice. He constantly complained about everything even when he lived with them. Grandma just couldn't take it anymore. After two years of being told how everything she did was wrong and not as good as his dead wife… they had him move into that assisted living place."

"Ugh. Horrible. Why is he so mean?"

I sigh. "Because he is. And, he's probably tired of living to be honest. Misses his wife and takes it out on everyone around him."

"I guess it's nice they pick him up for holidays, but sorry you have to deal with him." Ashley swishes her feet back and forth.

"Yeah. *This* year, he's not going to ruin it for everyone." I hold a finger up. "I have no qualms about putting his butt on mute. He can make all the faces he wants."

Ashley laughs. "Awesome. I was going to suggest you sneak away and come over, but Mom and I aren't really doing anything this year."

"No turkey? Seriously?" I put a hand on her forehead.

"Nope." She grasps my wrist to pull my arm down. "It's just the two of us. Since Mom's parents moved to Florida last January, there's no one coming. We're gonna fly down there for Christmas, but taking two trips is too much for Mom."

"Guess your other grands are still not coming?"

She looks down, flicking her pen. "Nope. They're going to Dad's. They don't want to see Mom and I'm not going to Dad's without her, even if she said I should. Not happening. If they're going to be crappy to her, they don't get to see me. Dad's barely sent me six emails since he left. Sometimes, I think he just set up a script to automatically send it on my birthday."

"Sorry." I scoot over and pat her on the back. "He doesn't hate you and he's not mad at you. He's just…"

"A living computer. I know." Ashley leans her head on me.

Her father's parents are still angry over Mrs. Carter getting custody of Ashley when they divorced. Initially, her family tried once or twice to 'put differences aside' for the holidays. Alas, according to the stories, the warfare that went on around their table made Great Uncle Hank seem mild. All he really does is complain and insult people. Hank has been dubbed 'The Ruiner' by Sophia even though he tends to leave her alone for the most part. She's quiet, meek, and overly girly—exactly how he thinks a girl should be. Sierra bears the brunt of his wrath, and I catch it, too. He largely ignores Dad, but constantly needles Mom. Two years ago at Christmas, she walked outside into the backyard and let out this Tarzan scream after he left. Mom has enough stress already from her job and wrangling the Littles… though my death *has* helped a bit. The sibs aren't at each other's throats anywhere near as much as they used to be—but her job's pushing her harder this year.

"Hey, why don't you guys come over here?" I ask.

Ashley twirls her pen around her finger. "I dunno. You think your parents would be okay with it?"

"Absolutely. My third sister and other-mother?" I ruffle her hair. "No question."

"Okay. Umm. Make sure first and I'll bounce it off Mom."

I logroll back to my former position—yes, I can be goofy, too—and grab my phone. A quick text exchange with Mom ends with an 'of course!' Grinning, I wave the phone at her. "We have clearance."

Despite the closeness of our friendship, Ashley's never been here for a holiday dinner before. Sure, she's spent an hour or two hanging out on the odd Thanksgiving, Christmas, Easter, or whatever, but she always had to go home for family dinner—or get carted off to some relative's house. These days, her remaining family is mostly either dead or living multiple states away. Her mother has one brother with a wife and kids, but he's in like Texas and they don't really have much contact. She has more relatives on the father's side, but none of them want anything to do with her mother after the divorce, which means Ashley ignores them.

Mentally, I give them all a giant middle finger decorated in blinking lights.

"Cool! Gonna call her." Ashley grins, pops up to kneel, and reaches for her... missing purse. "Umm. What the? Where's my bag?"

I sigh and push myself up to stand. "Be right back. My sister's kitten took it."

Ashley blinks. "Are you kidding me? She stole a scrunchie. How did that little kitten take my entire bag?"

"Trust me." I walk out, hang a right, and head for the stairs up to the kitchen.

Ashley follows, her expression one of pure curiosity. Sierra's in the living room on the PlayStation—shock, right?—no sign of Sophia. So, we go upstairs to her room. She's whispering to herself in a way that sounds like chanting. Uh, oh. Hypocritically, I pull her door open without knocking and peer in.

Sophia's kneeling on her rug in front of one of Mom's serving bowls full of pens, pencils, ripped-up bits of loose leaf paper with writing on them, some rulers, glue bottles—basically like all her school supplies. Her textbooks, papers, and notebooks surround her like she's made a ritual circle out of them. Ack! She's using crayons for candles. The 'rents would absolutely freak if they caught her with an open flame in her bedroom.

She holds her hands out over the bowl. "Flame consume the crayon of green. Teachers think homework is mean. Fire eats crayon of red. Much work do teachers dread."

Sophia blows a handful of glitter into the bowl—then snaps her fingers.

All the crayons stop burning at once.

Ashley gasps.

Sophia jumps with a clipped yelp, whirling to stare at us with the same face I must have made the time Dad caught me and Scott making love. Well, not exactly the same face. She's not blushing or screaming.

"Soph?" I ask. "What'cha doing?"

She clasps her hands in her lap, flashing the most adorable of cheesy smiles. "Just practicing."

"By doing what?" I walk over and stand next to her, examining the layout.

"Umm, trying to cast a spell on my teachers to get them to stop giving homework. Dunno if it will work, but what's the point of having magic if I don't use it to solve major world problems."

Ashley laughs. "War, hunger, and disease are major world problems. Homework isn't."

"Says you," mutters Sophia. "You're like old now and don't have it."

Ashley and I exchange a forced-serious stare for two seconds before we crack up.

"If only. Still have it, kiddo." I crouch beside her. "More than they gave me senior year. I had the most as a freshman, and since this is basically my freshman year in college, that makes sense."

"Aww, poop." Sophia hangs her head. "Seriously? What good is magic if I can't destroy something as evil as homework?"

I fold my arms. "Using magic to influence people to do things against their will is bad."

"I'm not forcing people to do anything." She holds up a finger. "I'm forcing them *not* to do something."

"You walk a dark path, young mage," says Ashley in an eerie voice.

Sophia sets her hands on her hips. "Would it be wrong to use magic to stop someone from killing people?"

"No, but assigning homework and killing people aren't even close on the scale of evil." I wander over to her bed.

"Fine," she huffs, then twists to look at me. "Do you have some kind of sixth sense that goes off whenever I'm doing something you think I shouldn't be doing?"

"Nope. Your cat took Ash's bag."

"If she did, it's under the bed." Sophia gestures at the spot. "Klepto?"

The little grey kitten appears on my sister's shoulder. "Mew."

"Aww. She's adorable," coos Ashley.

I get down to look under the bed, but pause, staring at Ash. "You aren't reacting at all to the cat teleporting?"

"Should I? Figured it's just a breed trait." Ashley skritches the top of the kitten's head. "Got a feeling she's not a Russian blue even if she looks like one."

Sophia laughs.

Sure enough, I find Ashley's purse under the bed along with a pile of other random things, many of which don't appear to belong to anyone I know. "Your cat has expanded her operation. She's stealing from the neighbors."

"No she isn't." Sophia flops on her back, holding Klepto up over her chest in both hands.

"There's stuff under your bed that isn't ours."

"She's not stealing from the neighbors. The stuff's from like Minnesota or something."

I facepalm. "Stealing from far away doesn't make it better."

"Didn't think it's bad because she's not taking anything valuable." Sophia makes cute faces at the kitten. "Just plastic jewelry, junk, and lots of socks. But only left ones."

"That explains *so* much," says Ashley in a spacey voice. "Teleporting kittens must have been around since humanity invented socks. There are always strays!"

Sophia babbles in baby talk noises at the kitten, and I swear the cat looks down at her with an expression like 'seriously? Stop.'

"What are you objecting to?" My turn to pat Klepto on the head. "You *are* a kitten, right?"

The little furball slumps defeated, hanging in my sister's hands.

"Any idea why she steals?" asks Ashley.

Sophia makes a series of contemplative faces. After a moment, she sets the kitten standing on her chest and pets her with both hands. "I think she's collecting items with emotional significance to their owners, because they make good focus items for spells. But... the socks, no idea. Maybe she likes them because they're soft."

"Your cat is nesting?" I grin and toss the bag to Ash.

"Guess so." Sophia shrugs.

Ashley fishes her phone out and calls her Mom to float the idea of them coming here for Thanksgiving dinner.

"Nice!" Sophia grins up at me. "Two more. We're going to drown Uncle Hank in estrogen this year."

Wow. That's as close as she gets to being mean to someone. A scary spark of inspiration dances in her eyes.

I point at her. "Do not enchant Uncle Hank. He's ninety-one this year and can't take it."

She moans. "But he's gonna ruin it again."

"Nope." I wink. "He won't."

"Ooh!" Sophia grins. "I can't wait!"

10

TMI

Tuesday night at about three in the morning, I'm having some nice quality time with a 'banana split' bath bomb. It's kinda become a habit of mine to fully immerse myself in the tub and hold my breath for somewhere between forty-five minutes and an hour. This late at night, it doesn't inconvenience anyone, though I've learned my lesson and lock the door.

When it opens midway into my soak anyway, it can only be Blix walking in on me. Sam would've knocked before he used a screwdriver to unlock the door—or at least made a lot more noise.

Sure enough, the click of tiny clawed feet goes by the tub.

I sit up.

Blix overacts a silent scream of fright and springs up to hang from the ceiling like something from a Looney Tunes cartoon.

"Question for you."

He abandons the 'fright' in an instant and glides down on his little wings to stand on the edge of the tub. "Mmm?"

"These two guys were saying some highly age-inappropriate stuff to Sierra the other day. Do you have any weird supernatural way to find someone if all I know about them is the names they use for the online game?"

Blix tilts his hand side to side.

"Sort of?"

He taps his ears, pantomimes using a controller, then puts his hands together and makes a diving gesture.

"If you hear their voice while playing a game you can go swimming?"

Blix slaps himself in the forehead. "Ugh." He huffs, then points at himself, at his ears, makes the game-playing gesture again, then walks a few paces across the tub edge and punts an invisible object.

"Oh, are you saying if you hear them while playing a game you can find them?"

He points at me, nodding.

"Great. Killgod97 and Snake69."

Blix raises an eyebrow.

"Light hospitalization."

He blinks, both eyebrows up.

"Yes, seriously. You didn't hear what they fantasized about doing to Sierra." I grumble. "Okay, they didn't know how young she is until she said something, then they stopped with that crap. But they still went way out of line. Okay, never mind on the hospitalization, but do something embarrassing."

He gives me a thumbs up and glides over to the toilet.

I lower myself to lie back under the water. Hmm. It might not be wise of me to become so casual about asking an imp for favors. I'm becoming entirely too comfortable consorting with daemons. Probably should stop that, but those jackasses crossed the line with my little sister.

There must be consequences.

THREE DAYS PASS IN RELATIVE QUIET.

Damarco doesn't show up anywhere near Seattle Central College, and he's not at the hotel. Admittedly, a chance exists I checked the wrong room. Didn't exactly memorize the number. Flying around outside the building peering in windows didn't let me find him. Maybe he went home to see Tiffany for the holiday? Still, worry this dude is going to kill a vampire and I'm going to be blamed for it keeps me up at night—metaphorically speaking.

I'm already up at night.

So, whatever time homework didn't eat, I threw at scouring the city for this guy. No luck. Worse, Glim's pulled a disappearing act. Shadows are *way* better at finding people than me, but he's gone off somewhere and never mentioned anything to me. Not that he *has* to. It could mean something came up suddenly, and he didn't have the chance, or it's personal. I'm not *too* worried about Damarco, though. If he got close to killing a vampire and it would put me in danger, I'm sure Coralie would appear and warn me. Did I mention it's extremely cool to have an Oracle's gratitude?

Eventually, Thursday arrives, meaning Thanksgiving. The reality that this is my first major holiday after death hits me hard again as soon as my eyes open.

I lay there on my bed, staring up at my ceiling, stuck in a tangle of bad thoughts. Mostly, my stupid brain is trying to make me imagine what the day would have been like if Dalton hadn't been there to bring me back. Would Mom have even tried to host dinner? I can just picture Great Uncle Hank saying something nasty about me being dead. He's totally the kind of guy who'd insist my death was my fault somehow. I shouldn't have dumped Scott or something to that effect. Dad would've punched him. Hank would've had a heart attack and died. The Littles would be scarred for life.

Ugh. Stop. I sit up and grab two fistfuls of my hair. It's long enough to drape into my lap—and will stay this way forever. Staring at it again makes me feel like the midpoint between my sisters. Sophia doesn't mind spending tons of time on hair care. Sierra just lets it do what it's going to do. Though we got lucky gene wise. All of us have straight hair neither too thin nor too thick.

I'm still fully dressed from last night's searching, even shoes. My butt got in the door about forty seconds before sunrise. Attempting to change for bed would have resulted in me passing out halfway into my nightshirt. No doubt, someone would have found me in an embarrassing pose. So, I flopped on the bed in my clothes and waited for the darn sun.

So, yeah. First major family dinner event after death. Grandma Sheridan sometimes invites us over for Easter dinner. My parents don't pay any attention to the holiday unless we go there, but last Easter happened before my change.

My door opens. Sophia pokes her head in, sees me awake, grins, and hurries over. She's completely dolled up in a fancy pink dress—though Aurélie would consider it dreadfully plain because it's modern, not from 300 years ago, and doesn't require a maidservant to help put it on. The kid's wearing a little bit of makeup and a pair of thin 'elven' braids that meet at the back of her head and trail down the length of her hair. She's even put hot pink polish on her toenails. Given Mom's 'no shoes in the house' policy and how we're going to be inside all day, no surprise.

"Who's getting married?" I ask.

"No one, dork. It's Thanksgiving. People are coming over! Gotta dress nice."

Sophia is a total paradox. For the most part, she is the picture of shy and quiet. She doesn't like dealing with crowds or rooms full of strange people. However, she *adores* being in a group of people she's familiar with, like what happens during big holidays. I think she's doing 'child' wrong. She gets more excited at having people around than about her Christmas presents. She's an extroverted introvert. The kid is lucky our parents had four. She'd have been miserable as an only.

Me? I've always been kind of 'meh' about family gatherings. Some of it is from Great Uncle Hank—I've mentioned he's kind of an asshole, right?—and some of it comes from being a moody teenager who had better things to do than sit around in a room with a bunch of older people, especially when they put sports on.

Like, New Years' Day, we usually go to the grandparents' house (Dad's side) for a baked ham dinner. Grandpa Wright invites some of his Air Force friends over, sometimes their wives or adult kids come with. It had been horrible before the Littles were born. Imagine pre-tween me, the only child in a house full of adults watching freakin' football, drinking beer, and talking about stuff that went way over my head. I used to *dread* going there for New Year's. Maybe I could write a physics thesis on the perceptual decompression of the time stream capable of causing eight hours to take four days to pass.

A tiny part of me briefly entertains the idea of hiding out in my basement bedroom all day and staying out of everyone's way. But… with Sophia grinning at me, bristling with eagerness, I can't. Seeing her reminds me how much of an effect on my outlook nearly dying had. In the matter of a few seconds, her excess energy and happiness rub off on me and starts making me thrilled to spend some time with the extended family. The grands are all roughly in their mid-sixties, so it's not like they're going to drop dead soon. Great Uncle Hank, at ninety-one, is an 'any minute now' situation. Honestly, it's mean of me to think, but the sooner he goes, the happier everyone else will be. Probably even him, too.

Still, I can't let him cast a shadow over my still having a family.

Sophia grabs my hand and pulls me out of bed. I laugh as she practically shoves me toward the downstairs bathroom. "You gotta get cleaned up and dress nice."

"Oh, do I now?"

"Yeah."

It's weird, but a little bit of the massive feeling of joy and relief at not being dead I'd experienced upon arriving home after waking up in a morgue comes out of nowhere. Sophia runs upstairs, leaving me to shower and change in peace. For being a vampire, my clothes are surprisingly funky. Then again, my bloodline is fully lifelike including sweat. Maybe that's why animals aren't freaked out by me? I still have a normal 'scent.' Neat.

Hmm. Oh, hell. The needle's already two ticks away from 'Full Sophia.' Might as well redline it. After showering, I wrap myself in a towel and scurry to my bedroom, then put on a dress. It's not as fancy as my sister's, definitely not pink—dark blue actually—but me wearing a dress at all is equivalent to Sophia putting on a frilly one.

Sierra putting on a plain dress is equivalent to Sophia wearing one of Aurélie's elaborate monstrosities.

Sierra *did* put on one of Aurélie's old timey fancy dresses when we sat for her painting. The world nearly stopped rotating.

I check myself in the closet door mirror. Okay. Looks fine. Like Soph, I skip shoes. Right as I'm about to walk out of my room, Sophia returns.

"Nice." She surveys my outfit. "Wait here. You are missing polish."

Amused, I sit on the edge of my bed. Soon, she returns and paints all my nails a shade of blue to match the dress. Wow. Not bad for a quick look at me then picking a color from her case upstairs. She blow-dries the polish to hurry it up. Once done, we head upstairs together.

It's overcast but not rainy.

That makes the upstairs uncomfortably warm to me, but not painfully so. Sierra is on the PlayStation as normal, trying to cram in her game time before the TV is commandeered for sports. She's thoroughly unimpressed with the notion of holidays and is wearing her usual print T-shirt and jeans. Apparently, Sophia has already guilted her into accepting polish on her toenails.

Sam's sitting cross-legged on the recliner, absorbed in his PS Portable. He's also gone for a normal non-holiday wardrobe of a T-shirt and jeans. His toenails do not have polish. Though, I'm honestly uncertain if he'd object to Sophia using him for practice.

I join my parents in the kitchen to help out.

"Wow, what's the occasion?" asks Dad. "You look beautiful."

"Just Thanksgiving. Figured since Sophia turned it up to eleven I might as well set the dial on six."

Mom laughs.

"Sorry I wasn't awake to help you guys out more."

Dad pats me on the arm while carrying a baking dish across the kitchen. "It's fine, hon. We know you have no control over that."

Mom zooms over and hugs me tight. Uh oh. She's having a 'we almost lost her' moment. Anything I say will only make her upset, so I merely hug her back, sincerely happy to still be here. To my surprise, she doesn't turn into a ball of emotion.

For the next almost two hours, we buzz around the kitchen like people working in a restaurant getting ready for the dinner rush. I trade occasional texts with Hunter wishing him a happy Thanksgiving, but we don't have a chance to get into a long conversation since he's kinda busy, too. The doorbell rings at 4:06 p.m.

"I got it!" calls Sophia.

"Knock yourself out," mutters Sierra, sounding oh so thrilled.

The soft sucking noise from the rubberized weather seal around the front door precedes Grandma Sheridan squealing at Sophia. Mom rolls her eyes, thinking no one notices. It's not that they fight or anything, but as a mother, Grandma Sheridan had been kinda strict with Mom. Less so with her little brother Ricky. However, as a grandmother, she is, as Mom puts it, 'indulgent.' For example, if Mom wanted something like a Nintendo system, she'd have been told to get a summer job and save up for it. But... Grandma Sheridan saw an ad for the Ps4, knew Sierra 'only' had a Ps3, and got both her *and* Sam Ps4s without them even asking her to do it. The bulk of the toys and dolls in the Littles' rooms came from her. Well, her and Grandpa Sheridan.

He spent a long time in the Air Force. He still sometimes flies commercial jets, but only part time. Not sure how much longer they'll let a sixty-four-year-old guy behind the controls, but I think he's decided to accept he's getting older and will finally retire. Where Grandma tends to shower us with gifts and cookies, he loves taking us places. Mostly historic sites or science museums.

Unfortunately, behind them on the porch is Great Uncle Hank in his wheelchair. He's Grandma Sheridan's older brother. He doesn't look any different than I remember him from last Christmas. Pale, wrinkled, spotted, wearing brown pants pulled up so high they almost count as a bra. As always, he's sporting a frown as sour as the smell clinging to him. It's a mixture of talc, Old Spice, stale clothing, stale care home, and... age, I guess. Can't blame him for it since he's ancient, but having a valid excuse doesn't make it a nice fragrance.

Grandpa Sheridan pushes him in the front door. He briefly glances at Sophia, gives her a terse nod of acknowledgement, then proceeds to frown at the room. He's not in the door for ten full seconds before he begins muttering to Grandpa about how 'plain' the house is and how Mom should've decorated better for a holiday.

Grr.

Sierra glances over at him with thinly veiled hostility in her eyes and continues playing her game.

"Oh, Sarah!" Grandma Sheridan whisks over to me at the archway between the dining room and kitchen. "You poor dear. Such a scary experience you had with that awful boy." She grasps my arms and fusses at me. "It's so good to see you're all right."

Grandpa Sheridan parks Hank by the end of the sofa and hurries over to me as well. "How are you holding up, kiddo?"

"I'm okay." I smile. "Was scary there for a while, but it's all past me now."

"Heard they got the bastard," says Grandpa.

"Dad!" calls Mom from the kitchen. "There are children present."

Grandpa chuckles, then whispers, "If 'bastard' is the worst thing I let slip tonight, consider me keeping it tame."

I chuckle.

"Oh, you poor dear." Grandma hugs me. "They scared the hell out of us when they mistook that other poor girl as you."

"Yeah, they—"

"Take yourself upstairs and dress properly, young lady," snaps Uncle Hank.

Sierra doesn't react.

"I said—"

"I heard you. I'm ignoring you," deadpans Sierra.

Great Uncle Hank emits a gurgling noise. "Didn't your mother teach you to dress properly? You shouldn't be wearing that, especially on a holiday."

Grandma and Grandpa put on fake smiles, trying to pretend his outburst isn't happening. Grandma's expression also has a hint of apology directed at Mom. They continue peppering me with comments and questions about surviving my crazy ex-boyfriend's knife attack while Hank needles Sierra over wearing jeans.

"What about him?" asks Sierra, pointing her thumb at Sam.

"I'm talking to you, little missy." Hank coughs. Sounds like a ball of goop the size of a rat does a flip in his trachea.

Yeah, the more I look at him, the happier it makes me I'll never get old.

Sierra pauses the game. Oh, shit. That's only slightly less dangerous than an Old West gunslinger unhooking the snaps on their holster. She stands, facing him. "So, let me make sure I understand what you're saying. It's okay for Sam to have on a shirt and jeans, but *the girl* needs to wear a dress?"

"Allie," wheezes Hank, waving as if trying to summon Mom. "What are you doing with this girl of yours? She wouldn't have this attitude if you raised her properly. You got it right with the little one at least. Guess it took four tries."

Sophia looks down, ashamed.

"Gah!" Sierra fumes. "Why do we keep inviting this asshole!?"

Mom flies past us into the living room. (Not literally flying. That's my thing.) "Sierra Renee Wright! Watch your language."

Sierra leans up on tiptoe, thrusting her chest at Mom, hands balled to fists at her sides, and shouts, "Go ahead and ground me. But I'm *not* gonna just sit here and take this sexist BS without calling him on it. This is 'improperly dressed' for a girl, but not a boy? I don't care if he's old. He's wrong. And he does this *every* year. I'll sit in my room all night and be *happier*."

Everyone falls into stunned silence. Sierra continues staring a challenge up at Mom.

The music from the PS Portable stops. Sam sets it on the sofa next to him, gets up, and walks without a word—or eye contact—past the Mom/Hank/Sierra cluster and goes upstairs.

Great Uncle Hank glances at him as he goes by, then looks at Sophia, Sierra, Mom, and me. Seconds later, he fixes his gaze on Mom and starts complaining about none of us having shoes or socks on. "You and your germ nonsense. That's the problem with the way you're bringing these kids up. They have no respect. Walking around barefoot like a bunch of ignorant primitives." He rambles in a partially coherent complaint storm, somehow blaming the rise of hippies and 'free thinkers' in the entire country on our mother's lax parenting abilities.

Mom pinches the bridge of her nose. Almost like a cartoon character, she turns red from the bottom up... a thermometer about to explode.

"Come on, Hank." Grandpa Sheridan hurries over and repositions the wheelchair to the inner side of the living room away from the front door, tucking him between the couch and recliner. "The game should be on by now." After settling the old one, he grabs the remote and attempts to change the TV from PlayStation to cable.

Sierra stands there fuming, so angry she's on the verge of tears.

I wrap my arms around her from behind. "Don't change. You wear whatever you wanna wear, okay?"

She nods, managing a weak smile.

The doorbell goes off again.

Sophia's still staring at the floor and doesn't leap into action to answer it. Seeing her reduced from excessive holiday joy to ashamed sadness in mere minutes infuriates me. Mom emits a frustrated sigh, like she can't figure out what to do with Sierra cursing at Hank, but puts it aside for now and answers the door.

Uncle Ricky, Mom's little brother, is there standing next to a pretty Chinese woman. He's twenty-six, a good deal younger than my mother. The woman's about the same age, I think. Her shimmery lavender gown bares most of her neck and shoulders, held up by a pair of silver metal butterfly-shaped clasps. The garment gets an 'ooh' from Sophia, improving her mood.

"Hey, Allie." Ricky hugs Mom. "Sare!"

I endure an overly energetic hug and back-pat from him. He's a *lot* nicer than Hank—then again so is moldy dryer lint—so I don't mind the attention and hug him back. Much to my surprise, he doesn't make me jump through the rigmarole of explaining my attack again. Some people in my position would be hurt he didn't think to ask about it, but I'm relieved.

"Everyone, this is Alyssa." Ricky puts an arm around the woman he brought.

"Hello," says Alyssa in a somewhat sheepish tone.

Even while offline right now due to the daylight, I can tell Ricky didn't mention anything about bringing her here ahead of time. From the looks on my grandparents' faces, they have no idea who she is either.

"Building a railroad, Rick?" Great Uncle Hank emits a wheezy chuckle.

Sophia peels her stare away from the rug, her nose scrunched in confusion at the remark.

"See?" says Sierra. "He's an asshole." She looks up at Alyssa. "Ignore him. He's a douche who still thinks it's like 1908."

That poor woman looks trapped between angry at Hank's crass remark, ashamed of causing a scene, worried her unannounced arrival is going to cause problems... she's basically got 'this was a mistake' written on her forehead.

Okay, Sarah to the rescue. I swoop over to her. "I absolutely *love* your dress! Hi, I'm Sarah. Ricky's niece."

We get into an easy conversation until Ricky finishes explaining to his parents that Alyssa is his 'serious' girlfriend. Then, he approaches us and redirects our conversation from girl stuff to my almost being murdered. Alyssa gasps.

"Glad you're okay." He grabs me in a pretend headlock and lightly grinds his knuckles across the top of my head. "Someone should've told that idiot a knife isn't the best way to a girl's heart."

For the second time in under a half hour, the entire house goes dead silent. Dad looks pissed.

"Uhh..." Ricky emits a nervous laugh. "Too soon?"

"Yeah, a bit," I whisper.

"Sorry."

I smile. "It's okay. I've dealt with what happened as much as it's possible to deal with it."

Rustling fabric draws my attention to the stairs. Sam walks down into the living room wearing one of Sophia's pink princess gowns. I think it's a Halloween costume from a year ago. Basically, he grabbed the most frilly, girly thing he could find quickly. Sierra bursts into laughter. At her sudden laughter, everyone else turns to see what struck her funny.

And for the *third* time inside a half hour, the house is silent—except for Sierra laughing.

Grandma Sheridan blinks rapidly. "Sammie? What are you doing?"

Great Uncle Hank makes a noise he's never made before. Ooh, is he maybe having a heart attack? Stroke? Ugh. I shouldn't joke about that.

In his usual blasé tone, Sam says, "Uncle Hank told Sierra she wasn't dressed nice enough. We had on the same clothes. So I dressed nicer." He walks past the couch so the old one can see him fully. "Is this formal enough for a holiday?"

Sierra stares at him, her mouth open in shock, her eyes a little wet.

Sophia's crying, but I can't tell if it's because she's trying to contain laughter, thinks he's adorable, is mad at him for going into her room, or senses the impending nasty argument the old one is about to start.

Great Uncle Hank gestures at him. "Good grief, Allie. Hope you're proud of yourself. The boy's gone gay."

"Hank!" shouts Mom.

Awkwardness clenches in my gut. It shouldn't really surprise me a guy this old thinks being gay is a negative thing, but now I'm dreading having him in the same room as Ashley. If he makes her upset, I refuse to be held accountable for my actions.

Dad climbs over the couch, since the rest of us are all kinda plugging up the space between it and the wall, and puts an arm around Sam. "So what if he is?"

"It's… it's…" Hank rapidly gestures at him, his fingers flopping about like a half-open pack of wrinkled hot dogs.

Mom leans over the sofa back, smiling nervously. "Are you going to wear the dress all night, dear?"

"Is Uncle Hank gonna be a butthead all night?" asks Sam with an expression of complete innocent sincerity.

Ricky laughs unexpectedly, but bites it back, emitting a noise like someone drop-kicked a chicken.

So done. I grab the sofa to stop myself from hitting the floor as I die laughing.

Mom and Grandma Sheridan get into a rapid muttering conversation with Great Uncle Hank, trying to futilely convince him there's nothing at all wrong with gay people and if he can't accept that, he should keep his opinions to himself. It's astoundingly rare for Grandma Sheridan to openly contradict Hank, which makes it all the more impressive to watch her defend Sam. Mom's further annoyed by his second accusation she failed at raising her kids, Sierra for being insolent (and not girly) and Sam for being gay.

As far as I know, Sam isn't. He's supporting his sister. And if he is, who cares?

Sam sits beside Sierra on the sofa, seeming in no hurry to change clothes.

I half expect Sophia to start putting makeup on him, but she resists the temptation.

Nuclear physicists could safely study the mechanisms of a chain reaction by merely adding Uncle Hank to any social situation. The argument soon engulfs everyone except for Sam, Sophia, and Alyssa. That poor woman stands with her back to the wall beneath the stairs, holding Ricky's hand. She looks like she's about to cut her arm off to get out of here.

The doorbell rings.

Since I live here and am not embroiled in the battle royale—and the closest to the door—I answer.

It's Dad's parents.

Gloria and Ken Wright both have PhDs and try to be as 'cool' as possible despite having woefully inept social abilities. They're basically the nerd-hippies from every Eighties college comedy film who live in a secret lair below the school accessed by a complicated rollercoaster setup or elevator hidden in a dorm closet. They would simply adore Professor Heath's lair, even if he doesn't have a strange little mine car elevator system to get in and out. He doesn't need that since he can fly. The Wright grands even drive a Volvo. Grandpa Wright's green plaid blazer and pink bowtie would legit cause any fashion columnist to drop to the ground clutching their chest. He's tall and kinda gangly, but has to be the second friendliest person in the room after Sophia. Grandma Wright is how I always imagined J.R.R. Tolkien's elves would look if they ever grew old.

"Sarah!" they chime together, and pounce hug me.

No big deal. Between the two of them, they're about 120 pounds. Dad had to get his skinny genes from somewhere, right? I'm thoroughly back-patted, squeezed, cheek-patted, examined, and hugged. For the third time today, I have to re-explain the Scott situation. As far as they know, he tried to stab me, mostly missed, and ran off after falling for me playing dead.

The Wright grandparents are still in the midst of squeezing me—having left the front door open—when Ashley's mother's car goes by out on the street, returning from their shopping. I don't bother closing the door since the two of them will be here any minute.

Their outpouring of concern over my near murder has injected a neutron absorber into the argument. My parents, the Sheridans, Ricky, and Alyssa stand there wearing awkward faces while trying to pretend a giant argument hadn't been going on seconds ago. Sam's making effeminate hand gestures while Sophia and Sierra laugh. He's obviously doing it on purpose to grind Uncle Hank's gears.

Just as the Wright grands notice Sam's in a pink dress and start asking why, Ashley and her mother appear at the corner, walking into the cul-de-sac.

Grandma Wright tells Sam he's adorable while Grandpa Wright asks why he decided to wear it, in a tone entirely curious and non-judgmental.

"Uncle Hank said a T-shirt and jeans wasn't fancy enough for

Thanksgiving dinner." He puts an arm around Sierra. "But he only yelled at her."

"Hey!" chirps Ashley as she bounds in the door, handing me a tray of homemade brownies.

Mrs. Carter smiles at me and tries to hand over two pies.

"Oh, wow. Mom!" I yell. "Pastry traffic jam."

My mother takes the pies and leads the way to the kitchen. Ashley follows us. Her mother tries to come along, but Grandpa Wright catches her in a conversation. I set the brownies on the kitchen table while Mom fridges the pies—a French silk and an apple.

"How bad is it?" whispers Ashley.

I spin away from the table, rolling my eyes up into my head. "Ugh. Not even fifteen minutes and it's already hitting the fan."

"Some people just aren't happy unless they're making others miserable," whispers Ashley. "Try to ignore him."

"Easier said than done." Mom squeezes both our shoulders. "Will you two give me a hand?"

"Sure, Mom."

Ash helps us in the kitchen as we put the finishing touches on the side dishes and arrange everything on serving trays and plates. Dad zooms in grumbling about Hank making him forget… and tosses two canisters of quick-bake rolls in the oven.

Doorbell.

"I got it!" chirps Sophia.

Well, that's good at least. Her mood's bounced back.

The long, rising squeal of delight in an older woman's voice tells me Aunt Jody has arrived. In years past, she's been the superhero who's kept Great Uncle Hank at bay. The woman deserves her own reality television series. She's crazy as a steeple full of bats, but means well. Aunt Jody's into stuff like pyramid power, healing crystals, essential oils, tarot cards, séances—though recent events have made me consider séances less crazy—and weird crap like dousing rods and astrology.

Yanno… I have killed an actual troll in an alternate dimension. Maybe there's more to her pseudoscience than—nah. The troll wasn't real. I'd been unconscious in a cave and dreamed the entire thing. Ben and Cody Peters lay sleeping right next to me and we all had the same dream at the same time via a three-way telepathic communication link.

That makes more sense than a legit freakin' troll.

One year, Aunt Jody had wireframe pyramid earrings as big as hen's eggs with crystal shards dangling inside them. Every time I look at her, the sound of them clinking comes back to mind. Today, she's got a pair of pink crystals hanging from her earlobes, miniature Himalayan salt lamps about the size of green grapes.

She's Mom's older sister, fifty going on twenty-one. Married some dude named Dale Wexler, but the guy disappeared before I was born. Depending on how much wine is involved, Mr. Wexler's fate changes from leaving her randomly, got killed by a robber during a gas station hold up, died in a car accident, died to cancer due to a vast military-industrial conspiracy poisoning the nation's food supply with mind-control chemicals, or died when his homemade rocket ship carried him at 400 miles an hour into the Grand Canyon.

For most people, alcohol loosens the tongue. There's some kind of adage out there about truth comes from the mouths of drunk people and children. In Aunt Jody's case, it doesn't really work. Her 'truth' gets wilder and wilder with each glass. My guess is the guy wasn't weird enough to click with her and bailed. Of course, if weird really does run in our family, maybe the guy really did pull a Wile E. Coyote with an ACME rocket.

Oh, wow. We could so totally mess with her if I convinced Blix to let her see him—but only her. Nah. That's mean. I do actually like Aunt Jody.

"Welcome the alien ambassador," calls Great Uncle Hank. "Didn't recognize you without the pyramid hat."

Aunt Jody waves at him while making a 'nice to see you too, Hank. Now go die in a fire' forced smile. With the food situation under control and nothing to do but wait for the dinner rolls to finish, everyone but Mom ends up in the living room sipping wine and munching from the party platter Dad put on the coffee table: two kinds of cheese, pretzels, tiny sausage slices, and some weird little crackers.

The couch is full, so I sit on the armrest nearest the door and mostly zone out. Football's on the television much to Sierra's discontent. All three Littles are sitting on the floor in front of the sofa. Sophia's politely *not* reading her Kindle. I've a strong suspicion Sam really is going to spend the entire night—at least until Hank leaves—wearing the dress.

Aunt Jody either doesn't notice the boy's in a pink princess gown or it's weird enough to seem normal to her. Mrs. Carter gawks at him for a few seconds but doesn't say anything. She's known us long enough to assume there's a deeper underlying story to everything that appears unusual.

Even though no one is near him or looking at him, Great Uncle Hank continues grumbling about everything: Mom's parenting, it's too warm in here, not enough decorations, food's taking too long, Sam's gone gay, Sierra's insolent, and so on. Apparently, the entire fabric of the country is tearing apart at the seams because a girl has jeans on. And yes, he's still complaining about how everyone but him have taken their shoes off. Good thing he didn't notice Ashley left hers at home. But hey, at least she's wearing a dress. You know, 'like a girl should.'

I frown.

Sensing the sunset imminent, I turn my head, hide my eyes against the inside of my left elbow, and fake sneeze. The Littles and 'rents know exactly what I did for two reasons. One: I don't sneeze for real anymore since I'm, well, dead. Two: in life, my sneezes never had so much energy. Most of the time I'd sneeze, it sounded like an angry cat spitting. Sophia makes these cute little squeaks when she sneezes. Sam and Sierra both sneeze like normal humans.

Anyway, I look back up. After coming online, the room pummels my senses. All the food has become much more intense in fragrance. Also, the scent of each person in the house is as clear to me as it would be to a bloodhound. Ugh. Someone turn the sun back on. Great Uncle

Hank's even worse with my nose cranked up. It's like I'm licking moldy drywall in the care home.

Maybe his attitude is revenge for living with that smell?

I glance over at him, second-guessing my animosity. Before I can think not to, I'm peeking into his thoughts.

She faked the attack for attention to get out of going to that school in California. Not sure why she bothered. The girl's not smart enough for college. What's a girl even doing going to college, anyway? What idiot thought it would be a good idea? No wonder the country's in ruin. Damn this uncomfortable chair. He glances at Sierra and Sam. *Bah, both of them are the LGB-whatever alphabet soup. And disrespectful.* He sneers in Mom's direction. *Allison's far too lax as a mother. Needs to use some proper discipline.*

By this point, I'm scowling at him. Apparently, since Sierra isn't sugary sweet and talked back to him, she must be a lesbian. Sigh.

He proceeds to mentally grumble about Grandma and Grandpa Sheridan not 'supporting him' in pointing out how children ought to be raised. He thinks they took Allison's side, letting her be too soft so her kids run wild. Simultaneously, he is annoyed they dragged him out of his room at the care home—he apparently hates any change to his routine—but he'd be upset with them if they didn't bring him to holidays. He's basically mad at everyone because no one else is demanding Sierra go 'dress like a proper girl' and disciplining Sam for his deviance. Since he's stuck in a wheelchair and has no real other way to express his discontent, he decides to crap his pants and sit in it all night without telling anyone so we all have to enjoy the bouquet.

Eww!

I poke him in the brain to put the brakes on his overactive colon until he's on a toilet, then break off contact before another disgusting thought can come up. Grandpa Sheridan gets a slight mental nudge to think he heard Hank tell him he needs the bathroom. He sets his drink down and wheels the old one off down the hall.

Crisis averted.

Ugh. I sit there trying not to look as bored as I feel. After dinner, the Littles, Ashley, and I will more than likely end up playing some kind of board game while the adults monopolize the TV for sports. At least *that* will be fun. And yeah, I came way too close to losing this family to begrudge the time with them.

My gaze falls on Alyssa. She's sitting on the sofa to my right, Uncle Ricky next to her on the other side. They're holding hands like lovebirds, but she does *not* look comfortable. Curious, I peek at her head. Not too deep, only what's right at the tip of her brain so to speak.

Most of her worry at the moment is due to insecurity about her relationship with Ricky. His former hesitance at bringing her around his family has her questioning if he's really in love or merely regards her as an exotic curiosity. She isn't sure if he brought her tonight out of a sincere interest in her meeting the family or only as a superficial gesture so she stays around longer. A few hostile looks from Great Uncle Hank have made her feelings of not belonging here worse. Also, she thinks Ricky's parents—the Sheridan grands— disapprove of him dating a Chinese girl. They haven't said anything, but she read disappointed surprise in their faces when he introduced her.

I don't think Grandma and Grandpa have any problem with anyone based on their ethnicity, though they have made a few racially insensitive jokes around me, older generation and all. I look at what's going on in Ricky's head, giving in to curiosity at the expense of ethics. The family threw that sort of ethics out the window when they brought Hank into the room.

Ricky is… happy. He *is* aware Alyssa's uncomfortable but blames it on Hank—no shock there. I probe a little more deeply and get the feeling he's totally in love with her. The hesitation Alyssa had been reading from him is real, but the reason behind it isn't worry he's only interested in her for sex. He doesn't know for sure if Grandpa Sheridan has a problem with non-white people or is tone deaf to sounding like a moron when he tells those kinds of jokes. Ricky had been worried they'd cause a scene and she'd leave him. He's also worried they won't accept her.

Oh, wow.

Well, since I'm invading privacy tonight, may as well at least superficially invade everyone's.

Grandma Sheridan feels guilty over Hank being a jerk, but she would feel worse leaving him alone at the care home. She is legit mad at him for shaming Sam for 'being gay,' though shares my opinion he's only wearing a dress as a show of support for Sierra. No matter what she does, someone's going to be hurt, so she errs on the side of not being the thoughtless person. Leaving Hank at the care home would be thoughtless on her part. What he says and does isn't on her conscience as much. The weird look she gave Alyssa appears to have been worry about Grandpa Sheridan making a stupid joke about Chinese people. She doesn't have any problem with Ricky seeing Alyssa. Alas, she doesn't understand why 'the sensitive generation' gets so upset at that sort of humor.

I smile at her. Even though she doesn't know why, she grins back at me.

Aunt Jody and Mom are talking as they usually do. No real reason to poke her brain since the contents of her surface thoughts are exactly what flows out of her mouth at any given moment. Even if she's alone, she doesn't have an inner voice. All her thoughts become words.

Sierra and Sam both stare at football on the TV with 'someone shoot me' expressions. It's tempting to whip out the board game now, but... food will be ready in less than ten minutes.

You know, I think Sam really *is* going to wear the dress all night.

11

THANKSGIVING MIRACLE

Mercifully, my mother beckons me to help move stuff to the table after only a few minutes.

Ashley rushes after me to help. She's far from unhappy to be here, though I get being in a room full of my relatives that she barely knows is kinda awkward for her. While we're ferrying serving platters from the kitchen to the table, Grandpa Sheridan and Great Uncle Hank emerge from the side hall. The old man's grousing about his belt going missing. Neither one of them have an explanation for how it could vanish right out of his pants while he used the toilet.

Hah. Bad kitty. Wait. No. Good kitty.

Hank spots me carrying the turkey and gripes at Grandpa Sheridan about how he or my father should be carrying it. Because, like, turkeys should be transported only by men or something. Okay, sure it's a giant freakin' turkey, but I'm plenty strong enough to carry it. He does not know this, however, so I force myself not to be mad at him for complaining about me again.

Eventually, everyone's taken their seats at the table. Grandpa Sheridan wheels Hank up to his spot on the middle on the side across from me. Ugh. They should put him in the corner of the table, so he's not so central. Or better yet, give him his own table in the living room like they used to do for the kids when we were tiny.

Aunt Jody and the Wright grands notice the huge oil painting Aurélie did of the Littles and me in early 1700s clothes. They think it's adorable and wonderful work.

"Did Jonathan do that with the computer?" asks Grandma Sheridan.

"No, Gran'ma," says Sam. "It's a real painting."

Great Uncle Hank glances at it, specifically Sam wearing a 'Blue Boy' outfit, and blurts, "So how long as the boy been gay?"

Ashley goes stone-faced.

No one acknowledges the comment, continuing their discussion about the painting like Hank didn't say a thing.

"Hmph," grumbles Uncle Hank. "Why are you wearing that, Allie? No wonder the kids are dressed like hooligans. You're too casual. No one cares about doing things right anymore."

Again, everyone largely ignores him. Alyssa looks at Rick with a 'wow' expression.

Mom's inches from stabbing someone. In fact, Dad takes the big knife from her and proceeds to cut the turkey. Rather than draw someone's blood, Mom has a giant sip of wine. Yeah. Tonight's going to be rough.

As food goes around, most everyone tries their best to pretend Uncle Hank isn't there. Alas, it doesn't last long.

"Ehh. Smells all right," mumbles Hank. "Quite clear you're only cooking to be nice. Evelyn used to put *real* love into her food."

The glare Mom gives him makes me hear that little *dun-dun dun* riff from *The Terminator* play in my mind.

Annoyingly, Grandpa Sheridan merely tries to shut him up by nodding.

Sierra leans closer to me and whispers, "How much longer until he dies?"

Sophia coughs. Fortunately, neither Mom nor Dad caught it. Though, given the look on my mother's face, maybe she did and chose to let it slide. Despite intermittent random grumbles from Hank about the turkey being too cold, too hot, too tough, not seasoned properly, the potatoes being lumpy, and so on, we all dig in. Normal conversation goes on in spite of him, with Sam and Sierra loudly complimenting Mom on the awesome food.

Sierra smiles at Sam, whispering, "Thanks for having my back."

He nods once at her and stuffs a giant forkful of turkey into his mouth.

"You better not spill anything on my gown," says Sophia in a playful-scolding tone.

"It's okay if you wanna go change. Point made." Sierra nudges him.

He shrugs. "Nah. This is really comfortable."

"See?" Sophia makes bug eyes at Sierra.

About six minutes into dinner, Uncle Ricky makes the mistake of establishing eye contact with Great Uncle Hank.

"Shame little Ricky's developed such immoral political views. You voted for the damn commies, didn't you?" Hank squints at him.

"This is neither the time nor the place to talk about that." Ricky forces a smile.

"Of course it's the time and place. Only see you twice a year, dammit." He smirks at Alyssa. "At least you've still got an eye for women. That poor boy of Allie's—"

"Hank!" I snap, silencing everyone. He glares at me—right up until I dive into his head, implanting a compulsion preventing him from speaking unless he's going to say something nice. "If you don't have anything positive to say, just stay quiet and stop dragging everyone down into the misery pit you refuse to climb out of."

His brain explodes with indignation at me—not only a woman, but a mere teenager—talking to him with such a tone. However, the mental wall I built refuses to let anything past his voice box. He goes red in the face, making a bunch of constipated expressions while jabbing his finger at me. It's tempting to smile at him, but my goal is not to kill him off with a rage-induced heart attack, merely try and salvage as much happiness as I can for what remains of Thanksgiving dinner.

Everyone stares at me. The grands are all shocked, as much at watching quiet little me bark at him as they are he's staying silent. I've never raised my voice in front of the family before (arguments over homework, picking up my room, and chores aside). My parents aren't shocked. They know—or at least suspect—exactly what happened. Mom's glower shifts to complete gratitude. Dad goes red in the face just like Hank, but he's trying not to laugh.

"Awesome," whispers Sierra.

It takes a moment for everyone to resume eating and talking. Great Uncle Hank, aka The Ruiner, keeps making weird faces at us, but says nothing more. For the first time in my life, a holiday dinner becomes a pleasant affair.

In between scraps of conversation with Ashley about random stuff, I look around at everyone. When he thinks no one notices, Uncle Ricky slips Sam some wine, pouring it from his glass into Sam's opaque plastic cup. My little brother eagerly sips it, then makes a 'why would anyone drink this willingly?' face. That gets me chuckling to myself.

"Allie," says Aunt Jody, "there is something really strange in the air here. Maybe you should set up more crystals."

I can't help but imagine Great Uncle Hank making a remark about how 'pyramid power' did nothing to help Jody's co-worker and friend who died of cancer a couple years ago. My aunt filled the poor woman's hospital room with pyramids of every size and material imaginable. To no one's surprise, they didn't help. He loves reminding her of that. Maybe when an old person is so close to death, the concept of dying becomes hilarious to them. It's not funny to anyone else, though.

Having been there and done that, I feel I'm qualified to have an opinion on dying.

Not long after I put Great Uncle Hank on mute, Alyssa finally shows signs of relaxing amid a conversation with the Wright grands about her career. She has some kind of office job for the US Forest Service. Ricky—who works in IT—gets into a chat with Grandpa Wright about the computers the Air Force had 'back in the day.' Sierra inserts herself into the conversation about old technology and how much has changed... and keeps up with them. Some of the stuff reminds me of the paper I had to write about old storage technologies, so I chime in, too. Dad's thrilled I'm interested in programming.

Hank continues to gesture and grimace, occasionally managing a strangled clicking sound, but he doesn't say another word for the remainder of dinner. Aunt Jody hits the wine a little hard, downing it the way Dad inhales iced tea.

Surrounded by the din of multiple conversations, I start to wonder if allowing so many people to see me, know I'm still around, could be a mistake. There has to be a reason every vampire but me lets their families and friends believe they'd died. Glim has a pretty good one, in addition to being turned into a vampire while overseas. Somehow, I suspect the number of vampires who let their family know they're still around is larger than anyone admits. But... sharing it with the extended family is pushing it.

"Real quick," says Grandpa Sheridan, holding up his wine glass. "I'd just like to say how grateful Mary and I are that Sarah's okay. Quite the scare she had."

Pre-vampire me would have wanted to crawl under the table at ending up in the spotlight with so little warning. I probably wouldn't have, but my voice would've gone bye-bye. However, it's impossible to take on an enormous multi-headed 'nope beast' part scorpion, part tarantula, and the size of a UPS truck when I'm armed only with a sword and not gain a little confidence.

"Yeah, that was freaky, but it could've been way worse." I pick up my iced tea. The 'rents probably wouldn't care if I drank wine considering it *can't* have any effect on me, but I didn't even ask. The stuff they got is too expensive to waste—plus it tastes awful. "I'd rather he didn't try to stab me at all, but all things considered, I'm happy the way it turned out."

Aunt Jody raises her glass in toast—shakily. She's also only wearing one earring now. Gah. Cat!

Grandpa Wright lifts his glass. "Good thing the cops put him down. The bastard's lucky I didn't find him."

"Ken," says Mom in a chiding tone. "Please don't swear around the kids."

He chuckles. "Sorry, Allie. I'm trying, but you know how it is. Spend enough time in the military and certain words become like punctuation marks."

Sierra smirks. "Mom doesn't like it when we hear words like bastard, or shit, or—"

I put a hand over her mouth. "Hey. It's not a tradition you need to end every holiday meal grounded."

Dad leans forward. "Usually, she snaps at Hank, but he's oddly behaving himself tonight."

Great Uncle Hank emits a low gurgle, glowering at Dad.

"She already snapped at him," mutters Mom.

Sierra pulls at my arm, but I keep holding my hand over her mouth.

"However." Mom nods at her. "He deserved that one."

"Wmm?" Sierra stops fidgeting, her expression shocked.

Mom shows Great Uncle Hank the F-you smile she usually whips out on opposing lawyers who annoy the hell out of her during a case if she wins. Oh, damn. She really is pissed. "Yes, it is quite nice of him to be pleasant. Can't imagine what came over him that he's decided to finally be respectful of others." She sips her wine, winking over the glass at me. "It's a real Thanksgiving miracle."

A LITTLE HELPFUL PRODDING

I t's amazing how much difference a little mental domination can make in a holiday meal.

Is *this* what normal families enjoy? No wonder people do Thanksgiving or Christmas dinners with guests more than once. Sorry for being morbid, but if Hank is still here next Thanksgiving, he's going on mute the instant my powers come online. No, I don't want him to die, but the man is really old so there is a real chance he might not be around in a year. It *is* sad to think about. If he wasn't such a hateful old bastard, it would bother me he spends most of his time at the home. Sure, the Sheridan grands visit him at least once a month. Then again, if not for his acerbic nature, he wouldn't be in the home at all. And even if he did go into a facility, if he wasn't such a butthead, we'd probably all be visiting him.

Ashley's mother makes epic pies. I simultaneously adore that calories do nothing to me and feel guilty for taking pie away from a living person. However, I claim a reasonable-sized piece of the French silk since it's basically what love would be if it existed as a solid material.

Aunt Jody's had enough wine to rob herself of the ability to speak.

Rather, everything she wants to communicate, she sings. Somehow, Mom can understand her

A second miracle happens tonight beyond Hank staying quiet. Rather, I should say *a* miracle happens tonight. The old guy staying quiet was an act of Sarah, not a higher power. The real miracle is that my little brother made it through dinner and dessert without getting any stains on the pink dress. The boy even poses with me and the Littles so the grands can take pictures, unfazed at being captured on film in a princess gown.

When Uncle Ricky goes upstairs to use the bathroom since someone's in the downstairs one, I slip away and follow him, waiting in the hall until he's finished. He stops short upon seeing me right outside the door.

"Oh, sorry. You should've knocked and let me know you had to use it." He smiles.

"It's fine. I don't need the bathroom. Wanted to talk to you alone."

He raises both eyebrows. "What's up, kiddo?"

"Noticed you're being Oblivious Man. Not a big deal, a lot of guys are. Alyssa is pretty insecure about how you feel toward her."

"What do you mean? Did you talk to her? What did she say?" Ricky scratches the back of his head.

"Nah. It's, umm, written right on her face. Girls can pick up on that sort of thing." I try to keep an innocent expression. Does this count as lying? "I know—am pretty sure you love her, but girls like being told clearly. Did you notice the way Gran and Pop looked at her?"

He flinches. "No, but... I had a feeling."

I put a hand on his arm. "Not like that. They were surprised, but she took it the way you're taking it. Really, they're okay with her. I'm thinking Alyssa is worried you are dating a Chinese girl as a way to annoy your parents. You gotta tell her how you really feel."

Rick takes a deep breath and lets it out gradually. "Yeah. You're right. I'll do it."

"Cool."

"When did you become so intuitive?" He chuckles.

"Just kinda happened out of the blue. Having Scott come after me with a knife put a lot of things in perspective."

He pats me on the shoulder. "Noticed you and the Littles didn't spend the whole night bickering."

"Nope." I grin. "One of those changes. It's trite but that whole 'you don't know what you've got until it's gone' thing is true."

"Hint received. I'll talk to her." He winks and starts to walk past me, but stops, looking back. "Oh, how the heck did you get Hank to shut up?"

"Umm." I shrug. "Probably so shocked someone my age basically scolded him like a little boy that he went mute."

"Heh."

I fume all over again, at what he said to Sierra and about Sam. "Seriously, what the hell is wrong with him? Why is he so nasty to everyone all the time? He was going to crap his pants and sit in it to make everyone else miserable."

Ricky laughs. "Nah. He wouldn't do anything like that on purpose. He's just old. Accidents happen."

"No, he really was going to do it on purpose."

"You can't know for sure."

Eep. He's right. I *shouldn't* be able to know. "Oh, yeah, well... the look in his eye. Sure seemed like he was really trying to blow up the living room."

"However you managed to do it, nice job." He pats me on the back.

I follow him downstairs. He goes straight over to Alyssa, who's in a conversation with the grandmothers plus Aunt Jody. Great Uncle Hank has been parked in the corner where he's still making constipated faces at everyone, but all the nasty things he thinks to say at any given moment stall before they make it to his mouth. Dad plus both grandpas are on the couch watching sports, belts loosened from the turkey feast.

One of the wings mysteriously vanished, and no one appears to know what happened to it.

Alyssa and Ricky slip away to have a quiet conversation. Great. I've basically become Dear Abby with fangs. Hey, what's the point of having infinite cosmic power if I don't save a relationship or two on the way?

The clatter of dishes is like a lasso of guilt around my neck pulling me to the kitchen. I walk in on Mom, Mrs. Carter, and Ashley starting on cleanup... so I join them. Something must be wrong with me. Despite this basically being work, it's still fun spending time with them.

13

EVERY FAMILY HAS SECRETS

My good mood crashes and burns soon after we finish cleaning up the kitchen.

Mom, Mrs. Carter, and Ashley head back to the living room, likely expecting me to be right behind them. An inexplicable sense of sorrow comes out of nowhere and I find myself standing alone in the kitchen, staring down at my toes. The din of voices coming from the living room all of a sudden sounds foreign, like I'd barged into some other family's house where I don't belong.

On autopilot, I wander out onto the deck behind the house and sit on the first step, hugging my knees to my chest. The sadness didn't come from a momentary out-of-body experience or anything. No, I understood exactly what the feeling meant. Not a stranger's house. I don't belong in *that* house, with the Wright family anymore. It's only going to cause problems for everyone.

A few minutes of solitary quiet later, the sliding glass door squeaks open. No need for me to look back since I recognize Mom's scent. She pads over and sits on the step beside me.

"I'm guessing you're not okay. Want to talk about it? I didn't see anything happen."

I pull my hair off my face, holding it down against the wind.

"Nothing happened. Just worrying about everyone seeing me... and some other stuff."

"Why?"

"You know... I'm not going to get older. Guess it wouldn't really have worked for you guys to lie to them and say I didn't survive Scott's attack when we had people over. Not so bad now, or maybe for a couple years, but they're eventually going to notice my appearance isn't changing."

She pulls me into a one-armed hug. "We're doing fine. It's not pleasant to think about, but your grandparents aren't going to be around long enough for your age to matter. Nothing we can't explain away with 'good genes and some cosmetics.'"

"Wow, that's so wrong." I cover my face in both hands to muffle a sad chuckle.

"It is." Mom sighs. "But it's how the world works. I don't want to lose my parents, but the day is going to come... The only thing we can do is make every minute count as much as possible... except for Hank."

I burst out laughing.

"And wow. Sam in a dress." Mom whistles.

"Yeah."

My mother cracks a grin. "It's cute on him."

"It is." I chuckle. "Daryl and Jordan would tease him about it, but he wouldn't care. He's protective of his sisters. Even ran *at* a vampire trying to get him off me."

Mom shivers. "Please let them grow up before you start another vampire war."

"That wasn't my fault. Honestly. I didn't do anything to cause it other than be Dalton's, uhh, offspring."

She squeezes me. "If the man didn't save your life, I'd ream him out for putting Sam—and you—in danger."

"I don't think he expected things to go as they did. Bad luck."

"All right. But, don't be glum, okay? Tonight has got to be the best Thanksgiving I can remember for a long time."

"I found Hank's mute button."

"Glorious."

"Any idea why he's like that?"

Mom shakes her head. "He always has been vocal and judgmental, as far back as I can recall. Mostly, it's the era he came from. He still thinks it's 1920. Enough about him, though. Please don't be sad tonight. Enjoy these times because they won't last long. Grandma and Grandpa used to host big holiday dinners when I was little. Aunts, uncles, my grandparents, even sometimes a neighbor... but by the time I turned seventeen or so, most of them had died. Just my parents, me, Jody, and Ricky. Felt so strange being used to holiday dinners always being a gigantic affair, and then... one day it's just our usual family dinner on fancy plates."

"Wow..." I look down. "If you're trying to cheer me up, you're going in the wrong direction."

"Sorry." She jostles me with a brief back rub. "Just saying, you have nothing to be down about... yet. At least let us die off before you mope."

I stick my tongue out at her.

She chuckles.

"What's going to happen if the Littles have kids someday?"

"Hopefully, they'll stay close so I can see them."

"I mean... should I tell their kids the truth about me?"

Mom mulls it over, gazing up at the stars. "Well, you could either let their kids in on your secret or make them forget about you when they get old enough to start noticing you haven't changed."

"If I let them in on it, they're going to grow up and maybe have kids and the same question repeats. The number of people who know about me turns into a pyramid. That's definitely going to get me in trouble with other vampires, maybe even the Persons In Black."

"You'll do fine, dear." Mom kisses me on the side of the head like I'm six. "You've always succeeded in whatever you made up your mind to do. This vampire stuff is no different."

I scrunch my nose. "Think so?"

"Sure. Some families have weird secrets they keep for generations. It's not too hard to imagine."

"Mom, do you think I'm the only person who this has happened to who's told their family?"

She kinda frowns in thought, then shakes her head. "Nah. Given the sheer number of humans who have existed since the outbreak of humanity, I guarantee it's happened before."

"You sound like Dad talking about how with billions and billions of planets, there'd have to be life on more than only Earth."

She tugs on my arm. "C'mon. Let's go inside. And, your father has a point. Statistically speaking, with so many planets, even a fractional chance of life developing on any planet would translate to it happening thousands of times."

"Please don't bring that up around Dad's parents or it's all we will talk about for the rest of the night."

"Yeah. True." She chuckles. "All good now?"

"Mostly."

"What's still bothering you?"

"You wouldn't understand."

She nudges me. "Says every teenager ever to their mother. Try me. I was your age once."

"This isn't a teen problem." I sit up straight. "I stumbled on a vampire hunter lurking around the school. He's after one of my professors. The other vamps found out I discovered a hunter and didn't say anything about it."

"Is that bad?"

I shrug. "Not really sure. This one elder who's a complete douchebag made it sound like I'm helping the hunter and trying to get vampires killed. He got the rest of them to agree it's my like 'rite of passage' or something to deal with this hunter because I'm the one who discovered him first. Wants me to kill him, but I can't just do that. If I don't get rid of him, they're going to blame me for any vamps he kills the same as if I destroyed them."

My mother stares at me for a long moment, her eyebrows clearly transmitting 'wow, okay, I wasn't ready for that.' "Certainly a pickle."

I laugh. "A pickle? Okay, Grandma."

She pokes me in the side. "How dangerous is this man?"

"No idea. I've never run into a 'real' hunter before. The last ones who tried to kill me were complete idiots."

"What?" Mom gawks at me. "Someone has tried to kill you already?"

"Oops."

"Yeah. Oops is right, young lady! If someone tries to kill you, you are obligated to tell me about it."

I spend a few minutes explaining the morons in the van with the stake-chucking crossbow. "So, yeah, idiots. It sucks. I could reveal myself so he attacks me... it wouldn't feel like murder so much to defend myself. But, giving him the first move is kinda scary. My best chance of winning would be to ambush him—and it feels so wrong. They didn't say I *had* to kill him, only get him to leave Seattle. Pretty sure they all want me to murder Damarco. Stefano's going to mock me if I don't, but I couldn't care less what he thinks."

"Who is Damarco?"

"The vampire hunter."

"You know his name?" Mom blinks.

I nod. "Yeah. Overheard him on the phone."

"Maybe you could try to trick him?"

Hmm. Maybe. Blix might help me pull him through the mirrorverse. But it wouldn't stop him from coming back to Seattle, and it would be as good as killing him to leave him stuck in there. Okay, bad idea. The guy appears to be reasonable. Maybe I *can* talk to him. He's obviously mistaken Professor Heath for someone else.

"Do you think the vamps will be mad at me if I found the one Damarco is really looking for and sent him in the right direction, assuming the vampire isn't around here?"

"You should be studying law, hon. That's a rather adept way to jump straight through a technical loophole in the ultimatum they gave you. But make sure the other vampire is not around here first."

I almost laugh. "Me, a lawyer? I'm *so* not confrontational enough. Besides, isn't night court like when all the weird people come out?"

Mom shivers. "Yes."

The door opens. Ashley pokes her head out. "Hey, what are you guys doing out here?"

"Just needed some air," I say.

"C'mon. Let's get back in there before everyone leaves." Mom stands, pulls me upright, and starts for the door.

"Mom?"

"Hmm?" She turns.

I hug her. "Thanks for making me feel better."

"You're welcome, sweetie. I know you've gone through a lot of changes lately, but you're still my daughter and I'll always be here for you."

"Love you, Mom."

"Oh, Sarah? You *are* planning to push Hank's mute button on Christmas, right?" My mother smiles at me the same way Sophia smiled right after she asked to keep Klepto.

"Yep." I grin. "Are you gonna ground Sierra for swearing?"

Mom chuckles. "Not this time. He deserved everything she said. Just had to put on a show of being upset, you know how it is. Though, I *do* wish she wouldn't use foul language."

"I don't understand why no one ever tells him to stop," says Ashley.

"It's probably a mix of knowing he'll ignore us, some kind of 'respect the elders' thing, and hoping if we don't pay him any attention, he'll stop." Mom steps into the kitchen, waits for me to follow, then closes the door.

I chuckle. "Yeah, but—"

Sophia appears in the archway out of the kitchen. "Sare! C'mon, we're gonna play *Descent!*"

"Looks like I'm being paged."

Mom gives me a 'go on' wave.

Ashley grabs my hand and drags me after Sophia. We run to the dining room which has been repurposed for a giant board game.

And yeah, Sam's *still* wearing the dress.

14

PIE

S am's in the process of unboxing the stuff for the board game, a whole bunch of plastic monsters and such plus map tiles. I start helping set up, but Sierra walks over to see what Sophia's doing by the front door. Oddly, my youngest sister is lurking by the glass like a nosy neighbor.

Maybe she's watching Grandma and Grandpa Sheridan leave with Uncle Hank. They have to go early because the home requires he be returned before ten. Not exactly sure what happens if they bring him back late. Does the place 'ground' old people? Or do they only have to listen to someone complain at them? Aunt Jody will be spending the night since she's had far too much wine to drive. This is not unusual. Jody will probably still steal Sophia's bed for the night like she's done the past few years, and the girls will share Sierra's. Or maybe Sophia will crash in my room.

Within a few minutes of my sisters congregating at the front door, they get into a mild argument. The sports guys on the TV plus conversation drowns them out, but I do notice Sierra calling something a stupid idea; however, Sophia keeps insisting.

I set down a red plastic dragon figure and walk over to them. "What's up?"

The girls look at me.

"I think Mr. Neidermayer is lonely. There aren't any more cars by his house. It's Thanksgiving. Can we bring him a piece of pie?"

Sierra rolls her eyes. "The guy's as big a dick as Uncle Hank. He's only going to be mean to you and make you cry. He hates children and hates happiness."

"Naw." Sophia faces her. "He's probably like that because he's lonely and everyone's mean to him all the time."

"Everyone's mean to him all the time because he's a dick to everyone." Sierra folds her arms.

Sophia looks up at me. "Hey... you can find out why he's mean."

I sigh at the door. While it's true I could read Mr. Neidermayer's mind now and figure out what makes him hate kids so much and keep Frisbees, balls, and whatever else strays onto his property, it feels like a waste of time. "Some people are just like that. He has been nasty to kids ever since I was tiny. Probably even before."

"But why?" Sophia flails her arms.

"Because he's an asshole," says Sierra.

Sophia gasps, blushing.

"I heard that," calls Mom from the sofa.

"Well... he is." Sierra sets her hands on her hips.

Mom gives her a 'knock it off, please' stare.

Ashley walks over to us, wondering why we're not at the gaming table.

"He has to be thankful about something." Sophia puts on an innocent smile.

"Yeah." Sierra laughs. "He's thankful he doesn't have any kids near him. You'll be wasting your time. He'll probably think the pie is a trick and just throw it out."

Sophia looks down, her smile fading. "You think it's a waste of time to be nice to people?"

Damn that girl and her guilt-fu. I put a hand on her back. "Okay, okay. Fine. Let's go bring him a piece of pie."

"Yay!" Sophia grins, then darts to the kitchen, returning a few minutes later with a slice of apple pie on a paper plate, covered in plastic wrap.

Slightly selfish of me, but whew... she didn't go for the French silk or pumpkin.

Yes, we had far too much pie in the house tonight.

The four of us—Ashley decides to join us—head out the door and cross the cul-de-sac to his house. It's a little chilly for them to be outside barefoot, but we're not planning on staying out here long. Going to Neidermayer's place makes me feel like a character in one of Dad's D&D games walking up to the lair of the evil wizard.

I can't remember the last time a child set foot on this porch. Even the Girl Scouts avoid the place.

Sophia pushes the bell. An old timey *ding dong* goes off inside.

We wait for a few minutes, but he doesn't answer. I don't even hear anyone moving around. Ack. I hope Blix didn't make the guy so angry he had a stroke. He's been a major dick to me my whole life, but I don't want him dead. The guy's nowhere near as old as Hank, probably around seventy or really late sixties, but it's still possible he had a sudden medical issue.

"Do you think he went to visit friends?" asks Sophia, all innocence.

Ashley stands up on tiptoe to peer in the tiny door window.

Sierra makes a face but resists saying he doesn't have any. Can't tell if she keeps quiet for Sophia's feelings or because she's afraid Neidermayer might hear her.

"I hope he isn't hurt." Sophia rings the bell again. "If he doesn't answer this time, we should have Dad call the police to check on him."

Grumbling accompanies the thudding of footsteps moving across the house toward us. A few seconds later, he yanks the door open, his face twisted into a sour expression. "I'm not hurt. Just don't want to buy cookies or whatever else you're selling. Go on back home."

Wow. No screaming at us. That's a surprise. Even odder is him trying to ignore us. Usually, the man has a supernatural radar sense that activates whenever someone under the age of twenty puts even one toe on his property. Then again, we didn't touch even a single blade of grass.

Sophia holds up the paper plate with pie on it, giving him this huge, hopeful smile. "It's a holiday and we didn't want you to be lonely, so we brought you some pie."

Ashley waves, smiling. Sierra's expression is somewhere between the forced politeness kids put on when the parents tell them to smile and a stare of 'if you make my sister cry, I will end you.'

Not wanting to risk it, I peek into his mind, ready to stomp on anything he might say or do that would crush Sophia. He's suspicious the pie's a trick—spiked with laxatives or something to prank him... but he thinks Soph looks too innocent for mischief. He's a little bit like Great Uncle Hank in his beliefs about little girls being pure innocence and little boys are always up to no good. A few seconds after she hit him with 'full adorable,' he grumbles mentally about how annoying children are.

Predictably, he finds children irritating because they are—usually —much happier than he is and hearing them makes him more keenly aware of being lonely. And well, sometimes small kids *can* be super annoying, like when they start singing at the top of their lungs, repeating the same line over and over. But, yeah... he's miserable because he's alone. I feel a little bad for sending Blix to torment him, but the guy did sic the cops on the Littles over a hot cocoa stand and he's been nasty to every kid in the area as long as I can remember. Just because the dude's sad he never had a family doesn't excuse his being a complete turd to me for eighteen years. Well, more like thirteen... he didn't bother me before I could walk or go outside.

Mr. Neidermayer clears his throat. "Thank you."

Sophia hands him the pie. "Happy Thanksgiving."

Ashley echoes her.

The two of them are throwing off so much sweetness they could cause diabetes at thirty paces.

He nods, mumbling something inaudible. Probably because his brain forgot how to say nice things. For him, at least, this is being super friendly. We wave and leave his porch, careful to stay on the paved walkway connecting to the sidewalk. He closes the door, watching us from the window until we're far enough away there's no chance we'll step in his grass.

My sisters walk fast, eager to get back inside before their toes go numb.

Sierra looks up at me as we scurry across the cul-de-sac. "Did you do that?"

"What?" I ask.

"He didn't yell at us or even say anything mean."

I shrug. "Not me."

"So weird," whispers Sophia.

"Seriously." Ashley whistles. "I thought you brain-zapped him. The guy's *never* that nice."

I shake my head. "Nope. No tweaking happened."

Sierra pokes my side. "You were staring at him like you went into his head."

"Just making sure he wasn't going to say or do something that would've hurt Soph. But I really didn't need to compel him."

"What's his deal?" Sierra hurries up onto our porch and holds the door for us to go inside.

"Not too complicated. Never had a family, so seeing kids makes him feel miserable about himself. He thinks children are irritating."

"Aww," says Sophia in a quiet voice. "That's sad."

"What, no past divorce or death or something?" Sierra shuts the door. "Or lost his kids and Soph's act of kindness breaks his icy heart and he starts smiling again, turning nice?"

I laugh. "Alas. We *watch* cheesy Eighties movies with Dad. We're not living inside one. He's not going to suddenly turn into the nicest old man in Cottage Lake because Cindy Lou Who gave him pie."

Sophia rolls her eyes at me.

"Come on already," shouts Sam from the dining room. "Descent time!"

Time to forget entirely about my problems and finally enjoy some holiday time with my family.

15

THE HUNTER IN THE OINTMENT

S eattle Central College has no classes on Friday, the day after Thanksgiving.

It's also super gloomy and raining hard enough I could legit take a shower on the back deck. Even though the cold wouldn't affect me physically, it bugs me mentally. We're only about eight degrees away from it being snow. Mom technically has the day off, but she's going nuts trying to prepare for an upcoming legal battle, so she's gone into the office.

To give Mom a break, I sacrifice a few hours to housework. The weather is *so* crappy I come online at random spots on the first floor, but shut down near windows. Sam jokes that the constant, brief red flashing lights makes me look like one of those old school toy robots with the LED eyes.

Sierra initially accuses Sophia of having something to do with the weather since rain this hard without thunder strikes her as strange. I try to fly around and dust the wall near the ceiling but give up after an unexpected motion of the clouds brightens the room and shuts me off. Yeah, I face plant the floor, basically belly flop.

And the bitch cloud goes back a second after I land, the flare of my eyes lighting up the carpet in front of me. Grumbling, I resume dusting but only as high as it's possible to reach normally. Once I finish as much major housework as appears obviously in need of doing, it's homework time. Well, homework and laundry. Ninety percent of doing laundry is waiting for the machines to finish.

So, yeah. It's a sorta-holiday, but I'm still busy. Doing my actual homework is a challenge as my thoughts keep straying off the subject material to Damarco. I really ought to be doing *something* about the situation. Sitting here in my house isn't going to resolve anything. Maybe it's possible to claim newness if I fail to stop Damarco from destroying a vampire, but obviously not even trying won't go over well. Stefano keeps calling me a weak little girl, so I'm ready to throw it in his face if he comes after me for not being able to deal with the hunter. Like, one second, he's making fun of me for being young and weak, then he has the nerve to criticize me for not being able to win a fight? Which is it?

Still, it's not night yet despite how dark it is out there. Most of the other bloodlines can't wake up until actual sunset regardless of light levels. As far as I know, Shadows are the only other vampires who can wake up before sundown. However, they can't tolerate *any* daylight. Glim said they don't even have to sleep at all. It has to be super maddening to remain awake constantly.

Damarco didn't appear to know some vampires can fly. He probably assumes no vampires can function before the sun goes down. Other than trying to attack one in their 'lair,' he wouldn't expect to find any vampires at this hour. But, how much does he really know about us? That distracts me from calculus to wondering about this Unspoken Order he may or may not be part of. Considering the other vampires regard him as a threat, it must mean they have killed enough vampires to be dangerous. This Order would have practical experience, but the question is how much? Do they understand the existence of different bloodlines or what each one is capable of?

The dryer buzzes.

I'm sure if Stefano Bianchi saw me using superhuman reflexes to 'do laundry faster,' he'd probably make fun of me. Bleh. Whatever. If I stepped on dog poop, damaging its shape would upset me more than his opinion of me. You know, some puppy put a lot of careful thought and consideration into forming it just right. Who am I to destroy their artwork?

Empty the dryer, transfer from washer to dryer, re-load washer with the next pile, carry folded stuff upstairs. Yeah, I'm having a great holiday. Seriously. For a girl who nearly died, being home doing tedious grunt work really is cool.

While upstairs, I notice it's 5:33 p.m. Mom's still not home and Dad's hanging out in the dining room with the Littles plus Nicole and Megan. From what I overhear, they're in the midst of a board game that takes exponentially longer with more players. Their six-player game has been going since after lunch and they're not even close to finished. Klepto's perched on the table by Sophia, gazing intently at the game pieces.

It's officially sunset (has been for about forty minutes) so it's possible for me to go out and look for Damarco, but... I head to the kitchen, waving on my way through the dining room. The kitten turns her head to keep staring at me. Might as well get started on dinner. Dad's having fun and Mom's at work. According to the schedule, tonight is stuffed shells with some broccoli on the side. Between my mother's recipe book and the internet, I can pull it off.

Not long after I have the cooked, stuffed, sauce-covered shells in the oven, Mom arrives home. The hard *thump* of her throwing her briefcase and stuff down by the front door makes me jump. Ooh, that sounds like a bad day. She hurries into the kitchen halfway out of her drenched raincoat—and stares at me. Yeah, she looks completely exhausted.

"Hey, Mom. Food ought to be done in like fifteen minutes."

She walks out, not saying a word, her expression blank. The downstairs bathroom door opens, no doubt she's hanging her coat over the tub to drip. While I'm cutting up the broccoli to go into the steamer, Mom returns to the kitchen and hugs me from behind.

"You cleaned the bathroom?"

"Yeah," I say. "House is all caught up. One more load to go laundry wise. The only thing you need to do tonight is relax."

She squeezes me and whispers, "Thank you." Whispering's probably all she can manage without her voice cracking under the emotional load.

"Are you okay?" I stop cutting broccoli and turn to look at her. Mom's eyes have gone red but she isn't crying.

"This case is driving me nuts. I keep telling myself it's the job I expected. Long periods of slow to moderate routine with the occasional complete hell. It's not the job that's killing me. It's this case."

"It'll pass."

"Yeah." She chuckles, and stands there holding me for a little while. "You are being such a huge help. I don't know what to say."

I shrug one shoulder and return to the cutting. "Don't need to say anything. It's the least I can do for freeloading. Most kids leave the nest around this age. You're stuck with me forever."

"Literally." Mom rests her chin on my shoulder, her arms still around me. "You're going to think I'm getting mushy, but something tells me we won't mind never having empty nest syndrome. I'm glad you're going to be here."

"Me too."

I bite my lip, still not sure what the future holds for Hunter and me. Not like we're going to have kids together, but he is still going to likely want a place for us. If my intense attachment to my childhood home is a permanent part of my vampire psyche, that's going to be awkward. For those last few seconds of my mortal life and the first like... *day* of my vampiric one, all I could think of was how much I wanted to be home with my family. Admittedly, the idea of going to California had already made me homesick even before leaving, but not strongly enough I changed my mind about attending USC.

Could being so focused on that notion have permanently laser-engraved a need to stay here into my very being? Sure as hell feels like it. This is probably how ghosts wind up haunting places. Hunter's house might be big, but it needs a lot of work. It would almost be cheaper for them to get a smaller place in better repair. Considering how his father was, good chance Hunter doesn't have the same fondness for his home like I do for mine. Maybe he'd be happy moving in here. No, that's silly. What guy wants to live in the same house with his girlfriend-slash-wife's parents? This isn't the Middle Ages.

And yeah, here I go assuming our relationship is going to last more than a year or two. We *are* still teenagers. High school sweethearts getting married and staying married for sixty years only happens in the movies… and the 1950s. And we weren't even really high school sweethearts. He crushed on me from a distance for four years. I didn't even speak more than five words to him until after we graduated.

Regardless, there are too many other more immediate things for me to be worrying about now.

"Really, I'm not unhappy." Mom finally lets go and backs away to sit in one of the kitchen chairs. "Just a high workload at the moment."

"Totally get that." I grin back at her.

"It took me over an hour to drive home. The rain is ridiculous."

I cringe. Driving in the rain sucks only a little less than driving in snow. Sure my car—Dad's old Sentra—is ten years old and an accident couldn't kill me, but the other people on the road aren't immortals. As long as it's dark out, my butt will be flying to school. Even if I need to put on a bathing suit and carry a plastic bag containing dry clothes, it beats traffic in bad weather.

Vampires years ago had it so much easier. Smaller cities, no cell phones with cameras everywhere. No airplanes. I start to laugh at the idea of a vampire being sucked up into a jet engine, but there's fire inside those things. Being chopped up into tiny pieces and burned might actually kill us. Eek. Okay, not funny.

"What are you laughing about?" Mom smiles. "You always do that."

"Do what?"

"Randomly laugh."

"I have silly thoughts… like wondering if a flying vampire ever went into a jet engine like a pigeon."

Mom cringes. "Probably not. You don't fly too high off the ground.

I'd have to imagine a vampire would be aware of airplanes if they flew close enough to an airport."

"True."

We talk about random weird stuff until the food's ready. The board game is *still* not finished, but it doesn't surprise me as much as I'm amazed at all three Littles wanting to keep going. Holy crap. Whoever invented the game managed to completely absorb the interest of three tweens for over six hours. I should check the board for a curse affecting their minds.

I eat a little to enjoy the flavor. My system is still reeling from the amount of food it had to deal with yesterday. They say everyone overdoes it on Thanksgiving, even vampires apparently.

Klepto appears on the table beside Sophia's plate. Before Mom can yell at her to get the cat off the table, the kitten noms a bit of her stuffed shell and teleports away. You know, normal cat owner problems.

After dinner, Dad herds the Littles over to the kitchen to do the dishes with him. I take the opportunity to get the last load of laundry going and put the previous one away. A family of six with four kids generates a crapload of dirty clothes.

It doesn't take me too long to finish off the last of my homework even with the distracting worry of having to deal with a vampire hunter. Technically, 'dealing with him' isn't what worries me. My stomach is doing backflips over the idea Damarco might find a vampire and destroy them before I get off my ass. Most of the time I've spent thinking about the situation has gone toward trying to come up with excuses to give Wolent when Damarco kills someone. *Actually* confronting him doesn't worry me anywhere near as much as my fear of facing vampire society after an epic fail.

If it's bad enough, they might pressure Aurélie into abandoning me as her protégé, which would leave my family vulnerable. If *that* happened, Stefano could—just to be a dick—threaten to kill them if I didn't separate myself from them.

Grr.

With that totally awesome thought weighing me down, I trudge upstairs. It's still monsooning outside. Hello convenient excuse. Really, I should throw on my bathing suit and go after him. It sounds totally ridiculous to go hunting in a bikini, but honestly, most of the time I get into a fight, my outfit ends up in shreds, anyway. Might as well start the brawl half naked. Of course, I'm assuming a fight between vampires using claws. Damarco is still alive. Pretty sure he doesn't have claws, so he won't tear my outfit to ribbons. Still, even for a vampire, wearing wet clothes sucks. Five minutes outside and I'd be as drenched as jumping in a lake.

Hopefully, he feels the same way about wet clothes and stays in his hotel. But, it's still the day after Thanksgiving, so he might not even be in Seattle at the moment. He could have gone home to wherever Tiffany lives.

Mom's watching TV in the living room while everyone else is still around the dining room table at the game. Whoa, the map tiles are 3D. Looks like a fantasy dungeon crawl. They're all playing on the same team, apparently, against monsters and such directed by an app on Dad's tablet. No wonder they're all into it. The game master is a computer so everyone is cooperating.

"What's bothering you?" asks Dad.

"It's..." I catch myself about to make up some nonsense.

My entire family has seen some supremely strange crap. Imps invaded our house. There's one living here. Hell, my sister has a teleporting kitten and some degree of ability with *real* magic. Sam watched me shred vampires who kidnapped him. Sierra and Sophia ended up stuck in an alternate dimension on the inside of mirrors and were nearly eaten by a multi-ton giant nope-a-saurus.

A vampire hunter is small potatoes.

"It's a long story." I flop in an empty chair. "So the other day at school, this guy was showing a picture around..."

With my entire family listening, I explain about Damarco. Specifically, my problem is I don't want to kill him but will be in a heap of trouble if he destroys any vampires around here. My parents both get pissed off when I tell them about Stefano putting me in this position to be responsible on purpose.

"He's probably hoping this hunter kills you," mutters Dad, scowling.

I lean my head side to side while thinking it over. "Nah. Doesn't feel right. It would make him happier for me to fail and get kicked out of the city or forced not to stay at home with you guys."

"Wow, that guy sounds like more of an a-hole than Uncle Hank," says Sierra.

"The vampire is mad at Sare for breaking tradition. Uncle Hank is a butthead because he likes being a butthead." Sam shakes his head. "He's worse."

Sierra looks across the plastic dungeon map at Mom. "You know, according to this article I read online, it's okay to cut toxic people out of your life even if they're relatives."

Mom sighs. "He's ninety-one. Won't be a problem too much longer. We shouldn't be mean to him. Besides, Sarah can keep him quiet."

We all laugh.

"That. Was. Epic," says Sam.

"Not as epic as you in a dress." Sierra grins at him. "I thought the old bastard was going to explode."

My brother looks up from his cards at her with a satisfied smile. "I'll do it again at Christmas if he talks to you like that again."

"Ooh." Sophia bounces in her seat. "If he does, let me do your makeup."

"Okay," says Sam, casual as anything.

Uncle Hank shoots Mom a look like she'd sold one of her kids into a life of piracy or something.

Mom fixed him with a steely glower before spinning to Dad. "Sam looks good in that gown, but don't you go getting any ideas—you're not borrowing any of mine."

My father fake gasps like an offended aristocrat. "How could you say that?"

Uncle Hank turns red in the face.

"You can borrow one of mine," I say, "But I think they might be a little tight on you."

Dad gestures at me. "See, she's supportive. Not going to do heels though. I don't have the calves for them."

Sierra and Sophia burst into laughter.

I don't care what the old bastard says, you're an awesome mom.

My mother gets stuck wanting to cry and laugh at the same time, and ends up just smiling at us while trying not to look at Hank.

"Mind control, duh," blurts Sierra.

Everyone looks at her for a second or two in silence.

Dad grins. "Are you trying to explain why the Kardashians are famous or suggesting how Sarah should deal with this hunter?"

"Aliens," deadpans Sam without looking up from his character cards.

My turn to be confused. "What?"

"The Kardashians are clearly aliens. So are most celebrities and important politicians. We're being farmed." Sam picks up the dice. "My guy is going to try and disarm that trap."

Dad emits an odd squeak.

"Sam, do you really believe the lizard people conspiracy?" asks Mom.

"No." He rolls the dice. "It's just funny to make Dad turn purple."

Dad bows his head, letting out a heavy sigh. "Not funny, Sam."

"At least he didn't say he likes Nickelback." Sierra whistles.

"What's wrong with Nickelback?" asks Sam.

Dad wails in anguish.

"Seriously, Sare." Sierra points at me. "Just mind control the hunter guy to go away."

"Can't." I frown. "He's got some kind of trinket protecting his mind. I don't even know what it is. Ring. Amulet. Bracelet... something. The vamps think he's part of some guild who have been hunting vampires for centuries."

"Whoa. He's seriously got a magic item?" Sam's expression lights up in awe.

"Wicked cool." Sierra gawks at me.

"It's wicked annoying." I rest my elbows on the table. "But yeah, basically… something like that. He's got an enchanted ring of defense against vampiric mind control."

Dad rubs his chin. "Sounds like you need a thief. You can be sneaky, right? Ambush him when he's asleep and steal whatever item he's got shielding his mind. Then, do the brain reprogramming thing."

"I'm not sure I like the sound of that." Mom gets up from the couch and walks into the dining room. "Are you suggesting our child break into someone's home and attack them?"

"I believe I did," says Dad. "But… this is a vampire hunter. He is a direct threat to her life."

"Breaking and entering, Jonathan." Mom chops both hands in his direction. "We're not talking a misdemeanor."

"She's got one foot into another world that doesn't operate on the same rules as the normal world. You know the old saying, anything the cop didn't see, I didn't do. Or in this case, anything the cop isn't permitted to remember, *she* didn't do." Dad taps a few buttons on the tablet as Sam reads off the result of his dice. "Trap is disarmed… but a stray flame has lit Koa's robe on fire."

Mom pinches the bridge of her nose.

"No!" wails Sofia. "Put me out!"

Koa must be the name of her character.

"Is that a legit attack or just cosmetic and funny?" asks Sierra.

"It's not funny!" Sophia fake sniffles.

"Umm." Dad examines the tablet. "It's not saying to do anything or giving damage, so probably just supposed to be funny."

Sophia 'wipes sweat' from her brow. "Whew."

"That's the other problem." I gaze up at the ceiling, frustrated. "No one has any idea how dangerous this guy is. Sure, I might be able to throw him around like any other normal person… but what if he has like special vampire hunter powers and kicks my ass?"

"Depends on what level he is. The supernatural feats don't kick in until he hits level thirteen." Sam swishes air from side to side in his cheeks.

I laugh. "This isn't a game, kiddo."

Sierra shrugs. "Soph could send Fuzzydoom after him."

"Ack!" Sophia gasps. "No way! He's impossible to control. Pleeeease don't make me unleash Fuzzydoom on the world!"

I can't hear a line like that without bursting into laughter.

"I'm serious!" wails Sophia. "It's too dangerous. There's no way to control him. I'm not sure it's even possible to pull him out of the mirror world into reality. Even if it is, I don't wanna know how to do it. He'll kill everyone."

"Aww, I know you're serious. No one's asking you to hit this hunter over the head with the pom-pom of annihilation."

Dad and Sierra snicker.

Sophia wipes her eyes and appears to relax. Her fear vanishes, leaving behind a look of contemplation. She's probably trying to work out a way to help me. Hey, at this point, I'll take any help I can get... even from a ten-year-old.

As long as she stays in the house.

And doesn't unleash the puffball of death.

NOTHING IS ILLEGAL IF YOU
DON'T GET CAUGHT

My present situation isn't going to be fixed by sitting around at home.

Even if only to lessen the sick feeling growing in my gut—wait, that could just be from dinner—I have to at least try.

"Gonna do some recon."

Dad nods at me. Mom gives me the 'be careful' stare.

"Don't die," deadpans Sam.

"Again." Sierra cringes. "Please don't hate me for that. I just had to say it."

I laugh. "It's fine. And funny."

Sophia and Mom don't appear to appreciate the reminder of what happened to me, but neither of them complain.

"Back soon."

I head downstairs to my room, change into my bathing suit, then pack a trash bag with a T-shirt, jeans, sneakers, a towel… and a little surprise for my father. Once I push aside the expectation going outside on a cold November rainy night in a bikini is going to be colder than hell, it's time to actually do it.

The rain is still falling hard, but it's no longer like a standing wall of water in the air.

Mom mutters about not even being able to look at me going outside without a coat in this weather. The Littles find it hilarious. Dad blinks at me.

"Oh, I forgot something."

"You forgot a lot of something," says Dad.

I reach into the trash bag, pull out a red necktie, and put it on like a headband. "Now I'm ready."

The Littles laugh themselves to tears. Dad gives me a thumbs-up while pretending to do the 'I'm so proud of you' lump in his throat.

Doing my best Rambo impression, I march down the hall to the kitchen and out onto the back deck. The rain is frigid... for a few seconds. It unnerves me how fast my body acclimates to the cold. Yeah, I *am* undead, but it doesn't mean the reminders are welcome.

Flying to Seattle in this mess is... wet. I should have brought two towels. My hair alone is going to saturate one. Luckily, it's not too difficult to find my way to the hotel despite the storm. Finding the room Damarco is staying in—or stayed in—isn't any easier tonight. Without smashing a hole in one of the sliding glass doors, going directly into a room isn't happening. Maybe I'm too nice, but wanton property damage still feels like something bad. Trying to avoid making a hard-to-explain entrance, I go up to the roof in search of another way into the building. A cube-shaped structure that probably contains the elevator mechanism has a plain steel door likely intended for maintenance workers to access the roof. It's undoubtedly locked, but I don't mind lightly breaking it. A doorknob is a lot less expensive than a whole patio door and casual thieves aren't going to scale the building to get at a roof access door.

Pulling on the knob with increasing strength eventually breaks the socket in the doorjamb, sending a metal bracket flying over my shoulder. I duck inside out of the rain, entering a concrete-and-steel stairwell. To my left, a doorway leads into a machine room with two cable spools and other various components that make elevators work. No cameras at least, good.

After removing the headband—only wore it to make Dad smile—I do my best to squeeze water out of my hair. When it's as dry as hands alone can get it, I open the bag and towel off. Hair's still damp, but screw it. It's been wetter coming out of the shower. After trading the bikini for my tee, jeans, and sneakers, I pick up the trash bag and hurry down the stairs to the ground floor.

The lobby isn't big. This hotel is not what one would call 'nice.' It's not awful either. A single thirtysomething guy sitting at the reception desk peers over at me. The instant I see him, it's pretty obvious he's either got marijuana edibles nearby or he sneaks out back every hour or so to smoke. This dude kinda looks like he should be working at Starbucks but just didn't have the motivation to stay hip enough.

We lock stares.

He's bewildered about where I came from, but dismisses it assuming *we* checked in before his shift started. By 'we,' he thinks my parents are here because I'm like fourteen.

Sigh.

Do the Zen thing, Sarah. Being mistaken for a kid is the least crappy thing that could've happened as a result of Scott stabbing me in the heart.

I walk up to the counter. "Hi. Umm..." Drat. Asking which room Damarco is in and saying I'm here to 'meet a friend' is going to get this guy assuming something really disgusting is going on. He already thinks I'm underage. Why else would a young girl ask what room a grown man she doesn't know is in? Chris Hansen is going to show up any second. Nope. Need a new line.

"Can I help you, miss?" asks the guy.

Oh hell. No point in playing games. I dive into his head and put him into the same mind fog I use for feeding. It's tempting to bite him, but, no. For one thing, he looks high. For another, we're in a wide open lobby with at least two cameras. Dammit! That's why my first instinct was to talk it out of him. Those cameras might be picking up audio. Gotta play this out even if I'm puppet-mastering him.

"I've got a delivery for a guy named Damarco. Rain soaked the form. Can't make out the last name. Did he book a room here?"

The clerk looks at his computer with all the life of an automaton at a Disney theme park. "I've got a Damarco Miller checked into room 508. You can leave the package at the desk."

"I would, but the sender needs a signature. Leaving the package without one could get me fired." And eep! Still checked in? Maybe he *didn't* go home for Thanksgiving. I prod the clerk to program a room key for 508 and give it to me. "I'll just go knock on his door."

After erasing our meeting from his head, I rush to the stairwell and up to the fifth floor.

The beige hallway is on the narrow side with the kind of grey carpeting so bland I can feel it sucking the joy right out of my soul. Doors occupy recessed alcoves at regular intervals, numbered in order. I jog past 514, 513, and so on until reaching Damarco's room. I'm seconds from jamming the plastic keycard in the reader when it hits me that *not* being an idiot is probably healthier.

Dalton could probably teach me a thing or two about sneaking/breaking into places. But, really… I don't want to become good at it. Dammit, I'm not a thief. Spy maybe. What I'm doing right now counts as spying, right? Unless Damarco is here. Not sure what it makes me in that case.

In an effort not to be an idiot, I put my ear to the door and listen.

Total silence. Not even bedbugs humping. Eww. The thought disgusts me mostly because my ears probably *could* pick them up. Speaking of humping, at least three couples elsewhere on this floor are doing it—or maybe one's upstairs. Meh. Who cares?

The doorknob mechanism beeps when I insert the keycard. No signs of activity come from beyond, so I pull the door open and step into a basic hotel room. A small bathroom is to my immediate right. The fragrance of man sweat, soap, and some sort of cologne hangs in the air. It's not warm, so he couldn't have used it *too* recently. However, he definitely didn't go home yesterday unless 'home' is a short drive away. If he lived that close, he wouldn't need a hotel, right? Even if only Tiffany lived in this area, she'd have let him stay there. They sounded close on the phone, enough for me to assume they are either related or married.

So, no. This guy is motivated enough to skip Thanksgiving to kill Professor Heath.

Wolent hasn't sent anyone after me. That gives me hope the hunter hasn't stumbled across another random vampire and killed them. He's also still renting this room, which means he hasn't caught up to the prof yet. Small miracles.

I creep past the bed and go straight for the small desk. Rifling among the papers, his luggage—and plane ticket—tells me flew in from South Dakota the day before I first noticed him outside my school. A spiral notebook contains various journal entries and comments regarding nine other vampires he apparently encountered back in South Dakota. According to his writing, the first two he attacked as soon as he identified them. In both cases, he nearly died and ended up for weeks in a hospital recovering. From kill three onward, he spent days and weeks surveilling the suspected vampire, learning their routine. Finally, once confident he remained undetected, he made his move, attacking them in their lairs (his word) ten to fifteen minutes after sunrise.

'Sleepers,' he kills with a katana—I smirk. But of course he has a Japanese sword, right? His notes describe using a crossbow bolt modified to carry a standard magnesium road flare instead of a metal point. The weapon has enough power to punch it into a human body without penetrating all the way through and coming out the other side. Painful, but not deadly to a living person. However, vampires are kinda flammable. From what I'm reading here, having a burning flare embedded in them caused panic and made them less able to defend themselves from a decapitating sword strike. Once their head came off, they'd be 'unconscious' plenty long enough for the flare to finish them off... and in two cases, Damarco helped the vampire along with gasoline.

Ack. In fact, I say "Ack!" out loud.

Damarco has written a little in the side margins about each vampire he's killed so far. He is certain they were all part of a pack that ran in Watertown, where he grew up. He blames the group of vamps for 'forty to fifty' murders in the same spree in which his parents died. Aww damn. The parents had been out for a date night, Damarco and Tiffany staying at their grandparents' house. Aha. She's his sister. Police found the parents' remains near their car at a scenic location overlooking Pelican Lake, and blamed what happened to them on bears.

The vamps he destroyed, he describes as all appearing between seventeen and mid-twenties, but likely decades old. He believes another nine exist, all scattering once he began hunting them down and succeeding. Also, the whole pack initially followed one leader, a man he believes to be Professor Heath.

Wow, this dude has seen *Lost Boys* too often. Gang of teen vampires with an older guy in charge?

Nothing in this notebook sheds much light on what he knows about vampires, but I'm getting the feeling it's minimal at best. The only information he has comes from direct observation. He makes occasional reference to 'the old man said' when describing what he thinks we can do. Wonder if this old man is a member of that Unspoken Order? Good explanation for how a random guy who believed in vampires and wanted revenge obtained a magical trinket to shield his mind. He had a mentor. Sounds like he came straight out of a movie. It's more likely Damarco found the guy the first time he tried to kill a vampire and only had a few minutes to talk to him before the old man bled to death.

My confidence is starting to improve. Maybe I'm dealing with *Kick Ass* instead of *Batman*. Damarco could be slipping by on luck as much as skill. As far as I know, Apex Tech doesn't run any vampire killing schools that advertise a certificate program in commercial spots during the cable 'up all night' crappy movie timeslot. Maybe they have a dual-certificate program. Kill vampires while preparing for a career in welding.

There's a small, framed photograph on the table showing a pair of kids standing in front of a couple I assume to be their mother and father. The image has a somewhat dated look to it and Damarco is definitely not the adult. He's probably the boy, who looks about eleven or so. The girl's closer to seven. That's gotta be Tiffany.

Dammit. They're adorable.

My willingness to kill Damarco was already weak. Seeing him as a little kid is going to make it nearly impossible. Sure, if he backs me into a corner and the only chance of survival is to kill him, instinct will override sentimentality. My goal, however, is to prevent allowing myself to end up in that situation. Hmm. I can't mind control him, but… does Tiffany have a magic item, too? Maybe I could fly to South Dakota and give her a compulsion to beg him to come home and stay with her.

It may or may not work. If she's fully committed to him tracking down and killing the vampire or vampires who murdered their parents, she might break out of the compulsion. Then, they'd realize they'd been manipulated and become even angrier.

I pace in circles muttering, "Dammit" repeatedly. Killing Damarco isn't right, but if he finds and attacks a vampire, it's gonna be me in trouble. Depending on how angry Wolent is, it could threaten my ability to simply exist in peace with my family.

Frowning, I stare into eleven-year-old Damarco's eyes, wondering if I have it in me to kill a man in cold blood purely so I can remain with my family. Not even their lives… my selfish need to stay with them. If not killing him meant my parents or siblings would die, this man would be deader than grunge music.

Not gonna lie, it freaks me out how easily I came to that answer. To protect my family's lives, killing a man doesn't even register on my guilt meter. Guess after ripping Scott's head off, my tolerance for violence probably increased a touch. Still, Damarco isn't acting out of maliciousness. This guy's lumping all vampires into the same box. Again, not a surprise. His only exposure to vampire kind consists of the 'pack' he chased around Watertown.

"Okay. How can I fix this?"

I almost flop to sit on the bed, but decide against disturbing it.

Confronting him and trying to talk is an option. Of course, it could easily escalate into me saying the wrong thing, him discovering I'm a vampire, and us skipping straight to butt-kicking, do not pass go.

He looked straight at me and didn't realize what I am. Maybe I could pretend to be a fellow vampire hunter and try getting him to talk? Yeah. The idea sounds good. With Damarco no longer a scary super-ninja assassin bogey man in my mind—and a plan that doesn't involve immediate violence—this entire situation is starting to feel manageable.

Time to get out of here.

Best case scenario would be for me to bump into him again at the college. If he catches me in his hotel room, it would be kinda hard to explain. No sooner does worry grip me than an ominous sense of not being alone comes out of nowhere. It's stronger than someone merely standing behind me. This feeling is more like I'm the last surviving teen at summer camp and the guy in the hockey mask is raising his machete to take my head off.

Eep!

I whirl to face the room, expecting to see Damarco walking in the door with a crossbow pointed at me—but no one's there. Whew. Maybe this fear is some kind of warning sense vampires have? Whatever the cause, time to get out of here. I do a quick scan of the room and feel confident nothing looks obviously like someone burglarized the place. Wait… would tossing his room scare him out of Seattle or only make him angry?

Meh. Not enough time to debate it. I'm seriously starting to freak out as though my death is seconds away. I hurry to leave, plucking my trash bag off the corner of the bed on the way past it, and step out into a tomb-silent corridor. The door closing behind me makes such a sudden, loud *whump*, it startles a shriek out of me as I jump forward, spinning around with my claws halfway extended.

Oh, crap am I on edge.

"Something is not right here."

Just as I start to let my guard down, motion out of the corner of my eye makes me turn.

A skinny dude wearing a wool hat and olive drab raincoat trudges down the hall away from me, hands in his coat pockets. No other doors made any noise, nor are any open. I look the other way down the corridor, then back at the guy, clueless as to where he came from.

The grim energy here feels like it's coming from him. Okay, maybe I don't have a VEWS—vampire early warning system. Something does seem off about the guy. The more I stare at him, the sadder I feel.

"Hey, you okay?"

He ignores me, not even flinching.

Worried, I rush down the hall after him. He disappears around a corner into the elevator alcove at the approximate midpoint of the corridor. By the time I catch up to that point, he's gone. No way the elevator picked him up already. It didn't make any dings or noise. Again, I catch a flash of motion through the little window in the stairwell door. The guy's going *up*.

I shove the door open and yell, "Hey, you all right?"

The man disregards me, walking around the top of the switchback out of sight. I run up to the landing, but he's gone. Worried, I jump into the air and fly around in a corkscrew following the stairs—but fail to catch up to the guy. The *clonk* of a door happens an instant before I reach the exit to the roof. The floor here is still wet from my earlier arrival. Whoa. This dude is creepily fast.

Without a care to the rain, I shove the door open and run outside. The downpour has backed off to a light drizzle, but the area appears dark—which is a shock. Nighttime hasn't actually *looked* like nighttime to me in five months.

The guy in the raincoat walks across the roof toward the edge, giving off a strong sense of totally being 'done' with it all. Oh, shit. He's going to jump.

"Hey, stop!" I shout, while flinging myself into the air and flying at him from behind like a human torpedo. "Wait!"

He keeps going, walking right over the edge, hands still in his pockets.

I scream, horrified at what's just happened in front of me—but maybe it's not too late. Accelerating, I dive over the side, hoping to intercept him before he hits the ground. I was mere feet behind him when he fell—but he's gone. Stunned, I hover a short distance below the roof, staring straight down at the parking lot and the complete absence of a squished body or anyone falling. Wondering if he's a vampire, I hastily search the skies. Other than a few birds, there's nothing else flying but me.

It occurs to me the night no longer appears dark. Everything's gone back to normal.

Or, abnormal rather. My normal. The city below me is as well-illuminated as broad daylight. Only the sky remains black and starry.

The adrenaline crash of thinking I watched a man kill himself makes me tremble. Sadness gets into a fistfight with relief. He died already, maybe years ago. There's no need for me to feel guilty at failing to stop him. Nothing I could've done.

"Holy crap," I whisper. "Being a supernatural creature is freaky."

17

A GIRL'S GOTTA BE CAREFUL AT NIGHT

I
t takes me a little while to collect myself after witnessing a spectral suicide.

Well, a few minutes and a phone call to Ashley that helps me calm down. Ash is awestruck since she's really into ghost stuff. Weird considering she's so damn easy to scare. Anyway, she's fairly sure the 'ghost' in the hotel isn't really what she calls a 'sentient haunt,' but more likely a latent impression. She explains how spirits who seem to be stuck re-enacting the moment of their death aren't actual spirits but a collection of phantasmal energy kinda like a 3D video recording of events. The emotional energy of death imprinted that moment into the building and surrounding land.

That *would* explain why he didn't look at me or even flinch at me trying to talk to him. My experience dealing with ghosts isn't exactly vast, but so far, the few I've met have been quite surprised at my ability to see them.

Once Ashley is sure I'm okay, she gently extricates herself from the phone call, citing homework. Whoa. Her professors must have seriously loaded her up. Must be bad since it usually takes something major to make that girl stop talking. Like, for serious. We could be on the phone and the multi-headed scorpion/wasp nope-a-saurus could walk by outside and she'd keep on talking.

Since I'm already close to the campus, figure it couldn't hurt to check things out there. With it being the day after Thanksgiving and the school closed, it's kinda silly to think Damarco would be haunting the school. Oh, that's bad... if a vampire hunter lurks some place watching for his target, is he on a stake out?

Anyway, it's not like going there to look around real quick is going to take much time out of my night. I'm already at the hotel, which isn't far away.

The rain has faded to an annoying drizzle so I don't bother changing into my swimsuit. Damp clothes aren't a big deal. Even flying at over a hundred miles an hour isn't too terribly wet. At first, I circle overhead at a high enough altitude that it's unlikely anyone on the ground will see me. People rarely look up. Also, it's dark—to them —and my flight doesn't make any noise louder than the ruffling of whatever I'm wearing in the wind. My sneakers don't have blinking lights in them either, which prevents me from causing a whole bunch of UFO calls to local news stations.

Wow. The world is lucky I'm not a mischievous sort of person. Vampires have so much ability to mess with people. Wonder if... oh, right. I think about the vampires from Portland I met while picking up the Rebecca doll. One of their 'fun' pastimes involved rearranging people's yard furniture and statues—into neighbor's yards. Fortunately, the stuff they did to amuse themselves had been relatively good natured. Frustrating, but no one got hurt. Though, Kara has a short fuse when it comes to abusive men.

I start to feel guilty over how lucky my life has been so far. My parents aren't rich, but we're not in any way hurting. None of us have had any serious health problems. Mom and Dad are awesome. Sure, I've been catcalled and butt-slapped a few times, but never suffered a serious assault. An argument can be made that ending up as a statistic, a murder victim at eighteen, is the exact opposite of lucky, but here I am, a vampire Innocent—probably the best outcome possible after someone kills me. Well, best outcome for a girl like me who doesn't care about being powerful.

Kara's stepfather beat the hell out of her and her mother, and fatally stabbed her when she tried to fight him off. Not quite like me though. She got it in the gut and managed to stumble around alive long enough to be found by some other vampires, who she still hangs with. Hunter's bio dad was the same sort of abusive shithead *and* his family's barely making ends meet. Sometimes, they wonder about having enough food. Less so now, but he had some rough spots as a kid. For me, going to the mall to buy a gadget or clothes on a whim never struck me as anything to think twice about.

Sigh.

Dad said it's not my fault what happens to other people. Not like I'm laughing at their misfortune. And hey, I did help get his mother a better job. Okay, no more guilt. I have a job to do. A few circles around the campus later, I'm certain Damarco isn't here. Though, he might be hiding in a place that can't be seen from the sky. For a school in the midst of the Seattle Downtown, it covers a fair amount of area.

I land in my usual manner at the Harvard Garage, jog across the empty upper deck, and take the stairs to street level. As casual as I can be while carrying a trash bag, I walk back and forth across the campus, checking all the spots where someone might hide, especially in the section of Howell Street between the main building and the math and science building where it's not an actual street. No sign of Damarco there, so I keep going east, eventually making my way to Cal Anderson Park.

Figure I'll follow the walkway past the reflecting pool, check out the baseball field south of it, then loop back around on Pine street to the south facing side of the performance hall. I head past the little castle tower type building at the end of the reflecting pool and follow the walkway to the right back toward civilization—as opposed to the park. Cutting through a small area of trees with cement picnic tables brings me back to the city street.

Straight ahead of me, a long stairwell goes up toward the glass arch in front of the school's bookstore. Left of the stairs, a recessed alcove ends at a beige garage door and smaller person-sized door next to it. Chain link fence between concrete columns blocks off an area under an overhanging second story. I cut left, intending to walk around the block the long way in case Damarco is hiding.

A man comes out of nowhere, grabbing me from behind as soon as I reach the sidewalk. He covers my mouth with one hand and lifts me off my feet, dragging me into the area with the garage door, away from the street. Oh, boy is this pervert in for a surprise. I don't struggle, since it's much better that passersby aren't looking. If no one witnesses what's about to happen to this guy, there are no memories to erase.

The instant we're out of view from the street, I grab the arm holding me in both hands and pull it away from my chest, slipping down back to my feet. In one smooth turn, I duck away from the hand over my mouth and swing him around by my grip on his left arm, hurling him at the wall. He bounces off the beige concrete with an *oof* and staggers toward me, eyes wide with anger.

We glare at each other. His rage starts to shift to confusion, but I grab him by the throat and ram him against the wall. He clamps his hand around my neck; we struggle back and forth... and I'm really having to work to fight him off. Holy crap this dude is stronger than he looks. Maybe he's confused because I'm not freaking out and screaming?

In a sudden, hard motion I'm not ready for, he flips us around and pins me to the wall. Dammit! I hate feeling like a victim. Expecting him to grope me at any second pisses me off enough to tap an inner reserve of strength. All vampires can use up energy for temporary increases in strength or speed. Gradually, I start to overpower him and push away from the wall. There might be some snarling involved.

"Whoa... hang on." The dude pivots to his right, flinging me against the garage door.

At least he's let go of me. I catch myself with my ability to fly before crashing into the steel, and drop to my feet, rubbing my neck where he mostly crushed it.

"You want me to hang on?" I rasp. "You tried to rape me."

"No. Chill out." He holds both hands up and sprouts fangs. "Not at all. Just hungry. Didn't realize you were one of us until your fangs came out. No wonder I couldn't charm you."

Realization hits me like a blast of frigid water... only this ice bucket challenge isn't going on YouTube. "You're a vampire."

"Yeah." He relaxes, his stance casual. "Sorry about that. Damn, you're really good at faking being alive. You even smell delicious."

"Thanks... I think." I chuckle. "Never been called 'delicious' before."

"Why don't we start over?" He offers a hand. "Ruben Lopez."

I study him for a few seconds. He's young, maybe early twenties. The black leather jacket and jeans outfit kinda gives him a bad boy look, or at least a 'bad pretty-boy' look, like someone in the background of an Eighties music video pretending to be hard. And yeah, he's paler than a person ought to be, but not exactly ghastly. Vamps who aren't Innocent can still fake looking alive, but it burns energy for them, kinda like when I make myself supernaturally strong for short periods. His paleness tells me he's likely in need of a meal.

"Sarah Wright." I shake his hand. "Guess you're new, huh? Didn't see you at the party. Figured all the vamps in Seattle know me by now."

"No, I just got here. Flew in from New Mexico last night. Boy, are my arms tired."

I groan. "You are not old enough for dad jokes."

He chuckles. "What kinda party did I miss?"

"Honestly, it's boring." I explain the soiree. "More like a monthly meeting among vamps around here. Surprised they're not collecting dues."

"Oh, one of *those*. Ugh." Ruben shakes his head. "Not for me, thanks. I couldn't care less about any political society. I'm never in the same place long enough to give a crap."

"Lost One?" I ask.

"If that's what the old dusty ones call people who ignore them, I guess. Still kinda new at this."

"Heh. Me too."

He sets his hands on his hips, sighing at me. "Sucks they got you so young. I couldn't imagine being stuck as a kid forever, no one taking you seriously. Really gotta be a pain in the ass. How many times do you get harassed for being outside alone at night?"

"*That* hasn't happened yet... thankfully. And I'm not as young as I look."

"Let me guess, you're like ninety, right?"

I grin. Someday, it'll be true... hopefully. "Nah. I meant real age. Was eighteen when I turned."

"Damn, girl. You look like you're maybe fifteen."

"Yeah, yeah. I know." I hesitate, looking Ruben over again. He fits the description of the 'pack' Damarco has been hunting. What are the odds they're after him, too? "You ever been to South Dakota?"

Ruben shakes his head right away with an ease that makes me believe him. "Nah. Lived in New Mexico. Since the change happened, I've been bouncing around the southwest, mostly. Got curious to see what green looked like, so I came up here."

"Ahh. Yeah, we have lots of green. And rain."

"So I see." He glances out at the city. "The one who made you, did they stick around to explain anything or take off like mine?"

"Somewhere in between." I chuckle. "How long ago?"

"Almost three years. Learning as I go. You?"

"Five months."

"Wow. You're pretty damn strong for such a newbie."

I flex my noodle arm. "Like, rawr or something."

Ruben laughs. "You out looking for dinner?"

"Not exactly. I'm out trying to dodge a storm of political BS."

"Ugh. I hate that crap. It's why I never stay more than a couple months in the same city. Keep moving around and the BS never builds up."

"Makes sense. I'm not too into the 'society' thing either. Just wanna keep my head down and be normal, but... it's complicated."

Ruben shrugs. "Life is only as complicated as you let it become."

We talk about random stuff for a few minutes while walking down the street to the corner. His sire ambushed him out of nowhere and left him in the sewer. He thinks the guy gave him the Transference for the lols or maybe a bet. Of course, Ruben is guessing because he's never seen the man's face. I tell him about waking up in a morgue cooler, which he finds both laughable and sad. He seems like a reasonably nice guy; however, I still don't say anything about staying with my mortal family or share any real details about Dalton.

"This your territory, huh? Easy to blend in among college students?" asks Ruben. "Guess I'll head a couple blocks north and get out of your way."

"Oh, I'm not here looking for food. No one's ever told me anything about 'establishing territories.' We're vampires, not feral cats."

He laughs. "Fair enough. Still, if you're feeding around here, I'll give you some space."

"Nah. Trying to find a vampire hunter."

Ruben starts to chuckle again, but ends up staring at me. "Say what? Around here? Already?"

"Yeah. The guy is after someone I know, but has the name wrong."

"This person you know, do they move around a lot?" asks Ruben.

"Every couple decades, or so I'm told. It's weird. The hunter doesn't look too old, late twenties maybe thirty. It doesn't make any sense, because the timeline is off. Heath has been in this area too long to be the same vampire responsible for killing the guy's parents." I fidget. Saying it out loud only makes me doubt myself more. Damarco appeared about eleven in the picture. If he's (assuming) twenty-nine now, his parents died less than eighteen years ago. Heath told me he'd been in Seattle for over twenty years. While he'd have no reason to lie to me about that, his word isn't proof.

"Strange." Ruben scratches at his cheek. "Hunters usually have apprentices. Maybe the guy you're tracking is the apprentice of another one this friend of yours killed?"

"Could be. But… I dunno. Doesn't seem right. Heath feels like too much of a kindly old grandpa to be a killer."

Ruben play punches my shoulder. More a touch and push than a punch, really. "We're all killers, Sarah. It's in our blood. And, we're all good at deception. Look in a mirror. You're great at fooling people into believing you're still alive. I legit thought you were mortal. Don't think that friend of yours hasn't mastered the sweet old man act."

I look down, not wanting to think the worst about Professor Heath, but this guy does have a point. It doesn't prove my assumptions about the professor are wrong. Maybe he went through a change or something. "Yeah. I do disagree with you on one point. We're not all killers."

"You're telling me you've never killed anyone?" Ruben raises both eyebrows.

"That's not what I said."

"Aha. So you have." He grins, then gestures at me. "See? Killer."

I fire a scowl off down the street. "It's not like that. Someone opened a door, and I freaked out when the sun hit me. I've never deliberately tried to kill a mortal."

"Interesting." Ruben's eyes sparkle with interest.

Ugh. Hope he's not about to ask me out. The last thing I need now is to get stuck trying to explain having a mortal boyfriend. Bad enough living guys think it's just an excuse. Never been hit on by a vampire before. No, wait… he's not looking at me like that. Can't read his mind, but his expression looks more like curiosity than love or even lust.

"Killed a Scrap once." I bite my lip, thinking about the caverns. "Maybe more than once. And also a bunch of vampires. That's different though. They're already dead."

"Whoa. Seriously? You killed vampires? And you don't have to go into hiding?"

I shake my head. "Nah. Justifiable self-defense. They attacked us."

He leans back, both eyebrows up, probably trying to understand how a girl who looks so young and hasn't been a vampire long at all managed to kill others. "You sound like an intriguing person, Sarah."

"Guess that's one word for it." I manage a weak smile.

"Gonna go eat someone." He winks. "Be careful out here and good luck with your political BS."

"Yeah, thanks." I wave.

He ducks into an alley and flies off. You know what stinks about being into books and movies? What my brain does with situations. Guy grabs me from behind, which makes me think he's a perv, only to turn out to be a vampire who mistook me for a mortal. If vampires could have children, this would make for one of those 'how we met' stories we'd tell our kids and grandkids over and over and they'd get so sick of hearing.

It also sounds like the start of a decades-long romance. At least, according to what happens to the characters in the books I usually read. Boy meets girl. Boy tries to kill girl—or the other way around. Somewhere in the midst of trying to kill each other, they fall in love. Ugh. Seriously. He's too pretty though. The Latino bad-boy charm, even though it's obviously fake—the bad boy part; he's a real Latino— is definitely there, but interest is not. I love Hunter.

Ugh. And that's exactly what the girls in the books think at first.

18

CATS AND DOG

D amarco went *somewhere* last night, but not to Seattle Central College.

I spent way more time than intended combing the area. If not for taking a meal from a cop, the trip to town would have been a complete waste. On my way home, I tried to find Glim, but he's still missing. That could end up being for the best. As much as his advice would be super awesome about this, he might opt for the simple solution and kill the guy. Or, maybe he'd just slap Damarco around until he's delirious, search him for the item shielding his mind, and then massage his brain.

Saturday afternoon when I wake up, my mind is still circling those thoughts. Could I pretend to be a vampire hunter and get close enough to him to find his bit of enchanted jewelry? There's always the spy movie thing where I seduce him into bed. If he gets naked, it should be pretty easy to survey whatever baubles he's got. Not those baubles. I mean metal ones. If I tore the magical trinket off him, then I could play with his mind before we had to do anything that counted as cheating on Hunter.

Ugh. The idea of getting naked in the same room with a man who isn't Hunter feels wrong, even if I'm only pretending. Do actors who film sex scenes feel that way? Where does the line between cheating and doing a job stand? Wait, bad comparison. Actors doing a romantic scene *both* know they're pretending. Damarco wouldn't. Then again, if I succeed, he won't remember anything happening. Not like I'd break his heart or anything.

I'd only dent mine.

Okay, Sarah, you really need to forget the seduction angle. Without mental powers, the seduction would have to be entirely acting. I'm a rotten liar, plus I look too young. Picturing Damarco making a disgusted face at me like I'm 'some freaky messed up kid' and telling me to go away gets me angry at him even though it's entirely in my head.

The bigger question at the moment is where the heck did he go? Professor Heath didn't give me a phone number, only an email address. But, he hands it out to all his students. Still, better than nothing. I hop out of bed, plop into the chair at my computer desk, and send him a generically worded email asking how his Thanksgiving was and hoping everything is well.

If Damarco killed the professor, he wouldn't still have the hotel room booked—and I'd probably have angry vampires dragging me to Arthur Wolent's mansion in North Hill. That one bodyguard of his is so huge every time he leaves the mansion grounds, local radio stations start receiving calls about Sasquatch sightings. Seriously, the dude's arms are bigger around than both of my legs together.

It doesn't make sense for Wolent to have bodyguards, anyway. The man's a Fury. Guess the real world follows video game logic on occasion. Anyone trying to go after him would need to fight their way past a bunch of lesser vampires only to get their butt kicked by Wolent himself, who's more powerful than any of the vamps supposedly there to protect him.

I don't expect Professor Heath to answer my email until sunset. No point waiting around for him. Wonder what the day has in store for me...

As if the Universe hears me thinking, someone galumphs down the stairs into the basement. Too loud to be the Littles. Not loud enough to be the 'rents. Oh! It's Ashley. We're supposed to go pick up a sick dog today. I make it to my feet right as the door opens.

She knocks while barging in. "Hey! Morning… or afternoon."

"Either one works. And Hey. Just got up." I hug her on the way over to my dresser.

"Yeah, figured. You ready?"

"Unless you want me taking the ride without pants, I need a minute."

Ashley falls dramatically onto my bed. "Pants are highly overrated."

"Seriously."

I change from the long T-shirt I sleep in to a cute top and—on a total lark—skirt while Ash rambles about the trip, mostly how happy she is Hershey is getting a permanent home. Out of nowhere, she starts laughing. Usually, I'm the one who gets a random funny idea and cracks up for no apparent reason.

"What?" I ask.

"Just thinking, you probably *could* go outside without pants and get away with it. Just make people not realize what they're seeing."

I roll my eyes. "Been there done that. Yes, it's possible. No, it's not fun."

She lifts her head. "Really?"

"Yep. Remember, my first night as a vampire? Ran outside missing more than just pants. And, I mentally influenced people not to pay attention to me without even realizing it. Gawd, talk about beyond embarrassing. If not for being so totally freaked out about waking up in a body cooler, I'd probably *still* be hiding somewhere out of embarrassment."

She laughs harder.

I really don't like that glint in her eye. Remind me never to play truth or dare with her again.

"How is it outside?" I ask.

"Grey but it's not raining."

I smile. "Good. Perfect weather."

We head upstairs, fill the 'rents in on our plans to drive round trip to Portland, and walk out the door. All three Littles have already gone somewhere. Since the parents are both home, Sam's most likely over Daryl or Jordan's while Sierra and Sophia probably headed to Nicole's. Oh, right. I remember something about Mrs. Pierce (Nicole's mother) taking the girls (my sisters plus Megan and Nicole) to the mall or movies today.

Ashley's Jetta is almost as old as my Sentra, but it's better she drives. My eyes don't handle daylight well. One random sunlight reflection from the windshield of an oncoming car and I'd be blind for a moment. Or worse, the clouds might part and the glare blinds me for a lot longer.

So, I play navigator. The app calculates about three and a half hours one way. Ugh. No wonder Ash didn't want to do this alone. At least they're counting this time as her being at work and paying her for it. Still cheaper than airfare for the dog. She writes down the time we start the actual drive, and takes a picture of her dashboard clock for extra proof.

We start off talking about the trip. The poor dog got hit by a car and his original owner couldn't afford the surgery to save his life. Fortunately, rather than just put Hershey down, they surrendered him to the vet in Portland who did the surgery that kept him alive. Ashley's vet place is going to do a follow-up surgery, mostly to repair a broken hind leg, since the people adopting him have agreed to pay the costs.

Apparently, he's in too brittle a state to be shipped via air—mostly since neither vet nor the new owners wanted him stuck in an airplane cargo hold—so Ashley offered to get him. I've never road tripped without my whole family before, and Ashley's never gone on a ride longer than forty-five minutes.

"We're like Thelma and Louise or something." Ashley grins at me.

"Please don't drive off a cliff. And you're not planning to shoot anyone, are you?"

Ashley laughs, shaking her head. "Nah. If we need to rob a convenience store, you can just mind-control the clerk."

I stick my tongue out at her.

Our conversation goes from dog surgery to vampire hunters and my experience meeting Ruben last night. She finds his trying to feed from me hilarious. Unfortunately, she reads the same books I do and begins teasing me that my time with Hunter is going to be over soon. When I deny it, she taunts me about how I sound just like a character in a book. At least she spares me an attempt at pointing out all the 'logical' reasons why it would make more sense for me to date a vampire. Honestly, however it ends with Hunter—be it breakup or him growing old and dying—I'm not sure I'll even want another relationship. Maybe, maybe not. I don't *need* a boy in my life to feel complete and there's zero chance of me having kids or a stereotypically normal life. Anyway, talking about vampires gets me worrying about Damarco again, and *that* topic takes over the conversation for a while.

"You think it would be wrong to like try and seduce him so I can steal his magic amulet or whatever?" I ask.

"Yeah." Ashley smirks. "You'd never be able to pull it off, anyway."

I fake gasp.

"Seriously. You're like too wholesome and cute. You have no idea how to act sexy. And you're a rotten liar. You trying to act sexy while you know you're faking it is gonna be beyond obvious."

At least she didn't tell me I look too young. To tease her, I start trying to talk sexy to her as if she were Damarco. Giggling isn't the response I expected.

"Wow, fail," I mutter.

"You're just being a goof." She gives me side eye. "Or were you trying to be serious?"

"Umm. Trying to be seriously pretending. But I couldn't stop smiling because it's you, so not only was I pretending to be in the mood, I was double-pretending since you're not even the intended target."

"My head hurts."

"Doesn't that usually happen when you try to think?"

She sticks her tongue out at me.

We're quiet for a little while.

"Wow. Driving is boring."

"Yeah." I look out at the countryside. The sky is clearing up the farther we get from Washington, but the sun is also setting at the same time. Despite the occasional prickle of 'too hot,' being outside today isn't too unbearable as long as I've got a car around me. "The driving part of the road trip is the least fun. But we're also not stopping randomly everywhere that looks interesting. Like the place with the 6,000 pound ball of twine."

She blinks. "A giant ball of string is supposed to be interesting?"

"How many times have you seen a ball of twine as big as a truck?"

"Umm. Zero."

"There ya go." I gesture at her. "It's something to say you've done."

Ashley turns her head toward me. "Have *you* seen the mega twine?"

"Yeah. It's taller than I am."

"Wow."

"Maybe it isn't anymore. I was like thirteen when we saw it. Dad thought it was cool. Sam wanted to roll it down a mountain and see how high it bounced."

She laughs.

Sunset happens with about an hour left in our ride. My eyes flare with light as I come online, tinting the dashboard red for a few seconds.

"You feel like driving on the way back?" asks Ashley.

"If you want."

"Yeah. I need a break. Six hours straight behind the wheel is too much. Besides, if you're driving, I can pay attention to Hershey."

"Sure." I stretch and wind up yawning out of reflex. "Is the poor guy so sick he needs constant attention?"

"Not really." She grins. "He's a dog. I *want* to give him constant attention."

We make plans to grab fast food after Hershey's in the car rather than stopping somewhere to eat. Our arrival is cutting it close to the time the vet office locks its doors. If we hit an actual restaurant, we'll miss it. And we can't leave the dog in the car while sitting down inside some place to eat.

It's a few minutes to six in the evening when we reach Portland. I play the role of GPS voice, guiding Ashley to the Rolling Meadows Veterinary Hospital.

"Heh. That sounds more like a retirement community than a vet. Rolling Meadows?"

Ashley waves dismissively. "Most two-word names sound like old people homes. At least it's not like 'Happy Valley.'"

"No, that would sound creepy. Like 'be happy... or else.' A place where they have to put 'happy' in the name is going to be anything but."

At 6:03 p.m., Ashley pulls into the parking lot of a clinic much bigger than I expected. The large two-story white building looks like an actual hospital. Unfortunately, it also appears to be closed.

"Crap," mutters Ashley. "Are you kidding me?"

"I haven't said anything. How can I be kidding you?"

"Not you." She gestures at the place. "Them."

She rushes to park in a no-parking area right by the front door, hops out, and runs to the entrance. Sure enough, it's locked. She stares at me with a 'we're breaking in' sort of expression, but stops herself before asking me to do something stupid. A look of mission in her eyes, she storms back to the car, grabs her phone, and 'fury dials.' Well, as much as someone can angrily poke an entry in their contacts.

She stands there tapping her foot, waiting for whoever she called to answer.

"Hi, Doctor Adams. It's Ashley. I'm at Rolling Meadows, but the place looks closed. Yeah, they're supposed to be here until six. It's only four minutes past. Not even a car in the lot." She listens, nodding intermittently for a moment. "No. No one called me. Okay. Thanks."

I get out of the car and walk around it to stand next to her. "What happened?"

She lets her arm hang limp at her side, sighing. "The doctor's going to call the person who was supposed to be waiting here. He said the clinic knew I was on the way and should have someone waiting here for me. They were supposed to call my cell phone if they had to leave, but no one did."

"Ugh. So what's the plan?"

"Right now? We wait for Dr. Adams to call me back. Since we drove three and a half hours to get here and it looks like their person left early, he's going to insist someone take a ten minute ride to open the damn door for us."

I laugh.

We stand around waiting for a little while, occasionally peering in the windows. Ashley gets her dramatic sigh on big time. The delay doesn't bother her, more that we might have to leave the dog here and will have wasted six hours of driving time. A mobile phone somewhere inside the building starts ringing. Ashley doesn't react.

"Someone's inside."

Ashley looks at me. "How do you know?"

"Either someone's still in there or they forgot their phone. I can hear a cell ringing."

"Oh. Maybe they're just in the bathr—holy crap!" Her eyes go wide as she stares up at something in the air behind me.

I whirl.

Four people drop down out of the air to land behind me—the 'Portland Lost Ones' as I've come to think of them. Kara, Mick, Andrew, and Emilio. Kara is simultaneously younger and older than me. She got her Transference at seventeen... fourteen years ago. And she actually *looks* her age. Maybe a year older. So she is both older than me by total time existing and *looks* older than me while technically dying one year earlier, relatively speaking. Oh crap. She still acts like a teenager, not a thirtysomething. Guess that kinda means I'm stuck in Angstville, too. Meh, whatever. Better than living in Curmudgeontown like Mr. Neidermayer. Hate to say it, but Mick, Andrew, and Emilio also fit the description of the vampire pack Damarco has been hunting for years. But, I mean, seriously... young twenties vampires dressed like punks. Not exactly rare.

"Fancy meeting you here," says Kara as she goes in for a quick hug of greeting. "Good to see you again. How'd it work out with that doll?"

"Creepy, but okay. She's at her new home and seems happy."

The local vamps all chuckle.

"You sound almost serious. Talking about the doll like it's alive," says Mick, the oldest. He looks mid-twenties but was around for Woodstock… even if he had been a kid.

"I am. The doll's got a ghost in it." I shiver at the memory of watching that woman die protecting her daughter. "Real dark energy."

"Damn." Emilio shakes his head. "No thanks. Glad you got the thing out of here."

"You guys aren't like following me are you?" I ask, smiling.

"Nah. Out lookin' for something fun to do. Saw you two standing here alone, got hungry, but realized who you were." Mick pats me on the back—hard enough to make me take a step forward.

I grimace-smile at him.

Kara moves past me to scope out Ashley. "Hey. Who's your friend?"

"That's Ashley." The cell phone going off again gets me to glance briefly at the doors. "Ash, meet Kara, Mick, Andrew, and Emilio."

"Hey." Ash waves. "Sarah told me about you guys. Nice to finally meet you in person."

Mick nods at her. "Right on."

"'Sup," says Andrew.

Emilio slides up to stand behind her, a broad smile showing off his teeth. "It is so nice to meet such a pretty woman. I hope you'll let me show you around the city. Please, call me Emilio."

His Spanish accent is not normally so strong. I half expect him to kiss Ashley on the hand.

She goes starry-eyed. Ugh. Really? Is he charming her?

"Hope you're here long enough to have some fun this time." Kara makes 'metal horns' with her fingers at me. "Maybe catch a show?"

"I would, but we're picking up a sick dog from this clinic to bring back to Seattle right away. We need to get him from this place as soon as possible and we can't leave him sitting in a car while we go have fun."

"Bring the dog along." Mick holds his arms out to either side. "I love dogs."

"He's too sick for that," I say. "Poor guy needs surgery."

"Aww, bummer," mutters Andrew.

Ashley starts asking Emilio random small talk questions, which he's all too happy to answer. It doesn't take them long to find a common interest: their fondness for Carlos Santana's music. Can't blame them. The guy's so awesome he even made Nickelback sound good. Seriously, though. Nothing against the band, it just makes Dad and Sierra laugh to pick on them.

Kara frowns. "Dammit. You gotta head down here sometime when you're not being someone's errand bitch."

"Hah. Not really an 'errand bitch' this time. Helping out a friend." I nod toward Ashley. Maybe it would be fun to hang out with people so completely different from my usual world for a while. "Yeah, definitely. How 'bout around spring break or a random weekend sometime."

"Cool. Cool." Kara nods. "So why you picking up a dog?"

Ashley and Emilio have moved on from music to the kinds of movies they like. Dammit.

"Ash works at a vet place back home. She's technically on the job."

The vamps—except for Emilio—blink at me.

"She works?" Kara grins, then laughs.

"Yeah, she's my best friend since like forever. Still, umm, mortal."

Kara, Andrew, and Mick make faces like I'd told them she's a serial killer.

"Relax." I hold my hands up. "She's in on everything. Notice she didn't freak out when you guys flew in?"

"Thought you were the same, what is it, uhh... Innocent?" asks Kara.

I nod.

"Weird you're hanging out with a mortal." Mick looks back and forth between Ash and me. "That's messed up."

"Hanging out with Ash isn't messed up." I frown at him.

"No, not that. Well, sorta that. But, I mean... the girl's alive and she's paler than you are."

As soon as I start laughing, Ashley gives us both the finger, but smiles along with it.

The echo of someone running inside the building grows louder.

"Here comes an audience. Time to go." Kara takes a step back. "Soon as you figure out when you're gonna come down here to hang out, call or email."

"Totally." I wave.

Mick, Andrew, and Kara zip into the air. Emilio keeps talking to Ashley. An early-twenties woman in dark blue medical scrubs runs up to the door inside. Her hair is dyed into a literal rainbow. Wow... that looks so cool.

She flicks the deadbolt, opens the door, and slouches, winded. "Sorry. Had a major poop-splosion to clean up." She shivers. "I swear, when a chihuahua gets the runs, it's butt becomes a long-distance weapon."

"No problem. Glad you're here." I walk closer, presenting myself as a distraction to keep her from looking up at the vampires flying off.

"Hi, Ashley. I'm Denise."

"I'm Sarah. That's Ashley." I point a thumb back over my shoulder. "Ash!"

"Oops. Gotta go," whispers Ashley.

"Don't be a stranger." Emilio steps back, gradually pulling his hands away from hers.

Crap times ten.

She keeps staring at him instead of talking to Denise.

"Sec." I back up, grab Ashley by the wrist, and drag her up to the door. "Ashley, Denise."

"Oh, hi!" Ashley shakes hands with her. "Sorry. Oh, my gawd! I *love* your hair."

Denise grins. "Thanks! And, umm, it should be me apologizing. Had to go to the bathroom, so I flicked the lock on the door. But, before I could get back out front, The Antichrist exploded all over the damn place."

Ashley and I both lean back, wide eyed.

"That sounds... bad," whispers Ashley.

"Nah. This little chihuahua is named 'The Antichrist,' but most of us call her 'Auntie.'"

"Who would name a dog The Antichrist?" I gawk.

"She's a biter, chewer, food aggressive, refuses to be housebroken, vomits all the time, keeps getting sick... Been through six different owners." Denise leads us down the hall. "Number seven seems to be the charm this time. Poor thing's here for a GI issue... hence the four-foot stream of liquid poop."

"Eww." I shiver.

"That's not too bad." Ash nudges me. "Dr. Adams had a bad encounter with the back end of a horse. He's got the picture hanging in his office. The barn wall has a person-shaped clean spot where he was standing when it splattered."

"Ugh." I gag.

Denise laughs.

The two of them swap disgusting animal poop/pee stories the whole time they deal with some paperwork at the front desk, then head back into the surgical recovery kennel area. Giant steel cages hold several animals in various states of medicated consciousness. Denise opens the door on one holding an adorable brown lab puppy. His entire back end is shrouded in bandages and he's catheterized with a poop-collecting bag, too. Aww, poor dog.

Ashley gingerly offers her hand. After a few test sniffs, Hershey machine-gun licks her fingers while making an eager nasal whimpering. Pupper, my heart doth melt for thee. The two of us stand there doing the 'aww' thing for a little while and skritching around his ears. He's in canine bliss despite being in obvious pain—and probably the doggy equivalent of higher than hell.

Eventually, Ash and Denise get the documents sorted.

"Okay, that's everything filled out. Hope you have a safe ride back," says Denise.

Not so subtle hint is not so subtle.

"Thanks." I smile at her. "And thank you for staying late."

"No problem." Denise walks us to the front door.

I carry Hershey out to the car, slide the kennel into the back seat, and head around to the driver's side. Ashley tosses the keys to me over the roof and gets in. Once I've got my phone balanced in a cup holder with the GPS app running, I back out of the parking spot and start driving us home.

Ashley leans into the rear seat, opens the kennel, and proceeds to comfort the dog. "You're such a good boy. Yes you are. Sorry for this long boring drive, but you're gonna have a real home soon. Just one more little operation."

The first food opportunity turns out to be a Burger King. I swing around to the drive through lane. Soon, Ashley's got a grilled chicken sandwich for dinner along with an iced tea, and we're back on the road. A few minutes later, once we're out of Portland on the highway —and I don't need to hawk-eye the GPS to avoid missing a turn, I finally lose the battle of willpower to keep quiet. "Ash, you, umm... probably shouldn't get involved with Emilio. He's a vampire."

"So? You're dating Hunter."

"Hunter's not a vampire."

"Duh. You are."

I squeeze the steering wheel. "That's different."

"How is it different? One vampire, one mortal. You're not being fair."

Dammit. She's crushing on him pretty hard. Her defensive tone usually doesn't come out this fast. "It's different because I trust myself not to kill Hunter and make him a vampire. I don't trust those guys not to kill you. Most vampires look down on the living. If he really likes you, he's going to turn you. The society vamps make fun of me for wanting to live at home with my family and for dating a mortal."

She keeps petting the dog, eyebrows furrowed, but doesn't say anything.

"Besides, you're not in love with him. You've seen him once, talked to him for like ten minutes. You're having a crush."

"It wouldn't be so bad," says Ashley in a distant tone. "We could stay together forever."

"Don't you want to be a mother some day? Can't do it if you become a vamp."

She fidgets. "That's not fair. You're a vampire and it's okay for you to date a living guy. Why are you having such a problem if I want to go out with a vampire? Be reasonable."

"I am being reasonable." A long sigh slides out of me. "Every damn day, I spend at least ten minutes agonizing over if being with him is a good idea. Wondering if it's selfish of me not to make him forget I exist. With me, he'll never have kids. I'm going to be stuck like this— looking like a goddamned fourteen-year-old—for the rest of time. What are people going to say if they see us kissing when he's in his fifties? They're going to call the freakin' cops."

Ashley's eyes redden. "You never used to worry so much about yourself."

"I'm not!" I half-shout. "I'm worried about *you* right now. Every damn time there's a vampire-mortal relationship, the human winds up turned undead by the end of the story."

She rolls her eyes. "That's fiction. You can't make life decisions based on made up stories. I only *just* saw Emilio. You don't know what's going to happen. You can't assume he's going to want to kill me and turn me into a vampire or that we'll even date long. This *is* me we're talking about. Six months is the longest I've ever managed to stay with anyone. Just because you're afraid you'll lose control and kill Hunter isn't a reason to tell me who I can and can't see."

I gasp. Her words hit me like a slap. Tears blur my vision, but not so badly I have to pull over. What are the odds she's right? *Am* I subconsciously worried I don't trust myself? It's hard to think about. I mean, no one's ever shown me how to turn someone else into a vampire. Even if I wanted to—which I don't—it's impossible right now. Suppose it's probably something simple like dripping my blood into the mouth of a recently dead person within a few seconds of their last breath. But I'm thinking like movie vampirism. What are the odds it really does work that way? It couldn't be *too* complicated since Dalton didn't have a lot of time to yank be back from the edge of death.

Silence hangs heavy between us. It feels like we're right at the brink of exploding into a full on shouting match. If we weren't trapped in a moving car, I'm sure she would've stormed off after my last comment. I hate feeling like my best friend is *that* mad at me.

Can't stop crying. As if the tension in the air between us wasn't bad enough, I'm freaked out over what she said. People never truly see themselves from the outside. Ash knows me better than anyone except my parents. Could she be right? Maybe she said it out of jealousy over Hunter and I having something she doesn't, but what if it really is obvious to her I am scared shitless of myself.

A real fight between us had to happen, eventually. Ashley and I have been super close friends for a long damn time and we've defied all conventional wisdom. Not once in the almost fourteen years we've known each other have we gotten into a real bad fight. We've never had a spate of not talking to each other or 'breaking up' as friends or even getting into a screaming match. Mostly, that's due to Ashley being overwhelmingly nice. Whenever conflict happened, she'd always cave in right away and go with whatever I wanted. Invariably, I'd feel guilty within hours and make it up to her somehow. And even with that relationship, conflict had been pretty rare.

Seeing Ashley—probably for the first time in her life—not being passive about something worries me. Either Emilio charmed her or she's panicking that she's never going to find anyone to love. I know it frustrates her since my attitude has always been not to care too much one way or the other if I ended up married or permanently single. This girl Natasha at school used to preach at Ashley for *wanting* a boy, suggesting Ashley shouldn't base her worth on the presence or absence of a man in her life. We both totally agree with the idea, but it has nothing whatsoever to do with Ashley's problem: she wants a family. That doesn't necessarily require a man either. She'd absolutely consider artificial insemination from a donor if she married a woman. She just wants *someone* to share a life with and have kids.

I suppose as long as Emilio doesn't kill her, they could still do the sperm donor thing. But, seriously... what vampire wants kids? The scheduling is all whacked out. Turning into a pillar of fire in broad daylight kinda puts a damper on coaching soccer.

Glimpses of memory from our childhood haunt me for the next

twenty minutes or so of silence. Over and over again, I think back to all the times Ashley and I had disagreements and she always just went along with my idea. Most of it was stupid stuff like us trying to choose between cherry or orange Italian ices or which movie to see in a theater. We've never really had a serious fight until now. This is the first time she's fired off a zinger like that at me.

I deserved it. Even if my protectiveness in this case is warranted, I still deserved a barb for exploiting her passivity our whole lives. It never seemed to bother her since she rarely put up much of an argument. Most times a decision came up, we ended up on the same page anyway. But… yeah. She spent her whole life trying to make me happy. And yeah, I'm overplaying it to make myself sound like a greedy, selfish bitch because it's how I feel right now.

The silence becomes unbearable. Hershey senses the mood in the air and whines.

"I'm sorry," I say.

Ashley looks over at me, her eyes red. Not glowing red like mine can get, crying red. "Me too. You're only trying to protect me. Thank you." She sighs hard. "You're right. I'm just crushing on him. Maybe he charmed me even."

"I shouldn't treat you like you can't make decisions on your own. You always just cave in and agree with me. I feel like crap for treating you like that so long."

Ashley shrugs. "It's okay. I can't think of any time when we had a disagreement where it bothered me to go with your opinion. Would've made me more upset to fight. If something really mattered, I wouldn't have caved in."

"Really?" I sniffle.

"Didn't that just kinda happen now?"

"Kinda. Yeah." I manage a weak smile. "So you really want to see Emilio?"

Ashley resumes scratching the dog's chin. "I dunno. He's cute and seemed friendly, but he doesn't know I'm still alive. He thinks I'm like you. Probably won't be interested when he finds out from the others."

"You heard us? Wow, I thought you were enamored."

She laughs. "I was, but my ears didn't stop working."

"Do you really think I'm afraid of killing Hunter?"

Her smile fades. "Umm. No, not really. I think you're afraid of hurting him. You really do love him now, but you're worrying it's going to end sooner than either of you want it to."

I squeeze the wheel tighter.

"Not like that. The relationship. Like you said, when he gets older, it's going to be awkward. You could always pretend to be his daughter in public, but it's going into all kinds of icky creepy territory I don't want to think about."

"Yeah." I change lanes to the left, going around a slow van. "You're right about me being worried. But not about losing control of myself and killing him. I'm scared that if he ever asked me to do it, I wouldn't be able to say no."

Ashley sighs the way she sighs whenever doomed lovers die in a movie we're watching. "If he ever asks you to make him a vampire, you could always erase yourself and leave. That won't make you feel any better but he'll still be alive. But, I guess if he asks for it, it's nowhere near as bad as murdering him."

"How can being a vampire feel simultaneously awesome and dreadful?"

"Huh?" She peers at me. "That makes no sense."

"I mean..." I thrust one hand forward. "It's awesome to be a vampire. Flying, immortality, mind reading... who wouldn't want powers? The downsides of it don't seem too bad. So the sun's a problem and I can't get pregnant. I've never been a beach bum and never even thought about kids. Not exactly one of my great life goals."

She pouts at me.

"Not saying your goals are bad. Just, not what I dream about. Or dreamed about. Whether or not I had any kids would've been up to the opinion of the guy I ended up with. *If* I ended up with anyone at all. Maybe I'd have collected cats."

She laughs. "Nothing wrong with that. But you definitely would've had guys. They just gravitate to you."

"I am no Bree Swanson."

"Nah. You're way more real. That's what some guys are drawn to. Bree is probably going to be the 'girl he cheats with' until she's too old to be hot anymore. Then she'll end up working as a phone psychic or waiting tables."

"Ouch."

Ashley scrunches up her nose. "Meh. You're right. Too mean. Sorry."

"Little bit. It's not her fault Scott was a dick."

"Yeah."

"What for now?" I ask.

"Hunter's going to hurt you."

I shake my head. "No he won't."

"Not like cheating. He's going to get old and die."

Sigh. "Yeah. I know. I'll take 'stuff I think about every day even though I don't want to for $200.' Cats get old and die, but you keep adopting more of them."

Ashley stares at me with a 'how could you say that' face for a few seconds, then starts crying.

"Sorry," I whisper. "I didn't mean it like that."

She wipes her face on her arms. "I know. You just made me think of Pixie and Doofus and Kitty. I'm not crying because you said what you said. I'm crying because I miss them."

"I remember Kitty." I give a sad chuckle. "That cat was *so* fat. Major chonk."

Ashley laughs. "Yeah. And he still could run fast enough to catch mice. Used to bring them back to me all the time... alive even."

"And you kept them as pets, too. How many girls our age wouldn't have screamed at the sight of a live mouse?"

"Just the two of us. At least in our school."

I snicker. "Still can't believe you named a cat 'Kitty.'"

She shrugs. "So? I was six."

We reminisce about her other cats. Doofus earned his name because he kept walking into objects. At the time, we thought it hilarious. Now, I'm pretty sure he had some kind of neurological problem. The poor cat died pretty young, only four or so. Pixie was the coolest cat ever. Pure white, soft as a rabbit... She'd been the oldest, basically her mother's cat before they had Ashley. She passed when we were twelve, outliving Doofus by four months. Kitty, despite his obesity, made it to nineteen. He'd been five or so when Ashley adopted him, and passed away last January during our senior year in high school. Ash had been so upset she stayed home for three days.

Talking about cats mutates into a theoretical discussion comparing Ashley progressing among a series of cats throughout her life to me doing the same with boyfriends over the next few centuries. We debate whether the name 'Guy' or 'Manny' for my imaginary future lover is a closer comparison to her having a cat named Kitty.

It's sad at the same time it's hilarious.

And it's totally Ashley.

19

NEAR MISS

Upon reaching Longview, I pull off Route 5 because this car is in dire need of a gas station.

"Where are you going?" asks Ashley.

"The Jetta is thirsty. Unless you want to steer while I push us home the last twenty miles, we need to stop and get gas."

"Oh. Yeah, that would stink."

Smiling, I head for a Shell station conveniently in sight of the highway. As soon as we stop, Ashley hops out and runs around the car to the pumps. A sudden craving for coffee hits me while I sit there staring out the windshield at a Starbucks across the street. Sure, the gas station has coffee, but it's a harsh, medicinal elixir of wakefulness that will do me no good. I desire yumminess, not the scorched essence of burnt dreams.

I get out of the car and glance at Ash, who's feeding a credit card into the pump. "Gonna hit Starbucks. You want anything?"

She whirls toward me. "What? You're gonna leave me alone?"

"Umm." I do a 360, but don't see anything scary. "It's just across the street and I won't be gone long."

"That's what they always say." She bites her lip.

"Okay. No big deal." I hold my hands up. "We can both go once the car's full."

Ashley pulls the pump handle off the machine and plugs it into the car. "It's all right. Go on."

"Nah. This isn't what flavor of ice to get. You don't always have to agree to what I want." I stand closer to her. "You're scared. I'll stay."

"Thanks," she whispers.

This is unusual timidity for her. I mean, this girl charged at one of those numbnut vampire hunter wannabees ready to kick his ass. Again, I look around, but can't find any obvious sign of danger. My concern is high enough it warrants a peek into her head to see what scared her. Unfortunately, she didn't see anything specific—but she feels watched. Her subconscious has latched onto something that makes her feel like an oblivious mouse about to be ambushed by a diving eagle.

A gas station worker washing the inside of the convenience store windows appears to be checking us out, but he's far enough away not to present any threat. Plus, he looks like a bit of a geek. Even before my death, I probably could've knocked him on his ass if he got handsy.

Since nothing down here looks ominous, I check the skies. Still nothing. Being far from home at night, just the two of us, would have terrified me before my change. Scary to think we have to be the adults now. No Mom or Dad here to keep us safe. However, it's dark, so I feel immortal. That's not unusual for a teenager, except I actually *am* immortal.

Like some kind of supernatural guard dog, I keep looking around while she fills the tank. Window-cleaner guy keeps watching us, but his expression is difficult to read. It's as likely he's staring at us out of lust as it is he's concerned about a pair of young women alone by the pumps after dark. After a few silent minutes of nothing happening, the loud *thunk* of the gas pump stopping makes Ashley jump. Being scared and not understanding why freaks her out more than seeing an actual guy coming at me with a weapon.

Once we get back in the car, she calms down, but not completely.

We hit the Starbucks drive-through to avoid having to get out of the car again. Mocha latte, come to mama. Ash orders a peach green tea instead of coffee since she actually wants to go to sleep later. The few minutes we sit in the lane waiting, it *does* feel like someone is watching me, but I still don't see anyone suspicious around. It could be Glim, or a Shadow keeping tabs on me. Their mere presence might be enough to rattle Ashley. But… he wouldn't conceal himself from me. Assuming this isn't merely the general unease of being on our own at night, whatever is causing us to feel this way has to be supernatural.

When we pull up to the window and I hand over money, Ashley whines at me. "You don't have to pay. I should be covering it since you're taking this ride for me."

"Don't worry about it. Stopping here was my idea." I take the drinks from the girl inside the window, hand Ash her cup, and resume driving.

The spooky vibe gets me talking about my visit to the hotel and the ghost. Most people would say it's not a great idea to bring up a story about actual ghosts to a girl who's already frightened to the point her hands are shaking during a nighttime road trip. However, Ashley's fascinated by that stuff, so it has the paradoxical effect of distracting her from real world fear.

By the time we reach her vet clinic at 10:04 p.m., we're convinced the apparition I saw had to be a latent image. She wants me to go back to the hotel sometime to see if it happens again and note the times. Great. That's my luck. Helping a friend drive a dog around has turned into a research project.

At least we're laughing and in a good mood when I finally cut the engine in the clinic parking lot. There's no one here at this hour, but she's got keys. We get out of the Jetta, me grabbing the kennel carrier while she goes for the door to let us in. Pretty impressive they trust her with keys considering she's only been working there since the summer and isn't even a veterinary technician.

She lets me in and locks the door behind us. We take the dog to the medical boarding room and gently transfer him to one of the cages there. Naturally, a handful of other animals start meowing and barking at us. Except for this one enormous bunny rabbit. It neither barks nor growls—that would freak me out more than a giant troll to be honest—though the fuzzball does have one heck of an haughty stare. Ugh, it's gotta be super lonely for them. Predictably, Ashley makes the rounds, talking to the animals one after the next while she collects water and a blanket for Hershey.

"Hey there, boy," says Ashley while hooking up his water bottle. "You're gonna feel better real soon and be in a forever home. Sorry I can't give you kibble, but you've had a bunch of work done on your insides. Don't worry though." She pats a small IV bag. "You've got all the food you need right here."

The puppy yips at her.

I bite my lip. The concept of a 'forever home' means something a little different to me. My earlier fight with Ashley comes back in the form of worrying about my siblings. I've been assuming the house I grew up in is going to end up being mine when my parents are gone. Not once did it occur to me the Littles might need the place. I'd certainly never kick them out so I could keep the house for myself, but me staying there while one of them raises a family is going to pretty much require everyone under the roof know what I am.

Nah, what am I saying? Mom and Dad aren't going to drop dead the instant Sam turns eighteen. In an alternate reality where I remained mortal, they'd still be living there as we all grew up and moved out. My becoming a vampire isn't going to change that. I'm the only one in the family who's got no chance of having a normal life. And no, this isn't me feeling guilty at all. Mom and Dad won't need to stay in a care home when they're old, because I will be there to help them until the end. At the moment, I'm planning to keep the house as long as possible. But who knows… when everyone's gone, it might be too painful for me to stay there.

"Sare? Why are you crying?"

"Umm." I snap out of my bad daydream. "Just thinking about not wanting Mom and Dad to end up like Uncle Hank, stuck in a nursing home and left there."

"Random." She grasps the puppy's head and gently tilts him to look at me. "There are puppies here. This is a no-sadness zone."

I chuckle, and don't bother mentioning a vet clinic has *plenty* of sad moments. Totally not the point of why she said that.

"Yeah, you're—" I pause at an aluminum scrape like the front door opening.

"What?" asks Ashley.

"Think I heard someone breaking in."

She gasps and starts looking around for a weapon.

"Wait here."

Ashley picks up a metal tray, brandishing it like a weapon, then nods.

I move to the doorway and peer out into the hall. Only a few lights are on, but to my eyes, that doesn't matter. Electric lights only make color more vibrant in those places. No one can hide from me purely in darkness. At least not without magic or a black smoke generator. Soft squishing, rubber soles on the smooth floor, echoes from the outer lobby by the reception counter.

This is a pretty nice area without much crime. Still, there's no such thing as a completely crime-free area. Well, okay, *technically* there is, but only because no humans live in those places. This could be someone looking to rip off computers or maybe hoping to find drugs they can sell in a storage area. Might even simply be vandals. I walk out into the corridor and head past the inner area with all the doctors' desks. Not used to the complicated layout of the building, I pick a door that goes into a pet exam room. No big deal. It's got another door for clients, so I keep going straight and step out into the lobby, not particularly concerned with stealth.

Even if this is an armed burglar, so what if he shoots me?

I emerge in an empty front room. Moonlight glints off the front door as it swings closed. Sneaker scuffing comes from the parking lot. Crap. They probably heard me open the inner door into the exam area. I run outside, but only catch a fleeting glimpse of a man sprinting around the corner of the building to my left. It's tempting to chase him, but there's no reason to. He didn't do anything worse than walk into the lobby. Besides, if I go after him, Ashley will be alone.

It really bugs me she felt watched at the gas station and now someone decides to break into the vet clinic. Last time I checked, Ashley hadn't gotten herself involved in spycraft, so I can't think of any reason someone would be after her. The two events could be completely unrelated. Or... maybe the Portland vamps are playing pranks on us. The stuff they do to mess with mortals is far more involved than giving us a little scare. Plus, they avoid being spotted.

Bleh.

I head back inside, pausing to check the door for damage mostly out of worry Ashley would get in trouble for it somehow. Surprisingly, the window's not smashed. None of the metal parts are bent either. Okay, so either the guy had a key—unlikely—or he's a thief skilled enough to pick locks. I suppose it could also be one of the Portland crew. Lost Ones are good at being sneaky. Like, to the point Dalton can make locks open supernaturally. He's never explained if they all can do it or if it's like claws: some of us get them, some don't. Same with flying. But, claws and flying are not limited to one specific bloodline. Certain traits are only present within different groups. All Innocents look lifelike, for example. All Shadows can conceal themselves from others' minds. Glim calls it invisibility, but he's not literally disappearing, only forcing brains to ignore him.

Hmm. No way to tell if the guys are playing with me or I merely scared the hell out of a real thief. Don't really care too much either. I hurry back inside.

Ashley peers around the tray at me. "What happened?"

"Guy heard me coming and ran off. I shut and locked the door again."

She exhales, sets the tray on the counter, and finishes getting the puppy settled in.

I hover nearby, staying alert for unexplained sounds elsewhere in the building in case the guy tries a window or back door.

"How ya doin' in there, Hersh?" Ashley coos.

He nibbles on her fingers.

"Aww." I smile. "Hope his new family gives him a better name. Chocolate lab named Hershey? If dogs pick on each other, this little guy is in for hell."

Ashley gives me a 'seriously' look, then her eyes widen. "So someone was really out there?"

"Yeah, but they ran off. One guy. Picked the lock on the front door. Probably a thief, but he didn't take anything. Wasn't inside long enough."

Ashley pulls out her cell phone. "Should we call the police?"

"If you want. I don't think there's much they'll be able to do."

"There are security cameras. Yeah, I gotta call them. If the big boss sees someone break in, you chase them out, and we don't report it, we'll get in trouble."

"Yeah. Umm, did the security cameras catch the imps messing with you?"

She laughs. "No, thankfully. No one here knows I spent hours stuck in a kennel. Or made a huge mess. The imps must have made the cameras fail. The entire time craziness went on in here, the recordings are all static."

"Yeah, they have that effect."

Ashley takes a deep breath and calls 911 to report the break in.

A LONE POLICE CAR ARRIVES ABOUT SIX MINUTES LATER.

Two cops get out, both athletic-looking guys. One's Native American, the other looks like a Ken doll brought to life. Since neither of them appears older than twenty-four, I'm guessing they're probably rookies stuck on the night shift.

"Hello, girls," says the Native cop. "I'm Officer Sandoval. This is my partner Officer Bartlett. So, what's this about a break in?"

"Someone tried to get into the clinic, maybe to steal stuff," I say. "I heard them coming in and went to check... but they ran out when I made noise."

"Nothing was taken or damaged," says Ashley in an apologetic tone. "We wouldn't have bothered you, but whoever it is picked the lock on the door to get in. There's a security camera system, but I don't know how to work it or where the machine is. Hang on. Let me call Dr. Adams. He's expecting me to call him when we're done here, anyway."

Officer Sandoval examines the door, his expression unreadable. "Why are you two girls here at this hour?"

I explain playing dog taxi to the cops while Ashley calls the vet to inform him Hershey is settled in fine... and someone tried to break in with us in the building. She agrees with whatever he says, then hangs up.

"The doctor is on his way," says Ashley.

Both cops nod.

For the next twenty minutes, we stand around waiting while the cops examine the door, the lobby, and ask us various questions about what we saw and heard. Eventually, an older silver Mercedes pulls up right next to the Jetta. A late-forties guy with a tall face, slim build, and a bit of grey creeping into his afro gets out and introduces himself to the cops as Dr. Timothy Adams, co-owner of the clinic.

We all follow the doctor inside to one of the offices in the back. It only takes him a minute on the computer to pull up the camera footage from the lobby. At 10:39 p.m., a man in a black jacket and jeans walks up to the door. He fiddles at the lock for mere seconds before the door opens. When he steps inside, clearly into view of the cameras, I gasp in shock.

It's freakin' Matt Damon.

Both cops whistle.

Dr. Adams laughs. "Wow. That poor guy. Looks just like what's-his-name from those Bourne movies."

"Holy crap, yeah." Ashley blinks. "No way it's really him."

He creeps across the lobby, ignoring the computers at the front desk. For no apparent reason, he stops short, seems to listen for an instant, then hauls ass out the door. Two seconds after he runs, I walk into view from the bottom of the screen, my back to the camera, and hurry outside. My 'oh, screw it' eye roll while reentering the clinic makes Ashley laugh. The doctor pauses the video after I re-lock the door and walk away.

"That is the strangest thing I've ever seen," says Officer Bartlett.

"Yeah, no kidding. We put out a memo on the guy, they're going to send us for counseling." Officer Sandoval laughs. "Can we get a copy of this video for proof?"

The doctor nods. "Of course. Email?"

Sandoval gives him an address, and Dr. Adams sends an excerpt of the file.

Finally, at 11:18 p.m., we can leave.

As soon as we walk outside, Ashley starts looking around.

"You okay?" I ask.

"Feels spooky again." She hugs herself, rubbing her hands up and down her arms. "You see any ghosts?"

Both cops look at us, shake their heads in disbelief, and get in their car. Officer Bartlett mutters something about why are all teenage girls into 'that spooky stuff?' Sandoval laughs.

"No. Nothing." I spin in place, searching for anyone spying on us. There are no real hiding places anywhere nearby except for a row of small decorative trees separating the clinic property from the lot in front of the dentist's office next door. The only way anyone could hide behind those trees is under cover of darkness. It's obvious to me no one is there.

"I feel watched. I felt watched when we got here," whispers Ashley.

"Probably because someone was watching us."

She sticks her tongue out at me. "That's not helping. Are you sure you can't see anyone? What about your ears?"

"Don't see anyone, and there's too much background noise from the city for me to hear a person breathing nearby."

Dr. Adams is the last one out of the clinic. He locks the door, then walks over to us. "Thanks again, Miss Carter. Really appreciate you taking the ride, and so does Hershey."

"Happy to help, Doctor Adams." She grins. "I know he's gotta be in pain, but he seems happy."

"He'll be a little happier tomorrow once we've got his leg back to rights. Speaking of which, I should go home and get some sleep. You're off tomorrow, right?"

"Half day. Coming in late to make up for the long ride."

He nods. "All right. See you then."

Ashley hugs me. "Thanks for taking the ride."

"Still am. You're going home right?" I squeeze her hand. "Not leaving you alone to the phantom watcher."

"Ack. Great. Now I'm never going to be able to sleep tonight. You really think someone is after *me*?"

"You could do worse than having Matt Damon stalking you."

She rolls her eyes. "That's totally not him. Someone's got a rubber mask. One of those high-quality ones like they use for movies."

"Yeah, probably. But who'd go to so much trouble to break into a vet clinic? Is there anything in there *that* valuable?"

"Some of those medicines are pricey, but there aren't enough of them to be worth it." She scratches her head, then pulls her hair over her face, sighing. "So weird."

"Yeah... weird is my theme song these days."

She laughs.

"You wanna drive?"

Ashley nods, so I toss her the keys.

We get in the car at the same time. After one more look around, I give her an 'all clear' nod, and she starts the engine. One puppy transported successfully... and one unexplainably strange night. As if I needed something else to worry about on top of Damarco. But honestly, he seems like a decent guy. He's not truly the problem.

I'm worried about Stefano most of all.

CONFLICT OF INTEREST

O nce Ashley is safe at home, I return to the hotel to see if Damarco is still even here.

We would've hung out for a bit, but the trip and stress of the thief left her exhausted and she wanted to go straight to sleep. Remembering the room number of 508 reminds me he's on the fifth floor, making it easy to fly a circle around the building and peek in windows. When I find him sitting at the little desk staring at the screen of his laptop, it's both a relief and a frustration.

He's still here, which means he hasn't killed Professor Heath. But he's still in town... which means I have a problem. For the most part, I enjoy school. Not to the degree Sophia or Sam do, but vastly more than Sierra. Only one aspect of school bothers me, and it's the feeling of having an unfinished assignment hanging over me. Like a research paper or essay I have to write, it gets under my skin and nags at me constantly. How some people can wait until the last minute and actually enjoy doing other things before they finish the assignment, I can't even fathom.

This thing with Wolent telling me to get rid of Damarco is starting to eat at me in the same way.

I land on the little concrete slab balcony outside his room and peer in.

He's in the midst of a telephone conversation with Tiffany apologizing over not being there for Thanksgiving and promising her they'll do 'something with turkey' as soon as he's back. She retorts by saying anything she does with him will be done with a turkey.

Ooh. I clamp my hand over my mouth to stop from laughing.

She sounds mostly playful, but it's obvious she would have preferred him home.

I concentrate on the screen and zoom in my vision. It's a good thing my hand is already over my mouth. The f-bomb I drop only comes out as a mumble. Damarco is looking at a photograph of Petra Stanovaya… the freakin' crazy Sybarite. It's kind of a private eye type photo of her walking out of a nightclub downtown.

"Still ain't been able to find the one I tracked to Seattle," says Damarco. "Montgomery, or whatever he's calling himself now. Couple of the students said the photo looks like a Professor Heath, but there's no one by that name in the school's roster. The office people don't know about him either. However, I think I've found another fiend around here. Gonna deal with her soon."

Oh, crap! Seriously? Wow… I don't necessarily mind Petra being destroyed. In fact, it would be difficult to argue the world wouldn't be better off without her. However, if Damarco succeeds in killing her, I'm going to land in deep shit. Even a vampire as sick as her has friends, and they will—with Stefano's help no doubt—all blame me. And that's before Wolent chimes in with however he's going to punish me for failing to do what he asked me to do.

Yeah, Petra's a bitch, but better she continues to exist than anything happens to my family.

Damn, talk about a total Catch-22. Maybe I could warn her? Nah. That plan has a couple of really big problems. Mostly, I don't want to go near her. The bitch would either attack me or think I'm trying to trick her. If she believed me, she'd kill this guy without remorse—or make him one of her captives and torment him for years.

It bothers me more than I can explain in words she still has captive people, but there isn't much I can do about it. Or… maybe. If there are mirrors in the place, maybe Blix could… nah. Messing with Petra risks my family. No vampire in Seattle would sympathize with 'mere mortals' and take my side.

Another possibility is Wolent might not care about her destruction. She doesn't involve herself with the organized society, pretty much ignoring them. Technically, Petra isn't part of the 'official' vampire political group here. She doesn't attend the parties, most likely because she's feels it beneath her or her cruel nature has made too many enemies. Still, Stefano wouldn't let that stop him from trying to make a big deal out of Damarco killing her. Wolent's exact words were *any* vampire. On a personal level, he'd probably understand, but Stefano would push the technicality.

Worse, this is Petra after all. She wouldn't simply kill or capture him. She'd find Tiffany and torment her first while making damn sure Damarco knew everything that happened to her, taunting him for not being able to help his sister. Ooh. I really want her to go up in flames. It's infuriating to be too weak to do anything about her, physically *and* politically.

I'm so caught up in the stew of conflicting emotions and possibilities it surprises me when Damarco jumps to his feet, closes the lid on the laptop, and hurries out of his hotel room. Oh, shit. He's going after Petra *right now*. I can't just sit here and do nothing.

Oh, hell with it. I stink at lying, but time's running out. Need to make contact with him before things get out of control. Well, *more* out of control. If I screw up and he attacks me, at least killing him in self-defense won't leave me saddled with the kind of crippling guilt that leaves me curling up in bed being ashamed of existing. I'll merely spend a few months crying and hating myself.

Assuming, of course, I can take him.

UNDERESTIMATED

Movies are full of vampires lying in wait somewhere above unsuspecting victims, ready to swoop down on them. They never show the monster's perspective in those movies. Makes sense as the directors want us to be scared of them. The best way to be afraid of something is not to know much about it. Show as little as possible and let the mind fill in all the awful details. They don't really do that anymore. Today's movies are all about the special effects. Makes me wonder if the old timey movies concealed the creatures as an artistic device or simply because the special effects of the time were so hilariously cheesy.

Anyway, as soon as a movie goes into the vampire's head, the monster becomes more relatable—or even turns into a joke. *Cough* sparkles *cough*. What's the vampire thinking right before he attacks someone? Does he loathe the monster he's become or does he take delight in it?

I can answer the question for me, at least. Even though my intention is not to attack Damarco, my stomach's twisted up in a complex knot that could win a contest at a Girl Scout event. Pouncing on people for food doesn't really bother me anymore since I've gotten used to it and the process causes no permanent harm. Once or twice, I've had close calls when attempting to feed on people already low on blood—probably because they'd recently donated or had some medical issues as I don't make a habit of trying to feed from people with obvious gaping wounds. Fortunately, vampires have the ability to sense how much is left inside a person. It's not like a gas gauge with a needle. As soon as their blood hits my mouth, I get a simple sense of safe or warning.

But, I've been avoiding this situation long enough. Nothing good is going to result from Damarco confronting Petra. I sincerely doubt this guy is some kind of extreme badass Navy SEAL commando or whatever. Even with a boost of Fury blood in me, I *barely* survived my encounter with her. And honestly, Glim saved my ass. No shame in that considering my age as a vampire. It had been as dumb of me to challenge her as it would be for Sierra to pick a fight with a pro MMA fighter. Okay, maybe not quite *that* stupid, but close.

My elevator is faster than the one inside the building.

Close to the wall to avoid being seen, I glide down and land in the alley behind the dumpsters, then race around to the street side near the front entrance. A few passersby give me weird looks for running. My attempt at an innocent smile probably comes off cheesy. Heh. Don't mind the freaked out looking teenage girl. I'm not fleeing a mugger; I'm merely trying not to kill a guy.

Damarco strides out the door, looking quite a bit more like *Blade* than *Kick Ass* in a long, dark trench coat he's certainly using to conceal a crossbow and a katana. The thought of a katana makes my left shoulder twitch. At least the guy doesn't have the strength of a vampire.

They say confidence gets you halfway to done. I'm hoping this guy's more than fifty percent attitude and isn't really as deadly as he looks. Whatever item he's got that's shielding his mind adds another layer of defense beyond protecting his thoughts. A vampire trying to zap his brain and being unable to would probably freak out, unsure what sort of 'creature' came after them. The shock might cause them to make a critical error in the heat of a fight. Already knowing about it will stop me from making that mistake and getting caught in an 'oh crap' moment of indecision. But this guy seriously looks like he would kick my butt.

Looks, however, aren't everything. Take me for example. Everyone thinks I'm harmless.

All right, I admit 'harmless' is a rather apt description of me... mostly. More personality than capability. Hey, mutilating Scott with my bare hands kinda made a statement. Then again, he always was quick to lose his head when he got angry. But still. I'm not *as* harmless as my appearance suggests.

And, there's no choice left. If I keep delaying, this guy is eventually going to either die or destroy a vampire. Gotta do this now. Hey, maybe he won't want to get into a fight in the middle of a public street. People claiming to be vampire hunters are usually considered crazier than vampires. Not like he could really prove anything, whereas I could.

Before worry makes me chicken out, I hurry after him down the sidewalk and follow him into the hotel's parking lot. He's heading for that same little car he drove the other day, probably a rental. Damarco senses me walking up behind him and turns to look.

"Hey." I raise a hand, waving, trying not to let my anxiety show.

"You seem kinda familiar." Damarco regards me with a head-to-toe glance.

"Yeah, umm... you were at SCC the other day. Look, I don't usually break cover, but it's kind of important."

He raises both eyebrows. "Break cover? Yeah, kid. Sure. I'm supposed to believe you're a cop?"

"Ugh, no." I roll my eyes. The exasperation is real. "You're here in Seattle to hunt down a rather interesting sort of problem, right?"

He chuckles. "I'm sure I have no idea what you mean."

I look around for eavesdroppers, then lean close to whisper, "You're a vampire hunter, right? So am I." Technicalities rule the day. I am a vampire, and I am hunting something. Not exactly a lie, even if my quarry is a more abstract thing than a person.

Damarco coughs. "Funny, kid. Where's the camera?"

Sigh.

"I'm being serious. We need to talk. Couldn't help but notice you scoping out Petra Stanovaya. Trust me, you're not ready to take a bitch like her on."

"Who the heck is that?"

"The woman you watched leaving a night club. The really pale woman. Her name is Petra."

He stares at me for an uncomfortably long minute, then folds his arms. "You're a hunter? What are you, fifteen?"

"Eighteen actually. And I'm still kinda new at this." Yay for skirting minor points of logic. What I say and what he hears aren't exactly the same. Still, it keeps me from feeling like I'm lying and ruining my poker face.

"What makes you think I ain't ready? You don't know anything about me."

I chuckle. "You don't have a tank or Apache helicopter. I've seen Petra in action. Not only is she really old, she's an absolute psycho with no hesitation. She's also got a messed up habit of not killing people right away. If you fail, she's going to keep you prisoner and torment you for decades… and probably go collect all your relatives and friends and do the same to them while she makes you watch. She considers torture and ruin an 'art form' and adores it."

Damarco does the 'looking around for eavesdroppers' thing, too. "It's easier for me to believe in vampires than you're eighteen."

"Whatever. Doesn't matter what you think my age is. I'm trying to stop you from getting yourself killed. And, honestly, there are a handful of really old ones around here. They're aware of you. It might be a good idea if you kept a real low profile for a while or even got out of Seattle."

He raises one eyebrow. "I'm supposed to believe there are multiple fiends here who have both discovered me and will attack, but some kid vampire hunter isn't in trouble?"

"Yeah." My cheesy smile doesn't sway him. "Mostly, I'm a joke to them." Another win for technicalities. That *is* a true statement. "They just kinda let me be since they don't consider me any kind of threat whatsoever."

"How'd you end up discovering them?" He leans against his car, giving me a 'this should be good' expression.

"Someone I used to love was killed by a vampire." I look down. Guess Mom was right when she called me a budding lawyer. I used to love Scott, and Dalton—a vampire—killed him. Of course, I didn't love him at the time he died, but that's splitting hairs. "Haven't successfully hunted any vampires, since they keep mind controlling me to go away." While I *have* killed some vampires, no 'hunting' was involved. The mind controlling to go away is a lie, but believable... and looking down, plus awkward fidgeting when talking about a murdered loved one isn't out of place. "Good thing I'm young since they feel sorry for me. Just wanna get the one who did it, yanno?"

Damarco slides a finger back and forth across his chin, likely deep in thought. Uh oh. Please don't go all Obi Wan on me and try to take me on as an apprentice. He's about to say something when a group comes out of the hotel. Four men and two women, all apparently office workers, stand and chat by the door for a little while before dispersing to three different cars. The whole time they talk, Damarco and I exchange glances while basking in uncomfortable silence.

As soon as we're once again alone, he says, "There are ways to shield the mind if you are serious about getting revenge. People think we're crazy, but vampires *do* exist."

"Yeah. I know. I've seen them." I rub my hands up and down my arms, pretending to be chilly. "You really think there's one at my school?"

Damarco nods once, then gazes off at the city. "Yeah. Vicious one, too. He killed fifty young women over a thirty year span."

"That doesn't sound likely. I mean, you thinking the guy who did it is the same guy who's here." I shift my weight from leg to leg. "There haven't been any disappearances from SCC or around the area. A killer like that wouldn't just stop. Most of the vampires I've tracked don't kill when they feed, so I'm trying to focus on the ones who do. There aren't many around here like that."

He shakes his head. "You don't get rid of a disease by letting the viruses exist. All the fiends need to be destroyed so it doesn't spread. If you're serious about there being multiple vampires in Seattle, it's amazing this place isn't overrun by now."

"A bite alone doesn't pass it on. I don't really understand how they make more vampires, but simple feeding doesn't do it. I've witnessed it a couple times and the victims don't change. Vampires are basically big mosquitos that can talk... and don't spread malaria."

He chuckles.

"And the bites don't itch." I smile.

"You make them sound almost tolerable. Are you sure one of them didn't get to you already?" He leans close, staring into my eyes. Despite me having no idea how much of a threat this guy could really be, my heart races at the proximity. Any second now, he's going to realize what I am... "Or you're just naïve."

Whew.

"Maybe. Or it could be I've just seen the nicer ones... except for Petra."

"Nicer?" He laughs. "They're all fiends. Some are just good at pretending to be human."

I feel so called out.

"Yeah, well..." I shrug. "Vampires have been around for hundreds, if not thousands, of years. If they *had* to kill to feed, it would be near impossible that they've managed to keep themselves hidden so well everyone believes them to be myths. Think logically here. It's in their interest to be as inconspicuous as possible. Leaving people alive when they feed isn't just a matter of being nice, it's self-preservation."

"Hmm." He rests his hands on his hips while making an 'I don't like it, but you have a point' smirk. "What about this woman, Petra?"

I cringe. "She's over a hundred years old. Used to be like an artist or something, but then she lost her mind and decided being a sadistic bitch equaled art. She doesn't kill people as much as destroy everything about their lives to the point they become suicidal."

"Damn. Sick bitch."

"Yeah, tell me about it." I look away to hide my facial expression.

Honestly, I wouldn't mind if that woman ceased existing, but if Damarco actually manages to kill her, it's going to bite me in the ass. I'm under no illusion it's anything but selfish of me, but my family has to come first.

"This fiend sounds like a serious problem."

I look up and make eye contact. Grr. Still can't get into his head. "She is, but she's managed."

He laughs. "You? A minute ago, you told me I needed an attack helicopter with missiles to stand a chance... now, you're saying you somehow dealt with her?"

"Not directly. I did the only thing I could: set other vampires against her so she behaves herself."

Damarco stares at me. "Other vampires? Exactly how many are there around here?"

"Umm, like five or six that I know." Subtle difference between 'know' and 'know of.' Hopefully, he'll *hear* 'know of.' My face is doing the thing it does when I lie—something of a guilty partial grimace. Quick, gotta explain guilt. "It's so frustrating I can't do anything about them directly."

"You know these vampires? Talk to them?"

Shit.

"Umm. Not exactly."

He points at me. "How'd you set them against each other if you didn't talk to them?"

"Well, it's like... you know how in medieval times you had land owners who'd sometimes get into little wars with each other? The vampires here do the same thing. They all have normal humans under their control and it's like chess pieces moving against each other. I did some stuff that made it look like Petra's minions interfered with the other vampires' operations. Started a micro war, and now they're all watching her."

He mulls this for a minute or three. "Interesting. That's not going to last forever."

"No, but it's better than being killed. You really should trust me on this. Confronting Petra head on, especially at her lair, is an *extremely* bad idea for you. Not only is she too powerful to fight alone, I've seen her take instant control of men. She's like some kind of succubus."

Damarco reflexively rubs his chest about where an amulet would hang. "It shouldn't be a problem. But if you're right about the fiend's power, it sounds like this calls for a lot more planning."

"More planning and a small army. Do you know any other hunters?"

He shakes his head. "Nah. Just me. Only ever knew one other."

"Can he help?" I ask, trying to sound upbeat while hoping for a *negative* answer.

"I wish. If Mac was still around, the fiend hiding out in the college would've been dusted already."

"Sorry. Mind if I ask how he died?"

Damarco's smile turns sad. "It's okay. Nothing worth making a movie out of. Cancer got him."

"Oh wow, that stinks. Guess you two were kinda close?"

"Kind of. Met him a couple years after I saw my first vampire. He got wind of what happened, felt bad about it, and wanted to help. Took us so long to track down the one responsible, Mac ended up in a hospital before we had a chance to confront the bastard. The fiend took the opportunity to slip out of town."

I nod. "Are you sure this Professor Montgomery is really the one you're looking for? Or he's even a vampire?"

"As soon as he left, the killings targeting young women stopped. He'd been the leader of a small group. The weaker ones stuck around though. Dusted a handful of them before they scattered. Ended up stuck with no idea where their leader went for a while until my sister took classes here. She spotted this guy in the hallway at night. Seemed to be a professor, but no one knew about him. The administration didn't have a record of any classes downstairs even though she saw plenty of students going there. One day, I get an email from her she's going to crash the class and find out who he is. Next day, she's forgotten entirely about the whole thing."

"Wow." I whistle. Okay, it's not beyond imagining Heath made her forget him or he's conditioned the school staff to feign ignorance to anyone specifically asking about him. None of it raises a red flag for me beyond a vampire simply trying to remain undiscovered. "I think if this professor is the same vampire you've been looking for, there would be a bunch of missing women around here, or a trail of bodies. There's never been anything in the news around here my entire life about a string of unsolved murders. Did you look into that?"

Frustration etches deep grooves in Damarco's forehead. "Nah. Not really. Kinda got angry when the fiend messed with my sister's head, ya know?"

"I can understand that, totally. Ticks me off when people mess with my family, too. Is she still going to SCC? Wonder if I've met her."

"Nah, she's out already. Graduated last year, but she transferred two years ago after she realized her memory had been tampered with. Didn't want to be anywhere near a vampire."

"Who does?" I flash a weak smile. "They can be really scary. Have you seriously been here for two years trying to find this guy?"

"Nope. Just a couple weeks. Came out here back then, but before I could find anything, I got a strong lead on some of his pack, which pulled me back home to deal with them. At least there, I didn't have to take time off work to do this crap."

I try to stare the desire to go home and be safe into his brain, but it feels like my forehead is smacking against a stone. "Not exactly a fun vacation, right? Petra's behaving herself as far as I know, and this professor you're after... he can't be the same vampire who killed those women years ago. Nuts like that don't change. You should look for a similar pattern of killings. And please leave Petra alone. I don't want you to die."

Sighing, Damarco stuffs his hands in his trenchcoat pockets. "Yeah, you got a good point there. Gonna need to think about how to handle this Petra situation, if at all. At least, it's going to require more observation. Thanks for the warning. Guess it's back to the drawing board tonight."

"Sorry. But... wasting time is better than you getting killed." I summon my most earnest expression using Sophia trying to sell Girl Scout cookies as a model.

"Don't I know it. Thanks, kid. You better get home before your parents freak out. Be glad you still got 'em."

"I am. Every day, I'm grateful to still be with them."

He seems sad for a few seconds, then shakes it off before trudging off to the hotel entrance.

Whew. I guess 'harmless and cute' really *is* a vampiric superpower.

VAMPIRE DELIVERY SERVICE

Talking to Damarco has ruined any chance of me killing him.

He's not a monstrous bogey man vampire hunter. Just a normal guy with the unfortunate luck a vampire murdered his parents and he saw it happen. That's an assumption on my part since he knows about vampires. I understand why Hitchcock never let the audience see the killer, or much of him. The unknown is frightening. Like, if anyone bothered to try talking to Frankenstein's monster, they'd have figured out he wasn't too bad a guy. Same with me and the scary vampire hunter.

Oh well, suppose it's time to get out of bed.

I open my eyes to Klepto perched on my chest, staring into my soul.

Gah. What is it about cats? One second they're adorable, the next terrifying.

"Mew."

"Hey there." I skritch her atop the head, starting the purr engine.

She doesn't feel at all abnormal. Certainly not like a collection of magical dust Sophia somehow put together into a real kitten. It might be hypercritical of me, but I don't think ordinary cats are supposed to teleport. Then again, ordinary teenage girls aren't supposed to fly either, so I can't fault the little furball too much.

The cat gets her fill of love after about ten minutes and disappears amid a small cloud of smoke—or vapor. Or something. It has no smell. Magic fog. Heh. That sounds like a product to clean bathrooms too good to be true. Two sprays of Magic Fog is all you need. Never scrub a toilet again.

If only.

Even from my basement bedroom, I can tell it's raining stupid hard today. The sound of it falling is epic. This is the kind of day where pants should be illegal, leaving the house forbidden, and doing anything other than curling up with a book and cup of tea the sort of social faux pas that would cause someone to be exiled from a community. Okay, doesn't *have* to be a book. I'll make an exception for video games and a cup of tea. Or coffee if that's your thing.

My collection of oversized T-shirts is legend. They are comfortable to sleep in and, for lazing around the house, turn into almost-knee-length 'dresses'. The bewildered expression of Marvin the Martian on today's shirt is a pretty good reflection of my current mood. Part of me worries delaying Damarco's confrontation with Petra and walking away is like the idiot who puts duct tape over a gas leak and considers the problem fixed, thus causing an even larger explosion hours later that wouldn't have happened otherwise.

He's not going to wait forever, or even very long. Who'd take the word of a kid for proof, even if I did give up some real information and talk about vampires with a completely straight face?

Ugh! I bury my face under a pillow.

Ten minutes or so of failing to suffocate myself doesn't result in an epiphany of what to do about Damarco. At least, nothing concrete. He let slip about his protection coming from an amulet. The best possible outcome here would be for me to somehow get that thing away from him, give him a compulsion to leave Seattle forever, and let him go alive.

I really, really, really don't want to kill this guy.

Some girls feel awkward talking to their parents about sensitive subjects: drugs, sex, bullying... how to get out of murdering a dude when a vampire elder orders you to. Not like this is embarrassing, so why not. Dad will probably come up with something ridiculous, but it should at least be worth the laugh. I'm expecting him to suggest another family road trip involving a van, blacked-out windows, and a CIA-style abduction and relocation.

Yeah, that's not going to happen.

Frustrated, I get out of bed and trudge upstairs. It's only about three in the afternoon, but it's so dark my vampireness is inches from going online already. I pause to look out the patio glass on my right. Rain is falling so damn hard it's blocking my view of the back fence and forcing saltwater-scented air in past the closed sliding door. Whoa. So glad it's a few degrees too warm for snow or Seattle would grind to a damn halt.

Yawning out of habit because my brain thinks it just woke up, I make my way down the short hall to the living room. Sierra's playing *Call of Duty*. Dad's typing away in his office. Sophia's nesting in blankets on the sofa, reading her Kindle. My ears tell me Sam, Ronan, and Blix are upstairs playing video games in the boy's room. I don't hear Mom anywhere. Ugh, did she seriously go to work today? I may have to compel her to use some vacation time once this case is over.

"Hey, Sare," says Sophia. "Morning. Crappy weather for a Sunday, right?"

"Yeah, but it's comfortable."

Sierra must be having a good run in the video game because she's smiling and doesn't look the least bit angry. I also notice she's not talking on the headset, though she is listening. Dad emerges from the little hallway leading from the living room to his office (and the downstairs bathroom), grinning at us in that 'it's time for a movie' way.

"Hey, Dad... question for you." I lean on the sofa back right above where Sophia is sitting.

"Shoot." He pauses to pull a DVD off the rack and walks over to me. "You guys up for a movie?"

Of course, the question is mostly directed at Sierra, since it would force her to relinquish the television.

"Sure. Let me finish this match first?"

"Great." He smiles and faces me. "What's on your mind, hon?"

I explain the Damarco situation, confronting him at the hotel, and the whole issue with Professor Heath, which I'm totally sure is mistaken identity. Sophia stops reading to stare straight up at me. Dad's inclined to agree with my opinion that *if* Heath had been responsible for the killings, he wouldn't have stopped.

"Maybe he only does it right before he leaves an area," says Sierra.

"Eek!" Sophia shivers. "Don't say scary stuff like that."

Sierra shrugs. "Don't worry. We're too little to be victims and Sarah's immortal."

"Not the point!" shouts Sophia.

"So I'm pretty sure the item in question is an amulet. When we were talking about mind control, he made this grabbing gesture at his chest." I mimic it. "Right where an amulet would hang."

"Easy." Dad smiles. "He doesn't suspect you're a vampire, so you can get close to him and rip the amulet off. Then, you could make him remember whatever you want."

"Dad, you're not taking into account the amulet might be warded against undead. What if Sarah can't touch it?" asks Sierra.

I laugh. "We're not inside a D&D game."

"No, but he's obviously got a magical amulet. Maybe the people who made D&D based it on real stuff?" Sierra grins at me. "Vampires exist, right?"

"The child has a point." Dad points at her with the DVD box —*Ladyhawke*. Oh, fantasy. Sierra's going to adore that.

Sophia tosses the Kindle onto the sofa beside her and scrambles out of her blanket cocoon. "I'll get Sam."

Before anyone can say a word, she runs upstairs. She's in the same mood I am, still wearing a nightgown. Today is too crummy weather-wise to get dressed. Dad's the trend breaker. Except for not having shoes on, he could be in a relaxed office environment. Polo and khakis. At least he's not his father. I love Grandpa Wright, but orange plaid burns my retinas.

Dad and I settle on the couch, tossing ideas back and forth regarding Damarco. When he suggests chloroforming the guy, I burst out laughing. Close enough to piling everyone in a van for a kidnapping road trip. Sophia, Sam, Ronan, and Blix come downstairs. The imp's out in the open as everyone presently in the house is in on the secret. We've brought Ronan into the circle of trust, though his and Hunter's mother is still unaware of vampires. I'm not sure she'd be okay with Ronan taking shortcuts to get here across a dangerous mirrorverse filled with bizarre creatures, but at least it keeps him out of the rain, and he won't get hit by a car. Fortunately, they don't live that far away so the distance compression of the other side results in the trip feeling like a walk down a long corridor. There honestly isn't too much opportunity for something nasty to find him before he's back in the normal world.

Soon, Sierra finishes the match and relinquishes the television for Cheesy Eighties Movie Time.

Though, this movie isn't cheesy. Sometimes, Dad deliberately puts on bad ones because they're unintentionally funny, but he's got plenty of classics. This one, I've seen before, but the Littles haven't. Guarantee Sophia will cry at some point.

Not quite an hour into the movie, Klepto pops into existence in midair a few feet above Sophia's lap and drops onto her. "Mew." While she pets the kitten, the fuzzball rolls onto her back and stares at me with beyond-cat sentience and a weird sense of smiling. Bleh. I'm reading way too much into that face.

Sure enough, the movie makes Sophia cry several times—but she adores the ending.

While the credits crawl up the screen, Dad floats the idea of a double feature and we start discussing which movie to watch next. Sierra chants 'Cheese' repeatedly, but not annoyingly loud. Sam wants science fiction.

"Cheese and science fiction." Dad scans his movie rack. "*Freejack… Ice Pirates?*"

The phone rings.

"Pirates made out of ice?" asks Sophia, her nose scrunched.

"No, they steal ice." Dad wags his eyebrows and jumps to his feet.

"I got it." I fly up off the couch and pretend to swim down the hall to the kitchen. Yeah, I'm weird. Still floating horizontally in the air, I glide up to the phone and pluck it from the cradle. "Hello?"

"Sarah?" asks Mom.

"Yeah."

"Just who I needed to talk to. Can you do me a huge favor?"

"As long as it doesn't involve overthrowing any banana republics or the assassination of foreign dignitaries."

She gives a tired laugh. "Nope. Just some papers I seem to have forgotten at home for the case I'm working on. It's a report from metallurgists that's crucial. No darn idea how I could've left something this critical on my home desk."

I chuckle, thinking of a furry thief. "Heh. I have an idea for how it happened. Not sure you 'forgot' it. What's it look like?"

"A spiral bound stack of papers about a quarter inch thick. Full of schematic diagrams of aircraft parts and enough math to choke John Nash."

"Wow. Okay. Give me a bit to look around. If I don't call you back in like ten minutes, I'm on the way. If I can't find it, I'll call you."

"Okay. Thank you, dear."

I hang up and fly back to the living room.

The Littles laugh at my 'air swimming.'

Dad twirls the remote around his finger. "Ready?"

"Mom asked me to bring her something. Wait or start without me, doesn't matter. It shouldn't take me long to run the file she wants to her."

"It's absolutely pouring out there," says Dad.

"I know. Gonna wear my bathing suit."

Dad grimaces. "Hon, 140 miles an hour is going to rip your bottoms off."

Sierra finds this idea utterly hilarious.

He does have a point. "Yeah, probably. I'll figure something out."

I fly upstairs straight to Sophia's room to raid Klepto's stash. Since I'm already horizontal, I set down on the floor pretending to be a spaceship coming in for a landing. Yeah, I'm eighteen. Really. The amount of junk under her bed is increasing. Holy cow. In another week, her bed will be pushed up from the floor. I shove aside a few plastic Easter eggs, dolls that clearly aren't Sophia's, fake gold coins, some really overdone costume jewelry—bracelets, rings, tiaras, and this way gaudy gold pendant like something a 'wizard' would wear at a fantasy roleplaying LARP or ren fest. Seriously, the grape sized ruby is so obviously plastic it's hilarious. Guess kitty got into someone's costume stash. Oh, there's Great Uncle Hank's belt. Someone's cell phone, a softcore romance novel, a steel coffee mug—wait. Hold on. Softcore romance novel?

I pluck the paperback out of the pile and stare at it. The cover shows a hunky bare-chested 'pirate' standing beside a barely dressed woman tied to the mast of a big sailing ship. Wait, she's not barely dressed... she's *not* dressed. Rope covers the naughty bits. *Conquests on the High Seas.* Hmm. I skim a few pages... and yow! This isn't exactly *soft*core. Eek. I'm going to ask Aurélie to erase the phrase 'moist pulsating love tunnel' from my brain. This is *not* the sort of book Sophia should be allowed to read. And seriously, *pulsating*? Does whoever wrote this have any idea how girl parts work? My face is already glowing red and I'm merely skimming. Please let her not have seen this or looked at it.

The book gets tucked under my arm for removal. No, I'm not going to read it—and Sophia for damn sure isn't either. I don't even want to hide it in my room in case the 'rents find it and think I'm into this stuff. It would be less embarrassing for them to find dirty pictures on my computer than this book. Oh crap. Does that mean one of our neighbors reads this stuff? How far away does Klepto's net of acquisition reach? What really worries me is how Sophia said the kitten is drawn to objects people hold value in. Eww. Now I don't want to even touch this book.

A little more digging through mostly socks, underpants, neckties, and a few of Sam's action figures finally unearths a thin spiral-bound book fitting the description Mom gave me. As soon as I see the words 'metal fatigue' and 'stress fractures' on the cover, I'm sure it's the right one. Bingo.

Okay, easy part done.

If I try to fly to Boeing dressed, my clothes are going to end up *drenched* like I'd gone swimming in them. That's super uncomfortable. Dad's right about the bikini. I'll leave here with it, but it'll vanish somewhere in flight. I go fast, but I don't want to literally streak across the sky. Hmm. Wetsuit? Nah, too much effort. Besides, it will look way bizarre to walk into my mother's office in a wetsuit. Oh, hell. I guess a normal T-shirt and shorts will do. Just have to deal with being wet. No need for socks or shoes. I'm not going to be in contact with the ground outside much.

I head to my room and trade the Marvin long tee for a normal one and a pair of denim shorts. This won't be *too* uncomfortable soaked. Next stop: the kitchen. After stuffing Mom's file—and the offending book—into three trash bags to keep the paper dry, I go out the back door onto the deck and it's like I've jumped into the shower with clothes on. For about six seconds, the cold paralyzes me. Then, it's gone like the rain is room temperature.

Dayum. Guess the Old Gods are in a bad mood today.

I leap into the air, climbing to about a thousand feet while accelerating toward Seattle. Hindsight tells me swim goggles would have been helpful. Pelting raindrops in my face make it almost impossible to see anything when flying at full speed, but I don't need to pay too much attention on navigation until I'm much closer to the Boeing complex. Hmm. There is so much water in the air, I can't tell if this counts as flying or swimming.

Even with my eyes mostly shut, my mother's workplace is obvious from the air. Slowing down to the speed of a fast run allows me to see again. I didn't bring my phone due to the apocalyptic rainfall, so I can't text Mom to tell her to meet me in the lobby. My best option is to head to the main entrance.

This late on a Sunday, there are only two guys at the front desk, security guards. Both of them stare at my chest, which is kinda obvious under a clingy wet T-shirt. No, I'm not an idiot—mostly. I wore a black one for this specific reason. They avert their gaze to my face after a few seconds, feeling awkward about checking out the boobs on a girl they're sure is too young to check out the boobs on. Guy on the left changes the subject in his mind by thinking about 'all the chemicals in our food' now being responsible for a thirteen year old having boobs as big as mine—not that anyone has ever called them large before. Grr! Dammit. I'm seriously going to mess a dude up if they keep making me younger. Then again, this guy's like sixty, so he thinks of twenty-year-olds as 'kids.' He and the other guard move on to being perplexed at a girl going outside in this weather wearing shorts. Looking at me is making them shiver.

"Can I help you, sweetie?" asks the older guard.

I poke their brains, compelling them to ignore my clothes or even notice I'm soaked. "Yeah. Can you please let Allison Wright know I'm here with the file she wanted?"

"What service are you with?" asks the younger guy.

"None. I'm her daughter. This report fell out of her case at home."

"Oh. Okay. Hold on." The younger guy checks a listing on his computer, picks up a phone, and hits a couple buttons. "Mrs. Wright? Got someone here saying they're your kid and they brought you a— oh. Yes. All right." He hangs up and smiles at me. "She's on her way down."

"Cool. Thanks."

I pace around in front of the desk, dripping. Mom appears in a hallway behind a set of double glass doors. Her expression is halfway between exhaustion and homicide. If she ever wore that face while walking into court, the opposing counsel would probably just give up before the judge said a word.

A beep comes from the wall beside the doors as she pushes one open and walks out into the lobby, her high heels clicking on the white tiles. All trace of corporate lawyer evaporates to worried mother and she starts fussing at me for looking like a drowned kitten.

"Good grief, Sarah. You're going to get sick."

"Relax, Mom. They don't see me like this." I wink and hand her the trash bag-and-duct-tape bundle.

She grasps it, pauses, then looks at me. "What else is in here?"

"Umm. You know how the kitten has a habit of swiping stuff?"

"Right…"

I explain the book I found. "Way too awkward to give it to Dad. I looked at a couple pages and whoa. Didn't want you guys finding it in *my* room. So, here it is. Far away from Soph."

Mom chuckles. "Okay. Thank you for bringing this, sweetie. I'd hug you… but."

"It's fine. I know I'm drenched. What time are you going to come home tonight?"

She looks at her watch. "Maybe another hour. Opening arguments are scheduled for tomorrow, so I need to make sure everything is ready. Imagine how much I panicked when this report disappeared."

"Yeah. That kitten seems to pick up on how much people like things. Maybe she sensed the report was important to you." I shrug. "Please don't be mad at the cat. Or Soph."

Mom sighs, frustration and fatigue heavy on her breath. "You found it fast, so no harm done. I'm happy it's back and I don't need to request a new copy. It would've taken days. Go on home and warm up. Looking at you is making my teeth chatter."

"Be careful driving in this crap. It's bad out there."

We do the European cheek kiss not-quite-hug to prevent water transfer. I hurry out the door while Mom disappears back into the salt mines. Well, that didn't take too long. I won't have missed too much of the movie.

Never saw *Ice Pirates*. Maybe I'll ask Dad to start it over if no one objects.

23

UNLIFE ISN'T FAIR

By the time I get home, my clothes are so saturated with water they need to be wrung out.

"Back!" I yell, while stepping inside. "Be right up, just gotta dry off."

"Okay," says Dad from the living room.

Luckily, the access to the basement is right in the kitchen, so I don't trail water all over the house on my way downstairs and straight to the mini bathroom. The drenched T-shirt and shorts go in the sink for now. It's tempting to take a warm shower, but unnecessary. My being cold is entirely a state of mind. After toweling off, I wrap myself in another, drier towel, and scurry to my bedroom to finish drying my hair.

I lock the door, grab a dry towel and attack the mane.

Coralie manifests beside me.

For an instant, I almost scream since I'm naked. But... she's a she—and a ghost. They probably walk in on people doing way more embarrassing things than simply drying off all the time. I open my mouth to make a joke out of the situation, but the intense look on her face keeps me mute.

"Go to Ashley's right away." Coralie's spectral body flares brighter as she leans toward me. "Her life is in danger!"

I actually take two steps toward my door stark naked... but manage to salvage enough presence of mind to grab my Marvin T-shirt on the way past the bed. I still do run out of my bedroom with nothing on, wriggling into the long shirt on my way across the basement to the stairs. Even if any of my family had been down there to witness me, all they'd have seen is a smear of paleness go by.

I'm out the patio door—leaving it open—and zooming to Ashley's mere seconds after Coralie warned me. Not a long trip, only four houses down on the street my cul-de-sac is on. To save time, I swing around to approach her bedroom window, which is already open. Like Supergirl, I fly in headfirst.

Ashley's sitting on the edge of her bed, held by a man in a black leather jacket with his face buried in her neck. She doesn't look so good, eyes lolled up into her head, delirious, even paler than normal, which is pretty much chalk white. My first thought is Emilio, and things have gone way too far too fast.

"Shit!" I shout while pouncing on him, grabbing his shoulders, and tearing him away from her.

He hits the floor on his face and slides into her dresser. Ashley emits a half-awake raspy moan and flops over onto her back, bleeding from the neck. Furious and in a state of panic, I soccer kick the guy in the head as he tries to get up, launching him into the wall before jumping on Ash and closing the wound as fast as I can. The son of a bitch didn't rip her throat out, merely a normal pair of punctures, but the instant the taste of her blood—cinnamon sugar—hits my tongue, I know he's taken way too much.

He definitely tried to kill her.

Snarling, I whirl to face him. "Emilio, what the fuck are you doing!?"

The guy staggers to his feet and blinks at me a few times, still in the throes of feeding euphoria. Also, it's not Emilio. It's Ruben. He braces a hand to his temple as if he's trying to get his skull to stop spinning. Forcibly peeling a feeding vampire away from their meal is roughly comparable to being in the midst of an orgasm and suddenly finding yourself at 10,000 feet falling to your death. The body's still coping with the endorphin rush of a super pleasurable experience when mortal terror hits.

"Ruben? What the hell are you doing here? Give me one good damn reason not to tear your balls off."

"Whoa…" He staggers to the side, hands raised. "What's wrong with you?"

"With me? What's wrong with *you!?*" I stomp toward him, extending my claws. "You almost killed Ashley!" I glance over at her— she's out cold. "Dammit!" I slash at him.

He shields his face with his arms, my claws slicing up the thick leather enough to draw a little blood. "Ack!" Ruben scrambles away from me. "Calm the hell down."

"What are you doing here?" I shout.

"Feeding. What's it look like?"

"Why her?" I jump at him, but he dodges.

"Curiosity. Been following you… had to know more about a vampire who's so close to appearing mortal. Saw the ginger with you and thought she looked tasty."

I glare at him… and a realization hits me—his leather jacket is the same one 'Matt Damon' had on in the video feed from the vet place. "Stay away from her!" I roar, diving at him.

He catches my wrists, holding my claws back from his face. We spin around a few times before he throws me over the bed. I catch myself flying and zoom right back at him. Ruben dives to the floor, going under me and springing back to his feet at the same instant I whirl to face him again.

"She's just a mortal," says Ruben, his expression dripping with disdain. "What do you care?"

"Ashley is my best friend!" I fume at him. "And what the frick is wrong with you? Feeding from her is bad enough, but there's no damn reason to kill while doing it."

Ruben smiles, shaking his head. "Wow, you really are new, aren't you? Guess it's not something they teach. It's way more powerful to drink them dry. Addictive even. The rush is unlike anything you can imagine. Makes heroin seem like aspirin."

"Disgusting…"

"And, the best part is, I only *have* to feed once a month. There's so much power. But there's no fun in doing it so rarely. Now, if you'll excuse me… you interrupted."

I emit an inhuman noise somewhere between desperate friend screaming 'no' and a tiger that had her tail slammed in a cage door. My flying tackle carries Ruben clear over Ashley's bed. We hit the wall, bounce off, and roll over each other on the floor.

"Get away from her!" I snarl, trying to dig my claws into his throat. Just need a grip on his spine to rip the head clear off.

His grip squeezes hard into my forearms, fighting to hold my bladed fingers away from his neck. "Find your own meal."

"She's not my food!" I shriek. "She's my sister! I'm not going to let you hurt her."

"Aww, piss off."

Growling, I slash at his face, tearing two slices down his cheek. He rams a knee into my side, throwing me to the left. We both leap to our feet; he's a little faster. In a fraction of a second stretched out in slow motion, I see him going high, coming in for a grab, so I dive at his gut. He grasps me by the shoulders and hauls me up off my feet. Too angry to think, I lapse into my 'electrocuted alley cat' combat style. With him holding me off the ground by my shirt, I've got all four limbs available to end this idiot. We're too close for proper kicking, so I try to knee him in the ribs while ripping his face off.

Ruben throws me around, swinging left and right. A few seconds into my frenzy, I feel like a rabid raccoon scruffed by an animal control officer who's trying not to hurt it. This dude is genuinely shocked I'm upset over Ashley. We struggle for a little while longer until he pins me against her closet and the shock of my bare ass slapping into the cold door stalls me.

He's holding me by two fistfuls of red Marvin the Martian T-shirt, which has pulled the hem up a little too high.

Mrs. Carter picks that exact moment to poke her head in. I

couldn't care less about the state of my wardrobe with Ashley's life hanging in the balance, so I ignore her and keep trying to claw this bastard's throat out.

"Sarah?" asks Mrs. Carter. "What's going on? Why don't you have any pants?"

Since my back is against the closet door, I take advantage of something solid to brace on. Flight lets me hang in midair and use both legs and arms to shove the guy off. Ruben sails across the room, bounces off the far wall, and lands flat on his chest atop Ashley's giant steamer trunk. I smooth my shirt back down.

"He's a vampire who tried to kill Ashley. Sorry, I'd have gotten dressed, but didn't exactly have a lot of advanced warning to get over here."

"Oh, okay," says Mrs. Carter like I'd told her we were going to watch a movie. She starts to walk off, but stops, backs up a step, and gawks. "What? Did you say 'kill Ashley?'"

Ruben glares at her. "Go away."

"Okay." Mrs. Carter smiles a placid little smile and hurries off down the hall.

"Stop mind controlling my friend's mother!" I shout.

He laughs. "You are too cute. Are you seriously bitching about a mortal blood bag?"

"Yes!" I dive at him again.

This time, a last second feint lets me rip four nice slashes across his chest. He screams in pain and finally takes a real swing at me. I manage to duck the right hook and retaliate with a shoulder-grab-assisted knee to the gut. It's like ramming my leg into a heavy bag. He barely notices. It really is kinda pointless to hit vampires there. All the stuff that takes the wind out of living people isn't important to us.

"Ow, dammit!" He grabs me under the arms and shoves me off. "You are seriously out of your damn mind."

"Stay away from Ashley!" I fume, standing between him and her.

"There's no point. She's already gone. Only a little blood left."

I spin, gasping, and stare at Ashley. She's still breathing, but I can tell her heart is struggling to beat. "No…" Hastily, I gather her up to carry. "Gotta get her to the hospital."

Ruben grabs my shoulders, pulling me away from her. I spin, grabbing his neck in both hands while growling like a feral animal. We're nose-to-nose. His eyes bug out in pain as my claws sink into his throat. Gurgling, he grabs my wrists and forces my hands away. Damn, this guy is stronger than me. At least the effort it's taking him to overpower me shows on his face.

Jaw clenched, he pulls my right arm up and looks at my fingers. "Claws? What the shit? I don't have claws. How'd you do that?"

"Just happens. Some of us have claws, some don't."

"Crap. That's not fair."

I surge at him, pushing him back until he hits the wall. "Unlife isn't fair."

He snarls past his fangs at me, struggling to hold my claws away from his neck. "You know, I hate hurting women. But if I gotta knock you senseless to finish my meal in peace, so be it."

A sudden reversal—pulling instead of pushing—lets me peel him off the wall and throw him to the floor. I jump down on his back, ripping and slicing, but his stupid thick jacket absorbs the brunt of it. Ruben nails me in the side of the head with an elbow, throwing me off him onto my back—and he jumps on top of me.

I score another slash to his shoulder before he grabs my wrists and pins my arms to the rug while straddling me, holding me down. I try to force myself upright, but can't budge him much. Desperate to protect Ashley, I snarl and thrash, flailing one leg in an attempt to get it up over his head and kick him away.

"Yeah," I grumble. "Unlife isn't fair… like how everyone is freakin' stronger than me."

24

CAUGHT RED-HANDED

Grunting between growls, I struggle to get out from under Ruben, inching across the floor.

He holds me down like an irritating older brother. Being I'm as freaked out as I've ever been in my life, his laughing at me is only pissing me off more. Despite having plenty enough strength to throw a 190 pound guy, the way he's sitting on my thighs and pushing my wrists into the floor is making it damn hard to move.

"Sare?" asks Ashley in a not-all-there voice. "What's going on? Why are you and Hunter screwing in my room when I'm here? Am I involved?"

"Not Hunter. This bastard tried to kill you!" I yell, rocking my hips while trying to throw this guy off me.

Ashley emits a fearful gasp. "Umm. Why don't you have pants?"

I sigh. Hearing her conscious does calm me down a little. "I'm in a fight with a vampire. Figured it would end with me naked anyway, so I decided to skip ahead rather than have my clothes get ruined."

She laughs dazedly, sounding like she's smoked *all* the weed.

"I'm kidding. But"—I twist my body hard to the left, causing Ruben to topple… and ramming my knee into his groin hard enough to send him sliding ten feet across the floor—"This guy doesn't have claws or a sword so I might get lucky and stay dressed this time." I contemptuously fling my shirt back down to cover myself.

Ruben grabs himself and squeaks, "Why do freakin' girls *always* go for the nuts?"

"Grab whatever from my closet." Ashley waves her hand like she's gesturing at the closet, only she's pointing at the wall.

I dart to the chair by her desk and snag the pair of hot pink sweat pants draped over it—with a unicorn on the butt. Wow, these are almost too girly for Sophia to touch. No time to care about what I look like. Anything is better than a freak gust of wind showing off my nether regions. Flight lets me jump into them with both legs at the same time. "C'mon, Ash. We gotta get you to the hospital."

Ashley attempts to stand—and falls straight to the floor.

"Crap." I rush over and pick her up. "Dammit, Ash. Hold on."

The instant I'm standing with her in my arms, Ruben grabs my right ankle and yanks me off my feet. I manage to toss Ashley onto the bed before eating rug, my hands still gripping the edge of the mattress.

"Why are you so fixated on a mortal?" asks Ruben, pulling me back by one leg.

I roll over onto my back and stomp at his face; he catches my ankle and pushes my leg high. So glad I took a mid-fight break to put pants on. "Because she's my goddamned best friend. Why is that so hard for you to understand?" Like something out of a Jean Claude VanDamme movie, I throw myself into the air spin-kicking him across the face with my left foot—since he let go of that ankle.

Ruben sails headfirst into Ashley's desk, knocking over roughly a thousand plastic unicorns. I stare down the length of my pink-sweat-pant covered leg emblazoned with rainbow lettering spelling out 'Girl Power.' The designer probably didn't mean it literally. He groans and pulls his head out of the hole it made in the particleboard.

"It's ridiculous how you're getting so upset over a worthless food sourc—"

I spring at him in a flurry of slashing claws. "Ashley's not worthless! You..." and I launch into a stream of swearing that would make Sierra blush. Actually, it would probably make the guys who taunted her online blush.

Ruben punches me in the chest. A loud *crack* accompanies a hit that sends me across the room and out into the hallway. I crash into the wall, knocking a few small hanging plates to the floor, and fall straight down onto my butt. If I still needed to breathe, I'd be gawping for air and likely unable to move much. The dull pain in the middle of my chest says it would've killed me had I been alive. Broken sternum crushing my heart. Oddly, it doesn't hurt much.

He shakes his head dismissively at me and turns toward Ashley.

Oh, hell no.

I run at him, leaping over the bed, grabbing him around the middle, and power-flying us both out the window into the backyard. He hammers his fist down on my back a few times before we hit grass. My anger is to the point I don't even slow down, diving into the ground as fast as I can make us fly with him trying to go the other direction. He manages to put the brakes on enough so his entire pelvic cradle doesn't explode on impact—but it still cracks.

The crash mushes my face into his stomach and sends me somersaulting past him. This time, I'm faster to my feet since he's favoring his left hip. A quick look around offers nothing even remotely close to a weapon, only a few lawn gnomes and a bird feeder. While I am angry enough to consider attempting proctology with the bird feeder, the squirrels would never forgive me. And, if I'm honest with myself, it really wouldn't help.

As he's struggling upright, I leap on him, sinking all the fingers of my right hand as deep as they'll go into his chest. He screams in pain, calls me a crazy bitch, and grabs at my throat. His legs give out, dumping him over backward with me on top of him. The next like twenty seconds or so melts into a blurry haze of random shouting, flailing, and being punched.

Though, I'm letting him have it just as much as he's giving me. Neither one of us possess any real training at fighting hand-to-hand. Sure, Dalton kinda filled my head with a primer on using knives and swords, but it only translates so much to claws. He's a bit stronger than me, though I've at least got some experience fighting other vampires. And, well, claws are a huge advantage over bare hands. It's surprising he hasn't tried to bite me yet. Fangs used as weapons—as opposed to feeding—hurt really bad. Like worse than extreme buffalo nibbles on the way out.

"Will you freakin' calm down already? It's just a damn mortal," rasps Ruben.

"She is not *just* a mortal!" I thrust my arm up through his grip on my wrist. My claws end up in his throat, his hand around my elbow. "I'm not gonna let you kill her!"

Ruben's eyes widen, like he's *finally* got it through his thick skull I'm going to end him if he won't leave Ashley alone. "You crazy bitch. You're like the vampire version of a vegan."

The comment is so off the wall it startles me back from blind anger to merely murderous rage. "What the hell are you talking about? You're trying to murder my friend."

"*You* don't like killing your food, so you demand no one else kill their food." He grabs my neck in both hands, squeezing. "Just like a vegan."

I rasp, "Are you seriously trying to strangle me, dumbass? I don't breathe either."

He flies us upright to stand, then flings me to the ground by his grip on my neck. A jolt of pain tells me my vertebra almost broke. For the second time tonight, I eat the floor—only this time it's grass instead of rug and I've got a mouthful of dirt.

"Bleh." I spit it out.

"You're still a baby. I didn't have a sire to teach me how to be a vampire, but even I know we shouldn't allow ourselves to become attached to mortals. They don't live forever." He gestures up at the window. "I've already taken enough to be fatal. She's going to die no matter what. You should let me finish. It would be cruel to let that cute little redhead die slowly."

Tears stream out of my eyes. Grief and rage blind me. I'm vaguely aware of tackling him, my claws throwing blood, strips of leather jacket, skin, and grass everywhere. It's like Ruben is a physical wall between me and Ashley and I have to claw my way past him to find her. Maybe he's hitting me or pulling my hair or something… can't tell. My entire universe in that moment is a tsunami of pain and wrath.

Thwoonk!

A flicker of bright red-orange fire touches something deep inside my psyche, snapping me back to reality. Ruben screams. I notice I'm on my back, Ruben on top of me. He'd been holding me down with one hand on my neck. His right arm is up, fist cocked, knuckles bloody. My face hurts. Something's sticking out of his chest. Smoke's pouring out of the hole around it. It takes me a second to realize I'm looking at a fat crossbow bolt. Ruben lurches up to his feet, frantically grabbing at the stick protruding from his chest. Thin jets of fire blow out some of the deeper claw wounds he suffered, a magnesium flare torching him from the inside out. He howls in agony, a glowing crimson flame inside his throat rendering his fangs in shadow. Smoke belches from his mouth. His cries of pain fade to a toneless rush of air that expels the ashen remains of his vocal cords.

A man in a dark coat rushes past me. In a flash of metal, the *whoosh* of a sword takes Ruben's head from his shoulders. His body teeters for a second, then collapses still to the grass. The man turns to look at me.

"Sarah, are you okay?" asks a voice I recognize.

I gaze up at Damarco… too late realizing my fangs are extended, my claws out and bloody.

His wide-eyed look of concern gives way to guarded suspicion.

Ahh, crap.

25

AIR AMBULANCE

We stare at each other.

The crossbow in his left hand is empty. He's frozen in place, too far away to swing his sword at me, not far enough to be able to reload before I'm on him. His eyes tell me he knows he's dead if I want to kill him. If he so much as twitches, I'd tear his throat out—or so he thinks.

"What are you doing here?" I ask, trying to calm down enough to retract my claws. Not working. Don't ask me if I'm freaking about Ashley or terrified of what this guy might do to me. Can't tell.

Ruben's body succumbs to spreading flames, collapsing in on itself like a deflating balloon.

Damarco holds statue still, his gaze fixed on my hands. "Tiffany called me out of the blue. Gave me this address. Said I had to get my ass over here because a vampire was trying to kill you."

"How could she even know that?" I, too, hold completely still, not wanting to spook him. This is some kinda screwed up Old West-slash anime katana-wielding demon hunter showdown standoff BS.

"Damn fine question," says Damarco, his voice barely over a whisper. He looks worried. Maybe he's wondering how he survived meeting me before. Could be, he thinks I'm toying with him now.

"Coralie," I say. "Hey... can we talk? Like not fight? I don't want to hurt you."

"Give me one reason to trust you."

Finally, my claws decide to listen to me and shrink back to normal fingernails. "My friend Ashley is going to die if I don't get her to a hospital right away. The guy you just destroyed took too much blood from her. That's why I was fighting him. I don't have time to explain everything to you right now or my best friend since I was five is gonna die." Tears roll down my face. "Maybe she's already lost, but I have to try. Meet me at Virginia Mason Hospital if you want the truth. I swear I'm not trying to trick you. Shoot me in the back if you're going to. I can't let her die."

He stares at me, but I don't wait more than a second before leaping to Ashley's window. She's still breathing, but her heartbeat's way off. For an instant, I freeze, wondering if it's too late. Glim's voice in the back of my mind describes the transference—blood and intent. Ashley's clinging to life by a thread. Any second now, her heart's going to stop beating. If I tore my wrist open and gave her my blood, wanting to pass along vampirism, it would 'save' her the same way Dalton saved me.

But Ashley... she wants to have kids some day. She wants a normal life. No. I can't do it yet. There's like a thirty-second or so window after death. Even if I'm too late to save her life, I have to at least try. I scoop her up in my arms and run out, down the hall, down the stairs, and out the front door. Screw anyone seeing us—as soon as we're outside, I take off.

The only thing keeping me from crying is knowing my tears will kill her. If I can't see where I'm going, any chance of saving her is lost. I couldn't un-live with myself for turning her into a vampire if it wasn't absolutely necessary, so there's only one possible option: break the sound barrier.

Or try.

Unfortunately, Mach 1 is *way* past my capabilities. That's potentially a good thing since I don't think Ashley could survive going too fast. The wind would rip her face off. Still, I set a personal speed record. There's a lot to be said for not giving a shit. In this case, I don't give a shit if we're seen, if I hurt myself overextending my ability to fly, or if the PIBs get mad at me.

I have to be faster than a medical helicopter.

I have to get Ashley to the hospital.

I have to do this. I can't fail.

In what feels like an instant, we're diving toward the hospital, heading for the obvious emergency arrivals area where ambulances pull in with critical patients. We come down so hard, a bone or two in my foot breaks, but pain is meaningless. The automatic doors open with a hiss. A few people inside wearing various uniforms look up at us. None of them appear shocked like they saw me flying, only surprised to see us barging in.

My stare bores into the brain of the nearest guy who isn't dressed like a janitor or a cop. "Ashley needs a doctor right away. Blood transfusion. She's A-positive."

26

MISSION COMPLETE... SORTA

Amazing the kind of priority help you can get at a hospital when using mental domination.

And yes, I know Ashley's blood type. Sure it's easy to make a joke about a vampire being obsessed with blood, but our junior year of high school, we organized a donation drive and they typed us all. I used to be O-negative. Not sure if I still count as even having a blood type or if my blood has gone to Crazytown.

Not until two doctors, three nurses and some other staff are well into the process of giving her a blood transfusion does my brain reboot out of panic mode. We're in a room down a hall from the ER. They've got Ashley in a bed hooked up to two IV bags, a heart monitor, and some other equipment I don't recognize. It's hard to force myself not to bother the doctors with questions. Their thoughts say there's maybe a twenty percent chance she's not going to make it. Another half a minute longer in getting here and she'd have been gone.

That finally breaks the dam. I slump into the nearest chair and sob into my hands. Dread hits me hard the instant I wonder if I'll have to give her the Transference. If the doctors can't save her, I still can. But... would she want me to? As much as it horrifies me to consider, the only answer is yes. Guilt comes from this happening to my best friend because of me. Not like I killed her, but my being a vampire exposed her to this danger. All this supernatural stuff is doing it's damndest to invade my normal life. As long as we've known each other, I'm confident she will have the same opinion I did about becoming a vampire... beats being completely dead.

Even though my hands are shaking, pretty sure I stayed relatively cool in the situation back at her house. However, like a dumbass, I threw far too much time at fighting Ruben. I should have hurled him out the window, grabbed Ashley, and raced to the hospital. Maybe he would've chased us. He could fly. If Ashley fell out of my arms during a midair brawl, she'd have died on impact.

Argh! Everything sucks. Did I waste too much time?

"Miss?" asks one of the doctors. He looks Indian, but has no accent at all. "Your friend is going to be fine. Likely, she will need to spend the night for observation. I'd like to make sure her heart didn't suffer permanent damage."

I lower my hands from my face, tears shutting off as if a faucet closed. "Really? She's okay?"

"Yes. Her heart didn't stop, so there shouldn't be any hypoxic damage to her brain. We've managed to stabilize her heart rate." The doctor smiles at me. He's a little too old to be 'fatherly,' but he's not quite in grandpa territory. Still, his expression is reassuring as hell.

"Thank you!" I lean forward and hug him around the waist.

He pats me on the shoulder. "Do you have a way to contact her family? I understand you're her friend, correct?"

"Yeah. My phone... not with me. Umm... Her mother's Leslie Carter." I give him the address and her landline number.

He hands the info off to a nurse. "How did she lose so much blood?"

Dammit. I can't think of a good excuse on the spot, so I delete the entire question out of his head, giving him the notion he already asked and got an answer that made sense to him. He might not be able to remember exactly what the answer is, but he'll think it sounded good at the time he heard it.

Satisfied, he looks Ashley over one more time, smiles at me, and heads off to attend other patients. I do mental surgery on the other doctor, the nurses, and the technician here so they all remember hearing a perfectly reasonable explanation for how a girl could lose so much blood without any visible wounds, even if they have no idea exactly what the explanation is.

And hey, Ashley got some color back, which isn't saying much, but the difference *is* noticeable. I sigh in relief, head bowed. My legs are pink? Oh, wow. I still have pants. High-speed flight and sweat pants don't usually get along. My giant Marvin T-shirt must've stopped air from getting under the waistband. One by one, the hospital staff finishes whatever they need to finish for her and leave us.

Soon, I'm alone with Ashley and beeping machines. I get up, hold her hand, and just stand there radiating gratitude to the universe for my friend being okay. Grr. The 'thief' at the vet clinic wanted to steal something alright, Ashley's life. What kind of sick bastard stalks a girl to feed on her until she dies? He must have been following us to Portland. Ashley sensed him at the gas station. But where the hell was he that I didn't see him watching us?

Matt Damon. Oh, crap!

Shadows can blot themselves out of people's minds entirely. It's not too much of a stretch to assume Lost Ones can alter their appearance in a similar manner. He must have made himself look like some random inconspicuous motorist. Or... no. The guy washing the window who stared at us the whole time.

A commotion starts out in the hall, a woman telling someone they 'can't go back there' unless they're receiving treatment or have a relative in care.

"Can you at least let her know I'm here?" asks Damarco.

Wow. He really showed up.

I lean out into the corridor, spotting him at the end of the hall by the arrival area. A nurse or orderly is blocking him. He notices me and points. When the woman looks at me, I stare into her eyes and give her a compulsion to let him in.

"Oh, sorry. Go on back." She smiles and wanders off into the arrival room.

Damarco shakes his head, snugs the lapels of his coat, and walks down the hall, pulling his bucket hat off and stuffing it in one of the coat pockets. He still has a wary look about him like he doesn't fully trust me, but also a sense of curiosity. I back into the room as he enters, until we're both standing by Ashley's bed.

"How is she?"

"She's going to be okay," I say, forcing my voice past the lump in my throat.

"So what's going on? Gotta say, I've never once seen one of you who didn't immediately try to kill me."

I take a few deep breaths to sort my emotions back to something resembling normal. "Nothing as complicated or sinister as you're probably thinking. Saw you at SCC completely by chance. I actually go there as a student."

"Seriously?"

"Yeah. Most vampires are not mindless monsters. We're kinda like people with a few extra bells and whistles." I lean against the bed and explain knowing the vampire he thinks he's looking for, doubting he's the one who murdered those people, and my following conundrum. "I didn't want to tell anyone you were here because I was worried they'd want to kill you. What you saw of vampires, it makes sense how you feel. You're just a regular guy in a bizarre situation doing what you think is best. You don't deserve to die for it."

"Well damn. I never thought one of you would say a thing like that. *Not* wanting to kill. It all kinda makes sense now."

"What does?"

He regards me for a moment in silence, almost pityingly. "After we spoke the other day, I became curious what you might've gone through at such a young age to be in the business of hunting. Little internet digging later, I find a story about an eighteen-year-old girl who everyone thought died, but turns out the hospital made a mistake and misidentified a body... which went missing. Tried to find anything about the supposed murder, but there isn't much out there.

Now, you'd assume a local girl being killed would've at least made page three in the paper. Nothing. Kinda suspicious."

Thank you, Persons in Black, for scrubbing the news. "Yeah... kinda strange."

"Way I figure it, that girl really did die."

I fidget at the bedding by Ashley's hand, gaze downcast. "Yeah. She did. I didn't ask for this. My ex-boyfriend stabbed me when I tried to break up with him. Just my luck, I had a vampire following me that night because he wanted to bite me. But, he also saw Scott attack me and tried to save me since he has a soft spot for kids. He wasn't fast enough to save my life, but he stopped me from dying for good. I woke up in a morgue and didn't even know what I'd been turned into at first. I guess most vamps want the change and crave the power. Me? I only want to be normal."

"Damn... You seem so human."

"Thanks." I chuckle. "You probably don't know this, but there are different types of vampires. Mine's the closest to still being alive, but I'm weak."

"Weak? You were holding the guy off pretty well for such a little thing."

"Heh. Thanks. I mean weak relatively. Other bloodlines get cooler superpowers than 'looking alive.'"

"Oh."

I brush my hand over Ashley's. Ooh. Feeling her skin gaining warmth makes me smile. "Anyway, I did kinda lie to you a little about knowing four or five other vampires. It's sorta true. I do *know* that many, but I know *of* about thirty or so."

Damarco gawks at me, both eyebrows up. "Thirty? Shee-it."

"Yeah. And quite a few are incredibly dangerous. When they found out I discovered a hunter in the area and didn't kill you right away or tell any of them about it, they got mad at me. There's this one guy who really hates me. He convinced the guy who's basically in charge to order me to kill you. Well, sorta. They want me to kill you, but he's reasonable and knows how I feel about murdering people... so he gave me the option to 'solve the hunter problem' in a way that doesn't require anyone die. You seem like a good, decent guy. I hate killing. Vampire or not, the only thing I want is to have as normal a life as possible."

He shifts his jaw side to side, thinking. "Normal, huh?"

"Because of that guy who has it in for me, if you destroy any vampires in Seattle, they're going to blame me like I killed them. It will make it impossible for me to stay with my family."

"Girl, they ain't your family."

"No, they are. Not talking about the vampires. I, umm... still live at home with my parents and siblings. They're all alive. Generally, vamps abandon their mortal lives and allow the world to think they died, move to another city, and reinvent themselves. I couldn't do it to my family, let them believe me dead. It would've crushed them. The vamp who hates me, Stefano, is upset I'm bridging worlds and still living with mortals."

"Damn..." Damarco's eyebrows both go up. "That's a new one. Your people know what happened to you?"

I nod. "Yeah. We're dealing with it as best we can. Swear I'm making it work. Most of us aren't a threat. We don't have to kill to feed. Yeah, I know some do, but they're monsters... and they deserve to be destroyed."

Damarco blinks in surprise, but nods. "Damn right they do."

"What happened to you and your sister? Can I ask?"

"Not much to tell, really. A fiend killed our parents when I was eleven and Tiff seven. To this day, I don't know why they left us be. We saw the whole thing. No one ever believed us. Thought we were 'disturbed' by the sight and making up stories. Me going around and trying to get someone to listen about vampires is how Mac found me."

"I'm sorry. That's horrible. I'd be completely destroyed if someone killed my parents." I fold my arms, shivering. "I'm already dreading losing them when they grow old."

Damarco finally stops staring at me like I'm going to snap any second and rip his throat out. He gazes over at Ashley. "Glad I got there fast enough to help. You two must be close. You fought fierce as hell."

"We're like sisters. I've known her since we were five. The vamp you saw me fighting was a sick bastard. An addict. He said feeding to kill is like more powerful than heroin. He deserved to burn. We're not all bad."

"You are the first one I've been tempted to leave be." He chuckles. "Maybe I'm too sensitive, but you still seem like a child."

Sigh.

"I'm eighteen. The change takes a few years off in the face. Maybe more so in my case because of my particular bloodline."

"Now that I know for sure you have real information… what's up with this Petra chick?"

I shiver. "Oh, she's a total bitch. I didn't tell you to stop out of any desire to protect her. I wasn't kidding about wanting to save your life… and your sister's. The world really would be better off without Petra, but it would take more than you to get rid of her. She came after me, threatened my family, and kicked my ass several times. I needed a lot of help to even fight her into a political stalemate. She probably still wants me to suffer, but she's afraid of my friends. Believe me, if I thought you could destroy her, she absolutely deserves it. But, if you kill any vamps here, I'm going to get in a crapload of trouble for not killing you."

"What about that one outside your friend's house?" asks Damarco. "You gonna catch hell for it?"

"I'm hoping they'll ignore him because he's not from around here and hasn't even been in the area long. Transient, and a Lost One. Besides, I don't care what they think. He wanted to kill Ashley, so screw it. *I* would've killed him myself."

"Love you too, Sare," whispers Ashley.

"Ash!" I grab her hand and squeeze.

"Yep. I'm here," she says in a hazy out-of-it voice. "Bow before my magnificence."

I laugh, tears welling in my eyes.

"Why do I feel like I got run over by a bus?"

"You were attacked by the vamp equivalent of a druggie."

She grimaces.

"Just rest, okay? You're in the hospital."

"Where's Mom?"

I bite my lip. "Umm. He told her to 'go away.' She's probably in Texas by now."

Ashley starts to laugh but stops, whining, "Ow."

"Okay, you've convinced me." Damarco shakes his head in a shallow, rapid 'I can't believe this' sort of way.

"Convinced you?" I peer back at him.

"That it's possible not all of your kind are mindless fiends. You're the most human I've ever seen. Not even pale... at all."

I shrug. "Being lifelike is my great superpower. It's not much, but I wouldn't trade it for anything. Maybe the Universe knew that the only thing I wanted was to go home to my family, be as normal as possible."

"All right." Damarco stuffs his hands in his pockets and exhales. "S'pose I'll trust you, but I still need to finish the reason I'm here."

Crap. Back to this. "The professor isn't a killer. He's like super mild. Yes, he teaches a class at SCC, and Tiffany probably did run into him. He most likely looked into her thoughts, saw you, and realized she'd tell you about him in hopes you'd destroy him, so he made her forget. There's no possible way he's a killer. If he was, don't you think he would've simply killed her for discovering him instead of making her forget?"

Damarco takes my hand, opens his mouth to say something, then stops, glancing down while examining my fingers. "So warm and lifelike."

"Umm, thanks?"

"Are you describing Sare or a sex doll?" whispers Ashley.

I sputter, blushing.

"Hah." Damarco laughs. "Perhaps not the wisest choice of words on my part. Sarah, I think you are maybe too naïve to see the true nature of vampires."

"Really? Even though I am one?" I blink at him.

"As you said, you're new and the most human. They are masterful liars. The one who attacked your friend has already left three bodies around Seattle. At first, I blamed the professor, but when no vampires entered or left the school, it seemed another was responsible. My search located Petra, but she had nothing to do with the most recent victim. By then I figured I had at least a third vampire in the area. Didn't have the first clue where to find this guy until Tiff called me with your friend's address. Guess he didn't have a fixed lair."

"He said he moves around a lot." I keep squeezing Ashley's hand. "The guy seemed friendly the first time I saw him, too. But so do some serial killers."

"I can't let them continue. Any fiend I can stop is a fiend I have to stop."

Oh, come on. So close. I stare up at him—and sense guilt. He's legit going to leave me alone since he watched me fight to protect Ashley, but has decided to destroy all the other vampires who don't share my lifelike appearance.

Holy crap, I have to stop him.

I blink.

Oh, shit! I'm seeing his thoughts. The gates of his consciousness are unguarded. I slam those suckers wide open and storm into his brain, leaving him standing there with serious derp face. Okay… umm. Now what? I could erase his memories of vampires entirely, but Tiffany would talk about them and know something happened to him. After what happened with her and Professor Heath, she'd know exactly what happened and would coach him to remember. Her influence would definitely peel away any replacement memories I wrote into his brain. It's damn difficult to make someone forget their parents' murder. I'd have to replace the killer with a random mugger. Better yet, find the news about it and make his memory match the official story. Less chance of a break that way.

But no, I can't make him forget vampires entirely, not without going to South Dakota and erasing Tiffany's mind as well. Far too much effort. Besides, Damarco's destroyed about half of that pack he wrote about. The others might be after him, so taking away those memories will leave him vulnerable and would basically be another roundabout way for me to kill him.

Can't do it.

Ooh. Better idea. I create a memory of him learning Professor *Montgomery* already left Seattle, and he couldn't find any information about where the man went next. That will both get him out of the city as well as maybe give him the chance to pick up the trail of the real vampire nut job he's looking for. Geez, I really hope he's not right and Heath is tricking me. Can't be. The guy's way too nice. Plus, there hasn't been a spate of unsolved murders around here. Or even missing college-age girls. Even if he's dumping them in the Sound, there'd have been stories of disappearances.

I burrow deeper into his past, searching for how he came to blame Heath for this. In an older memory, I peer out of Damarco's eyes, standing hidden under branches behind a chain link fence at the edge of a parking lot. He uses binoculars to observe a group of nine 'punks' in front of a dive bar, gathered around a black Mercedes that just pulled up. An old man in the rear seat is visible for only a few seconds while talking to the apparent leader of the gang. Okay, he does kind of look like Heath, but only in that they're both late forties white guys. The dude in the car has dark brown hair. The prof's rocking salt and pepper. Also, car dude has a longer face and somewhat larger nose. He's basically the permanently grumpy butler from a stuffy English movie about stuffy rich people.

Whew. *Not* Heath.

I draw the memory closer to the foreground in Damarco's head. Making it feel like the guy stayed in view for a full two minutes. He's going to remember the face as if this guy stood over his eleven-year-old self personally the night his parents died. No more mistaken identity.

Finally, I implant the urge to go home and spend time with Tiffany. Evidently, they're still living together in the house they grew up in. She's dating and will probably move out if things go well with the relationship.

Yeah, he needs some family time. Forget Seattle.

I grin and ease back out of his mind. Suppose it's reckless to let him remember me, but he is sincere in not wanting to attack me. Who knows, it might come in handy having a vampire hunter in my contacts list.

Whew. Problem solved. He's going to go home, not destroy any vampires, or die.

Wonder how he misplaced his amulet? Did he take it off on purpose? Did he *want* me to make him forget me so he would have no temptation to kill me? I peek back into his head. Oh, wow. He doesn't even realize it's missing. I swim deep into his memories, searching for the moment the old hunter lay dying in the hospital and handed it over to him. Damarco knows there is an order of vampire hunters but has never tried to make contact with them. Eventually, I locate a memory of him standing by the bed of a late-sixties guy with long white hair. Oof, the poor guy looks bad. He's near skeletal thin and clearly at death's door. Damarco glances down at a hand rising from the mattress.

Wrinkled fingers peel back to reveal… a gaudy fake-looking gold amulet with a ruby the size of a grape. It's the sort of thing a cosplayer would make out of foam for a grand wizard outfit.

My jaw hangs open.

"You little fuzzy thief!"

FOG AND KITTENS

M rs. Carter rushes into the room while I'm still trying to process Klepto yoinking Damarco's amulet.

She grabs me by the shoulders and shakes me. "Why is Ashley in the hospital? What exactly were the three of you doing together, and how did I end up in Walgreens without my car or knowing how I got there?"

"Umm. Ashley's going to be fine. You didn't see Hunter. We weren't messing around. A crazy vamp from out of town decided he wanted to drain her. We weren't humping, I was trying to kill him."

Damarco robotically turns on his heel and walks out. Crap.

"Oh." She smiles, relieved. "What about Walgreens?"

"The other vampire gave you a command to go away. Not sure how it translated to Walgreens, but it's why you walked there."

She frowns.

"One sec." I rush after Damarco and give him a small prod not to go anywhere tonight. He will simply return to his hotel room and have a nice rest. That done, I hurry back over to Mrs. Carter.

"Your parents know you're okay and your father wanted me to tell you they can re-watch *Ice Pirates* when you get home."

I almost shout 'F *Ice Pirates, Ashley almost died*' but screaming obscenities might be frowned on in a hospital. Besides, Ash is sleeping. Dad might have been saying it as a joke to calm me down or perhaps they don't understand what happened.

"How… umm… how did you get the message to come here and why do my parents know I'm okay?"

"Sophia. Something about talking to a ghost."

"Ahh." I nod. "Coralie. Wow. That's super nice of her to keep my parents from worrying."

We sit in the visitor's chairs by the bed and I explain everything related to Ruben and the attack on Ashley. Based on the strange way he stared at me before he left, my guess is the guy developed a weird fascination with me since he'd never seen an Innocent before, and while stalking me out of curiosity, he'd seen Ashley and thought she looked yummy. Mrs. Carter hugging me to death for protecting her daughter makes me feel guilty as hell. Like I'd started a fire that nearly killed Ash, then put it out, and Mrs. Carter is praising me for saving Ash's life. My overactive sense of responsibility is lying to me. I know it's not my fault Ruben was a blood-addict psycho, but if I hadn't been searching for Damarco that night, he'd never have seen me and followed me to Ashley.

Sigh.

Okay, I'm bending over backward to feel responsible for this. The guilt is just me freaking out at nearly losing her. She completely fell to bits when I 'died' last June. The two of us are so damn close it's scary. The reality of Ashley almost dying falls on me like all the stone in the Hoover Dam. I wind up in tears while Mrs. Carter holds me and tells me it's not my fault and everything's going to be okay. Eventually, I calm down, but not before my eruption of tears causes a nurse to come sprinting over to check on Ashley and make sure nothing happened to her.

A few minutes past nine, a different nurse gently shoos us out due to visiting hours being over and Ash not being in critical danger. Mrs. Carter offers me a ride home despite knowing I can fly. That tells me she doesn't want to be alone, so I accept. The ride is long and quiet since she's not going fast. Neither one of us says a word, but it's clear she appreciates not being alone. She drops me off at home, assures me she's okay, then backs around in a turn to drive the short distance to her house.

I head inside. It's too late for a re-showing (or a showing… still not clear on if they waited for me or watched it anyway) of *Ice Pirates* as the Littles have school tomorrow. Sierra's playing a game I haven't seen before, guiding an elf around a fantasy forest. Guess she needed a break from shooting people. Sophia's bundled up on the couch with her Kindle, smiling at me like a kid who did something helpful and she's proud of herself.

"You…" I point at her.

"Yep." She giggles.

Sierra pauses the game and scoots around to face us. "What did she do this time?"

"Sare needed to find a way to get the magic amulet away from the vampire hunter." Sophia holds up Klepto. "I have a fully functional long range stealth attack kitten with warp capability."

"Mew," says Klepto.

No wonder the little bugger looked at me with such a self-satisfied grin.

"Awesome. You two solved most of my problems." I zip over, hug the kitten, and pet Sophia on the head. "Wait. Got it backwards." I hug Sophia and pet Klepto on the head.

The girls laugh.

"Most?" asks Sophia.

"Damarco doesn't realize the amulet is gone."

"The kitten has skillz," says Sophia. "That's skills with a z."

"Mew." Klepto licks her paw.

"Right, but I have a problem. He's eventually going to notice it's missing. When he does, he will question everything he thinks happened. And, knowing my luck, he'll assume all the true stuff I told him is mind control and regard me telling him I'm no threat as a lie. I gotta put it back on him before he realizes it's gone."

"Wow, you're just gonna give a valuable magic item back to the guy?" Sierra blinks. "It could come in handy."

"Not having it could get him killed. It could also cause him to come back to Seattle, try to kill me, or try to hunt other vamps, which would get the rest of them mad at me and mess with everything. Do you want them to order me to go away?"

"No!" shouts Sophia.

Dad looks up from his book. "When you open a door to chuck a hand grenade into the vault, it's a good idea to close the door again before the grenade goes off."

"Huh?" ask the girls.

"He means I need to put the amulet back. Open door, mind control, close door."

Both girls say, "Ahh!" at the same time.

Klepto vanishes in a puff of mist. She reappears a few seconds later with the amulet hanging from her mouth.

"Thank you." I pat her on the head again, then hold the trinket up to look at it. "Wow, this thing looks fake."

Dad gets up, walks over, and palms the amulet. "It's heavy enough to be real gold. But yea, that's rather gaudy."

"The gem though. Looks plastic."

He holds the amulet closer to his eye. "Nah. Glass. Hollow, filled with blood. Not a ruby."

"Eww," says Sophia.

"Vampire blood..." I look down at myself. Still in a long Marvin T-shirt and pink sweat pants, barefoot. Amazingly, Sierra hasn't teased me for the exceptionally cute sweats. Probably because Marvin is hiding the butt unicorn. "Be back soon."

"At least it stopped raining." Dad heads back to his chair. "But, it usually doesn't last long when it comes down that hard."

"Fly safe, unicorn butt," says Sierra.

Or not. Marvin is slacking.

Chuckling, I smirk at her. "I was waiting for someone to comment."

She shrugs. "You can't expect to wear something like that and not suffer some degree of light mockery."

"They're cute." Sophia gives me the thumbs-up. "Girl power on the legs is a bit much, but I like the rainbow streaming from the uni's horn."

Yeah, in an alternate timeline where Sophia was the eldest daughter, she and Ashley would have aligned and destroyed the world in an explosion of pink and rainbows.

I TAKE THE OPPORTUNITY OF FLYING BACK TO SEATTLE TO STOP AND grab a bite.

It's not too late yet, so it's a little bit of a challenge to find someone on their own. My lucky dinner guest looks like a corporate type. Nice suit, heading to a black Beemer. No, it's not the vampire Damarco saw at the dive bar. This guy's only like thirty. Not a damn clue why his blood tastes like mac and cheese, but I can't really complain.

Once I finish feeding—the brawl with Ruben wore me out—I race to the hotel and land on the balcony outside Damarco's room. He's in bed and the lights are out, but in that strange sort of way people can sense things, I know he's not asleep yet.

A few light knocks on the glass gets him to sit up. He looks at me confused. I wave. We stare at each other for a moment longer before he gets out of bed and walks over to open the door in a white T-shirt and red boxer briefs. Since he's not completely losing his mind at the sight of me, I don't think he's realized the amulet is missing. The guy's probably worn it non-stop since the old man gave it to him. Maybe I subconsciously didn't want him to notice it and made him not realize? Could be.

"What are you doing here? Hope you haven't decided to change your mind. The others tell you to finish me off?"

"Nope." I smile. "Just wanted to make sure you were okay. And… now that I have my head screwed back on straight, thank you for helping me protect Ashley."

He purses his lips, scratches his head, then shrugs as if to say 'it is what it is.' "So a vampire's happy about me dusting another vampire. First time for everything, I suppose."

"Yeah. Like I said, we're not all clones or on the same team. Vampires screw with each other more than they screw with the living. And… as far as I'm concerned, any who kill without remorse deserve whatever you do to them. If you keep your head down, hunt only the psycho ones, and don't try to go public and prove to the world vampires are real, the rest will probably leave you be."

"Right… Well, that's something. How is your friend?"

Warmth spreads over my chest. Only a little of it is from my recent meal. "Looks like she'll be okay. The only reason she survived is a matter of like twenty seconds. If you didn't kill him when you did or if I didn't fly her to the hospital…"

"Rough. Glad it worked out. Some people get lucky."

I absentmindedly rub my thumb over the spot where Scott's knife went in. Lucky's one word for it. "Yeah. Oh, Damarco?"

He looks up.

We make eye contact.

And he's on the last train to Derpville. Dammit, Dad. That song gets stuck in my head every time he listens to it. No idea why he even does since the Monkees were already 'old' when he was a kid. Okay, fine. I listen to Iron Maiden sometimes and it's old people music, too. Guess I shouldn't throw stones.

Anyway…

I implant a memory of me thanking him for helping protect Ashley, hugging him, and leaving. As soon as he's wearing this amulet again, my ability to touch his mind will go away. It's vital he never knows he took it off—or had it stolen. Otherwise, he may doubt everything. Given how he used to think all vampires were fiends needing to be destroyed, it will likely mean he'll doubt his opinion of me as a 'nice girl,' considering it a trick.

Once I'm completely sure he has no conscious memory of missing the amulet, I reinforce his desire to go home and enjoy a nice normal life for a little while. Okay, moment of truth. Possibly stupid of me to put this thing back on him and take away my ability to tweak his brain… but as Dad said, that door needs to be closed before the grenade explodes.

While Damarco stands there staring into the fifth dimension, I float up off my feet so I can put the amulet over his head, tuck it under his T-shirt, and let myself out via the patio door. A second after I leap into the air, a shrill woman's scream from directly above me nearly makes me soil myself. The only reason the sweat pants remain clean is I haven't eaten real food in a while. There's nothing in me to soil them with.

I flip over and stare up at a woman in a peach colored bathrobe who's stepped out on her balcony to vape. Her shocked scream peters out to an astonished gawk at me hanging in midair. Oops. I zip up and telepathically leap into her brain. She screamed because she thought she witnessed a suicide jumper. Easy to remove. This woman never saw me.

I'm almost jealous of her. She's forgotten entirely about seeing me, but my heart is still racing from the shock of the sudden loud noise. That startled me worse than someone sneaking up and popping a balloon behind my head.

Anyway, time for me to go home.

To avoid any other unwanted delays, I fly straight up until I'm well out of easy visual range of anyone on the ground, and face toward home.

"Engage," I mutter—and zoom up to full speed.

Gawd. I am such a nerd.

NOT QUITE DEAD

O n the flight home, I end up stuck somewhere between feeling relief and dread.

Unless something unusually weird happens, the vampire hunter situation is dealt with in a way that should make Wolent happy while also letting me avoid having to murder a pretty decent guy. Becoming a vampire came with certain undeniable truths, one of which being I need to consume blood and bite people. It doesn't mean we're all heartless killers. For me, it had the opposite effect: life has become *way* more precious. Even the idea of giving the Transference to people bothers me since they have to die first—despite all the awesome power it gives them.

Yeah, I know… as squishy as Sophia.

Maybe becoming a vampire only amplifies what's already there? Vampires like Ruben probably had some deep inner temptation to be a killer in life, but hesitated for fear of being caught and punished. Undeath freed him from any care what mortal authorities did. Or maybe he'd been addicted to drugs, unable to control the drive to chase the next big high. As a vampire, his addiction shifted from chemicals to the rush he got when he drained someone to death, a compulsion so deeply ingrained in his being he couldn't resist.

Aurélie could have been—don't wanna say self-absorbed here—but she probably enjoyed being beautiful in life. Me? I guess I've advanced to the next level of nice. Still don't think I'm as bad as Sophia. Like, I wouldn't cry for a whole month if a hamster died.

Just an hour or two.

Okay, maybe I'd be glum for a whole day.

Sigh. Week.

Anyway, the dread that's mucking up my relief is coming from worrying about the Ruben situation. Wolent specifically said any vampire Damarco killed would be my fault. This doesn't bother me *too* much since I had been trying to kill him anyway to protect Ashley. Self-defense is one thing, but some of the vampires around here— Stefano especially—would no doubt laugh at me for protecting a mortal. To them, it would be like getting into a fistfight because I thought it cruel to bite a poor, innocent hamburger.

It doesn't make sense to me how some vampires can feel so superior to normal people, since at one time or another, every vampire had been human. To me, it's like someone works for twenty years at a place, then gets promoted to a manager... and treats all the other employees like they're some kind of inferior creature. Dude, remember where you came from. Amirite?

Maybe living for a couple centuries causes mental problems in the same way political talk radio does.

But really, those vampires who have giant sticks up their butts could use Ruben's death to make trouble for me. Why do they have such a problem with me staying home? So what if a handful of mortals know the truth? It's not like my family has any plans to go public or interfere with vampires. Stefano and the few who agree with him are either some kind of bloodline purists who think Innocents are second-class vampires, or they're totally into cruelty for the sake of cruelty.

Even though Ruben had been an outsider, and it's quite possible none of those elders even knew he existed—or died, with each passing minute, the anxiety a political shitstorm awaits me powerful enough to threaten my family grows. By the time I'm over Cottage Lake (the town, not the actual lake), it's nearly made me sick to my stomach. Fortunately, no normal food is inside me or someone out for a late walk would be in for a disgusting surprise.

The sight of snow on the ground distracts me from my mental wandering. What the hell? When did it snow? There's a decent coating already, though it hasn't concealed all traces of lawn and road yet. But, no snow actually fell that I remember. Worse, when I left the hotel, the ground had been clean. Why is there only snow on the ground in my neighborhood?

Uh oh. What did Sophia do now?

Worry makes me fly faster to my cul-de-sac. The big living room window of my house is lit up, the curtains aglow in warm yellow light. Much to my astonishment, the Christmas tree is up and twinkling. Mom usually insists we wait for at least the second week of December to decorate, so it's unusual to see the tree up so soon.

I glide down to land on the little strip of sidewalk connecting the driveway to the tiny front porch, right in front of the window. Mom and Dad are on the couch, the Littles are all kneeling or sitting on the floor, each with a present in their lap. In defiance of what appears to be a Christmas Eve scene, my siblings all appear glum. Sophia's crying. Sierra has an expression like the only thing stopping her from throwing the gift in the fireplace is us not having one. Sam's frowning. The parents both stare at the rug, holding hands. Mom's eyes have a red tinge around them, but she's not currently crying.

What the hell?

I rush inside, but no one looks up at the door opening.

"You didn't get me what I wanted," says Sierra in a tone part bratty part weepy.

Not once in eleven years has the girl ever complained about a gift. While she's not as unmaterialistic as Sophia, she's always been gracious in regard to presents, even when Aunt Jody gives her ugly sweaters or socks. Plus, she hasn't even taken the ribbon off or torn the wrapping paper to see what the box contains. How can she know it's not what she asked for?

The parents cringe.

"Open it, sweetie," whispers Mom. "Santa knows you've been asking for that, too."

"I wanted Sarah back!" blurts Sierra. "This isn't her."

Sophia sobs harder. Sam's lip quivers. Mom lapses into crying on Dad's shoulder.

What the hell. "Guys? I'm right here."

None of them look at me.

"We should open this stuff and pretend to be happy," says Sam, his voice lifeless. "Mom and Dad *did* get this stuff for us. They'll be sad if we don't."

"Hey!" I yell, running over to grab Sierra in a hug.

My arms pass through her like she's a ghost. Not even her hair moves.

"Guys! I'm not dead!" I shout, then try to kick the coffee table—but it's not solid either.

Oh, shit. My family aren't ghosts—I am.

Sophia stares at the gift in her lap, torn between being too sad to open it and not wanting to disappoint the parents. She starts to tug at the ribbon, but ends up twirling it back and forth around her finger, her expression heartbreaking.

"Mom! Dad! I'm right here. I'm not dead." I try to grab them, too, but my hands pass through them.

The Littles all end up crying, even Sam.

Oh, no. What's going on? Who is messing with me? How did I end up in an alternate reality where I stayed dead? Or… is this the future after vampire elders make them forget my return? I drop to my knees, shaking my head and muttering 'I'm not dead' over and over a few times before the pain of hearing my family suffering such grief boils over and I shout, "I'm not dead!"

… and wake up in my bed.

The echo ringing in the air tells me the shout happened outside my dream as well as in it.

"Holy crap! Just a dream… hopefully."

I scramble out of bed and grab my phone to check the clock. It's 2:44 p.m., Monday December Second. The first Monday after Thanksgiving. I haven't jumped forward in time. It's merely the next day after tweaking Damarco's memory. Guess being consumed with worry about how the vampires will react to Ruben's death right before sunrise gave me a hell of a nightmare. Overcome by a need to go squeeze the heck out of my family, I start for the door—but stop short when a small flash of light explodes in front of me.

Klepto appears and drops into my arms. "Mew."

"Hey you." I hug the kitten. "Thanks again for the assist."

"Mew." Klepto purrs.

Clutching the kitten, I run out of my room and go upstairs. All three Littles are in the kitchen foraging an after-school snack. I gather them into an ambush hug all at the same time.

"Uh oh. Unicorn butt's gone emo," says Sierra.

Sophia grins and hugs me back.

Sam smiles.

Mom's at work—probably in actual court at the moment—and Dad's in the office typing away, the keys sounding like a machine gun.

"Mew," says Klepto from somewhere inside the multi-hug.

"You okay, Sare?" asks Sierra. "What happened?"

"Fine, now… just a bad dream." I squeeze them all again and let go. Klepto leaps from my shoulder to sit on Sophia's head.

Wow, so I've survived my first Thanksgiving as a vampire. Had some rough moments, but all things considered, it went well. The case Mom's working on must have stressed her past the point of no return since she didn't do the thing where she asked everyone around the dinner table to name something they felt thankful for. I used to hate it that, thinking it lame as hell. A teenage girl was too cool to have to deal with being so Hallmark cheesy, especially in front of people.

But yeah… I'm thankful Dalton was there to give me the Transference, thankful my family doesn't have to deal with losing me, and beyond thankful I still have them all in my life.

Even Great Uncle Hank.

fin

ACKNOWLEDGMENTS

Thank you for reading the eighth book in the Vampire Innocent series!

I'm grateful to all the readers who have told me how much they enjoy following Sarah and her family through her crazy new life. This series first came about when I decided to test the waters of self-publishing and decided that with my other series books wrapped up with a small press (that I have since gotten my rights back from) it would be a good idea to have a series of my own. The idea to do a semiserious vampire story kinda came out of the blue and to this day, I can't say what made me think of it.

I do know that it would not have reached eight books deep without the support from everyone reading. Thank you for all the feedback, encouragement, and reviews!

Additional thanks to Lee Hargrove for editing and Alexandria Thompson for the cover design and interior art.

Special thanks to Ann Anderson Noser for helping out with some veterinary info.

ABOUT THE AUTHOR

Originally from South Amboy NJ, Matthew has been creating science fiction and fantasy worlds for most of his reasoning life. Since 1996, he has developed the "Divergent Fates" world, in which *Division Zero, Virtual Immortality, The Awakened Series, The Harmony Paradox, and the Daughter of Mars series* take place. Along with being an editor at Curiosity Quills press, he has worked in IT and technical support.

Matthew is an avid gamer, a recovered WoW addict, Gamemaster for two custom RPG systems, and a fan of anime, British humour, and intellectual science fiction that questions the nature of reality, life, and what happens after it.

He is also fond of cats.

Visit me online at:
Facebook: https://www.facebook.com/MatthewSCoxAuthor
Amazon: https://www.amazon.com/author/mscox
Pinterest: https://www.pinterest.com/matthewcox10420/
Goodreads: https://www.goodreads.com/author/show/7712730. Matthew_S_Cox
Email: mcox2112@gmail.com

OTHER BOOKS BY MATTHEW S. COX

Divergent Fates Universe Novels

Division Zero series

- Division Zero
- Lex De Mortuis
- Thrall
- Guardian
- Harbinger
- The Shadow Fixer
- Neuroshock

The Awakened series

- Prophet of the Badlands
- Archon's Queen
- Grey Ronin
- Daughter of Ash
- Zero Rogue
- Angel Descended

Daughter of Mars series

- The Hand of Raziel
- Araphel
- Ghost Black

Virtual Immortality series

- Virtual Immortality
- The Harmony Paradox

Prophet of the Badlands Series

- Prophet's Journey
- Prophet's Mercy

Divergent Fates Anthology

(Fiction Novels - Adult)
The Roadhouse Chronicles Series

- One More Run
- The Redeemed
- Dead Man's Number

Faded Skies series

- Heir Ascendant
- Ascendant Unrest
- Ascendant Revolution

Temporal Armistice Series

- Nascent Shadow
- The Shadow Collector
- The Gate to Oblivion
- The Queen of Discord
- The Burning Alchemist

Vampire Innocent series

- A Nighttime of Forever
- A Beginner's Guide to Fangs
- The Artist of Ruin

- The Last Family Road Trip
- The Phantom Oracle
- How Not to Summon Demons
- Ordinary Problems of a College Vampire
- A Vampire's Guide to Surviving Holidays
- An Introduction to Paranormal Diplomacy
- A Vampire's Guide to Adulting
- How to Stop a Vampire War in Six Easy Steps
- Ancient Vampire Death Cults and Other Annoyances
- Hunting Vampires for Fun and Profit
- A String of Seriously Unlucky Events
- The Summer of Completely Usual Strangeness
- Demonic Crisis Management for the Modern Vampire

Standalones

- Wayfarer: AV494
- Axillon99
- Chiaroscuro: The Mouse and the Candle
- The Spirits of Six Minstrel Run
- Sophie's Light
- The Far Side of Promise anthology
- Operation: Chimera (with Tony Healey)
- The Dysfunctional Conspiracy (with Christopher Veltmann)
- Of Myth and Shadow
- The Girl Who Found the Sun

Winter Solstice series (with J.R. Rain)

- Convergence
- Containment
- Catalyst
- Catacombs

Alexis Silver series (with J.R. Rain)

- Silver Light
- Deep Silver
- Silver Quarrel
- Silver Crucible
- Silver Heart

Samantha Moon Origins series (with J.R. Rain)

- New Moon Rising
- Moon Mourning
- Haunted Moon

Vampire For Hire series (with J.R. Rain)

- Moon Master
- Dead Moon
- Lost Moon
- Vampire Destiny
- Infinite Moon
- Vampire Empress
- Moon Elder
- Wicked Moon
- Moon Blade

Maddy Wimsey series (with J.R. Rain)

- The Devil's Eye
- The Drifting Gloom
- Dark Mercy
- Primal Wrath

Samantha Moon Case Files series (with J.R. Rain)

- Blood Moon

Immortal Operative (with J.R. Rain)

- Broken Ice
- Broken Wing

Four Elements series (with J.R. Rain)

- The Elementalist
- The Black Rose
- The Wakefield Curse

Witches series (with J.R. Rain)

- The Witch and the Hangman

Zeb Clemens series (with J.R. Rain)

- The Beast of Devil's Creek
- Wanted: Undead or Alive

Young Adult Novels

The Eldritch Heart Series

- The Eldritch Heart
- The Cursed Crown
- The Sapphire Soul

Evergreen Series

- Evergreen
- The World That Remains

- The Lucky Ones
- Nuclear Summer
- The Nuclear Frontier
- The World We Make
- The Threat Unseen

Progenitor Series

- Out of Sight
- Out of Mind

Diary of a Teenage Fey

(Short story series)

- Elder Horror
- The Hag of Barrow Falls
- Babysitter's Nightmare
- Lharakki
- Bauble for a Soul
- Simulacrum
- Amorphous
- Manticore

Standalones

- Caller 107
- The Summer the World Ended
- Nine Candles of Deepest Black
- The Forest Beyond the Earth

Middle Grade Novels

The Adventures of Ubergirl series

- My Dad is a Mad Scientist
- Aliens Ate My Homework
- The End of all Halloweens
- Dr. Infinity and the Soul Smasher

Tales of Widowswood series

- Emma and the Banderwigh
- Emma and the Silk Thieves
- Emma and the Silverbell Faeries
- Emma and the Elixir of Madness
- Emma and the Weeping Spirit

Standalones

- Citadel: The Concordant Sequence
- The Cursed Codex
- The Menagerie of Jenkins Bailey

www.ingramcontent.com/pod-product-compliance
Lightning Source LLC
Chambersburg PA
CBHW031425200626
46814CB00016B/2190